No Game No Life

9

LOOKS LIKE
THE GAMER
SIBLINGS
ARE SKIPPING
A TURN!

YUU KAMIYA

"We request an audience with you, O King of Immanity, O Spieler. We— are *Ex Machina.*"

Mysterious Light, with its ever-so-dependable non-euclidean geometry, decided to drop in and make their phones flash!

If anything, this wouldn't make the cut using *Pixelation*. However! Our friend Mysterious Light puts it **in the clear for broadcast!** Therefore, this content is **definitively wholesome!! QED**!!

It was merely a wish...for her host, the Shrine Maiden, her friend... to *smile*. That's all it was, the humblest of songs... And yet.

THE TEN COVENANTS

The absolute law of this world, created by the god Tet upon winning the throne of the One True God. Covenants that have forbidden all war among the intelligent Ixseeds—namely.

1. In this world, all bodily injury, war, and plunder is forbidden.
2. All conflicts shall be settled by victory and defeat in games.
3. Games shall be played for wagers that each agrees are of equal value.
4. Insofar as it does not conflict with "3," any game or wager is permitted.
5. The party challenged shall have the right to determine the game.
6. Wagers sworn by the Covenants are absolutely binding.
7. For conflicts between groups, an agent plenipotentiary shall be established.
8. If cheating is discovered in a game, it shall be counted as a loss.
9. The above shall be absolute and immutable rules, in the name of the God.

10. Let's all have fun together.

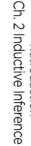

CONTENTS
09

No Game No Life

YUU KAMIYA

9

YEN ON

NEW YORK

NO GAME NO LIFE, Volume 9
YUU KAMIYA

Translation by Daniel Komen
Cover art by Yuu Kamiya

NO GAME NO LIFE Volume.9
©Yuu Kamiya 2016
First published in Japan in 2016 by KADOKAWA CORPORATION, Tokyo.
English translation rights arranged with KADOKAWA CORPORATION, Tokyo, through Tuttle-Mori Agency, Inc., Tokyo.

English translation © 2019 by Yen Press, LLC

Yen On
150 West 30th Street, 19th Floor
New York, NY 10001

Visit us at yenpress.com
facebook.com/yenpress
twitter.com/yenpress
yenpress.tumblr.com
instagram.com/yenpress

First Yen On Edition: October 2019

Yen On is an imprint of Yen Press, LLC. The Yen On name and logo are trademarks of Yen Press, LLC.

Library of Congress Cataloging-in-Publication Data
Names: Kamiya, Yu, 1984- author, illustrator. | Komen, Daniel, translator.
Title: No game no life / Yu Kamiya, translation by Daniel Komen.
Other titles: No gemu no raifu. English
Description: First Yen On edition. | New York, NY : Yen ON, 2015–
Identifiers: LCCN 2015041321 |
   ISBN 9780316383110 (v. 1 : pbk.) |
   ISBN 9780316385176 (v. 2 : pbk.) |
   ISBN 9780316385190 (v. 3 : pbk.) |
   ISBN 9780316385213 (v. 4 : pbk.) |
   ISBN 9780316385237 (v. 5 : pbk.) |
   ISBN 9780316385268 (v. 6 : pbk.) |
   ISBN 9780316316439 (v. 7 : pbk.) |
   ISBN 9780316502665 (v. 8 : pbk.) |
   ISBN 9780316471343 (v. 9 : pbk.)
Subjects: | BISAC: FICTION / Fantasy / General. | GSAFD: Fantasy fiction.
Classification: LCC PL832.A58645 N6 2015 | DDC 895.63/6—dc23
LC record available at http://lccn.loc.gov/2015041321

ISBNs: 978-0-316-47134-3 (paperback)
       978-0-316-47138-1 (ebook)

10 9 8 7 6 5 4 3 2

LSC-C

Printed in the United States of America

SKIP START

Okay, it's time to recap. You may object, asking, "Where'd that come from?" Unfortunately, you have been overruled. Stories always need recaps. Just look at those Games of the Year that subject you to an annoying recap with every load screen. I hope that puts you in the mood to tolerate at least one recap. If not, go ahead and skip it.

Our setting is Disboard, the world on a board. A world where all violence has been prohibited by the Ten Covenants and everything is decided by games. Into this world came a brother and a sister from Earth, who are good at nothing except games.

No, that was a bit too much of an understatement. Let me rephrase.

A brother and a sister, Sora and Shiro, both socially incompetent shut-in losers, who build up their kung fu at failing at life.

Together, they are " " (Blank), the two-in-one gamer who reigns undefeated in every sort of game. Otherwise, they are pretty much useless. They then appeared in Disboard—specifically, in the Kingdom of Elkia. This is the last country of Immanity, the human race, which has been pushed back into its last city, on the brink of extinction. So Sora and Shiro were like, *Well now, let's see here...* and casually grabbed the throne. And they started playing games against the various other races of the "sixteen seeds," or Ixseeds, who have various totally broken abilities like magic and superpowers. It's too bad these two don't get along with the class's honor students like Love and Friendship and Justice. They're always hanging around with those troublemakers like Fraud and Cunning and Trickery. So they beat Flügel, Werebeast, Siren, Dhampir, one after the other. Then they beat Old Deus—the gods themselves. Yet, they didn't enslave or subjugate or oppress any of these guys. Instead, they took them under their wing. The Kingdom of Elkia turned into the Commonwealth of Elkia. It's history's first multiracial commonwealth, and it's spreading like wildfire.

This all happened in the span of a few months. This steady build brought Elkia from its knees to the top of the world. Which also means it's now considered one of the greatest *threats* in the world. But whatever. Continuity is power. Even in the case of horrible human beings, credit must be given where credit is due.

...Anyway. Perhaps you've heard of the second law of thermodynamics: the law of increasing entropy. That law that says things would rather dissipate than concentrate. Hey, it's not a hard concept to understand. I bet everyone's had some experience with it.

It's the mystery of how your room would rather get super messy than stay clean.

It's how you struggle to gain favor with your crush, but then you make one wrong choice and suddenly, you've lost them. You work like a horse to earn money, but then gamble it all away on junk. When playing a game, you have to actively try to win, but losing takes no effort at all. You get the point. Basically, it's easier to destroy than to build, easier to lose than to keep.

Now, all you dear readers who have skipped to this point: How about I segue from a recap into a spoiler? You know Sora and Shiro? The law of entropy applies to them, too.

————*They lose everything.*

Yes, everything. The throne, the position of agent plenipotentiary—

everything. Everything starts crashing down from that one phone call. Who would have thought they'd get a call in the middle of a fantasy world with no reception? Who would have thought they'd get a call at all? It's not as if they ever had any friends. So they pick up gingerly and this is what they hear:

"We request an audience with you, O King of Immanity, O Spieler. We—are Ex Machina."

■■■

Now we return to the Kingdom of Elkia in the Commonwealth of Elkia, back when it was alive and well. The stately Elkia Royal Castle stood tall in the center of the capital, and it bore a placard. This enormous placard dangled from a spire, as stately as the castle itself, and it announced:
CLOSED FOR BUSINESS.

In the Elkia Royal Castle that was now closed for business... Scratch that—the *Bl4nk Productions* Castle, as the wooden board nailed onto a stone slab would have it. In any case, the castle was now deserted, with every last one of the staff having been given time off. The only sounds that echoed within its walls were the footsteps of a young redhead, Stephanie Dola, better known as Steph, and—

"Okay, stop!! Holou, you really think you're gonna be a star like *that*?!"

"…If you don't have the drive…just quit…!"

—likewise from the LESSON ROOM indicated by the wooden board on the assembly hall—

"I know not even the meaning of the word 'drive'! If I may quit, then quit I shall!!"

"Gahhh!! We say quit, and you just go ahead and do it?! Kids these days!"

"…This is why…no one, respects…your generation…!"

Thus was the tearful declaration of the uncomprehending little girl, and the weary sighs of the two from that very same generation that no one respects.

The former was Holou, a little girl with a floating inkpot that was roughly the same height as her body. She was a god—it was impossible to mistake her for anything else. To be more precise, she was an Old Deus, Ixseed Rank One.

The latter were Sora and Shiro, a brother with an "I ♥ PPL" shirt, and a sister with white hair and red eyes. The two of them were—though one would desperately like to mistake it or hide it—the monarch of Elkia.

Steph was glaring at these two horrible excuses for human beings, bewildered by the sheer spectacle of them bringing a god to tears.

But Sora continued his rant, completely oblivious. "Tomorrow's supposed to be your *big debut*! The hell are you thinking performing steps like *those* today?!"

If you were wondering what it was that Sora and Shiro had to close the castle for, here is your answer. They were now in the business of producing a pop idol: Holou, the Old Deus.

Steph hung her head as she questioned the siblings' sanity.

"Holou hath acted in accordance with thy requests! If thou hast objections, ye must state them in full!!"

Ignoring her, the seated Sora and Shiro sighed once more at Holou's protests.

Suddenly, they got up and broke into song and dance.

Steph was at a loss for words. It was perfect.

"*Hff… Hff…!* Like *that*! Y-you get it?!"

"…W-we can't, keep this up… *Please*, just get it."

Sora and Shiro collapsed onto the floor, out of breath.

"That *accorded not with your description*!!" shouted Holou, stamping the floor.

In a way, making a god stamp her feet was kind of an achievement. Sora and Shiro snickered.

"Merely following the music is the work of an amateur! A pro *expresses* herself in order to rouse the audience!"

"...Not that there, is an audience... But I guess this is the, console version... And, it's not like you play...when people are, watching."

The two of them had achieved the top scores even in music games and karaoke. Holou, as a god, was perfectly capable of replicating what she saw right down to the letter. But—

"There's no point in ripping off others! Express yourself! You're not a machine. Sing from the heart!"

"Thou shalt explain the meaning of 'expression' and define this 'heart' from which thou wouldst have me sing! And clearly!"

Holou wailed at these incompetent producers who only gave vague instructions.

...Incidentally, Steph had been calling Sora's and Shiro's names all the while, for a total of four times.

"C'mon, Holou! One more time! '(Save Me) Godly Summer ☆,' from the top!"

It seemed there really was only one name the two of them would respond to. In light of their continued disregard, Steph drew in a deep breath and shouted:

■■■

"PRODUCERRRRRRRS!!"

"Hmm? Oh hey, didn't see you there, *manager babe*."

"...You can just, call us 'P'... Mmkay?"

Sora and Shiro turned deliberately toward Steph, now that she had addressed them correctly.

"I thought you were jok— Well, no, I honestly didn't..."

Nothing Sora and Shiro said could ever be written off as a joke. Steph, of all people, must have known that by now. And yet, with what little hope she had, she asked them why they had vacated the throne, given leave to all their attendants, and closed the castle.

"But still, I have to ask. You're *closing the administration*? Do you want to destroy the country?!"

Her cry, in other words, was a plea to locate the whereabouts of the monarch's misplaced minds.

"Whaaat? You want us to work our staff twenty-four seven? Talk about a corporate scandal..."

"Is it not preferable to a rumor that the boss is insane?!"

But Sora had been so focused on Holou's song-and-dance routine that he merely answered.

"Do you know, Sir, what people are calling you two?!"

As Steph snapped her finger at them, Sora and Shiro wondered:

—*Wait, what could it be?*

Perhaps "the monarch of national resurgence, who has vanquished higher races one after the other and overcome the gods themselves"...?

But it wouldn't end there. Sora and Shiro imagined the kind of slander that would be mixed in.

"They call you the *Discredited King*! They trust you even less!!"

"What, that's all? ...Hey, wait, that's actually kind of a cool name!"

"...Nah, it's...kinda lame..."

The brief bit of stress dissipated with Steph's answer; Sora was hyped up, while Shiro felt let down. The fact remained that they didn't give a shit, which irked Steph to no end.

"Look at all you've done, only to be *scorned rather than celebrated*. Do you know why this is?!"

It seemed to offend Steph more than it did Sora and Shiro.

—*How to explain it...?*

They ruminated on this intractable problem before Sora's expression turned mysterious—

"We trick people into falling in love with us and bet Race Pieces without asking anyone. Just how do you expect anyone to be like, 'Oh yeah, I trust you!'? We're obviously just frauds, perhaps even lying bastards."

"*Ah-haaa!* ♥ I'm *so* glad you're aware of all this! ♪ Now *do* something about it!"

—and he asked back just why anyone should trust him. Steph answered with what could be described as a song and a dance. She twirled with the grace and sensitivity of a ballerina.

"I understaaand, people can't change just like that. You just have to take little steps, one at a time—so you can stop being a fraud who won't even let *me* in on what's going on! How about we start with you telling me why you closed the administration?!"

Her ballet dance gradually became more heated, until it transformed into a break dance punctuated by a shout.

—*Holou could learn a thing or two from her,* Sora and Shiro both thought.

"Why we closed the administration...? No real reason... There just wasn't anything to do."

There's no useful move for Elkia to make at present.

But this first reason failed to convince Steph.

"What do you mean there's nothing to do? What about the commercial associations? They were just getting started!"

...Commercial associations... Mmm... What was that again?

"The traders and lords who've been fattening themselves up on all the new resource export! Don't you remember the other day? You two got them all to play a game by the Covenants to shove your papers down their throats!!"

"Oh yeah. Don't worry, I remember. Those pretentious douches, right?"

He didn't lie. He remembered. He just didn't mention that he'd forgotten.

Sora and Shiro thought the same thing.

—*This is what I hate about nation-building strategy games.*

They knew well that the idea of a multiracial commonwealth would be hard for people to swallow. Then on top of that, they had to deal with the people's reactions to this meteoric rise and reformation. The economic and legal stuff wouldn't be able to keep up, and it was just one domestic pain in the ass after another. Not least among which were these nouveau riche smart-asses and all the uproar they caused.

"So. What about them? We dealt with them, didn't we?"

"The *way* you did was like adding fuel to the fire! Don't you see people are just getting more upset?!" Steph pointed fiercely to the two siblings. "It's time for you to show your leadership as the monarch! It's a test of your personal charisma!!"

And in such a time, for the monarch to be one like this... Steph's face seemed to say, All right, forget it. She worried that if the castle—the de facto seat of the Commonwealth—was to be shut down, then even the advisers—

"...If there's, one thing...we don't have...it's...charisma...!"

"Why do you think we stay inside all the time? Chew on that!!"

The two had not the slightest confidence they could be loved—However! They sneered boldly in their conviction that they would be hated, *and furthermore—*!

"Thus, we have demonstrated beyond all doubt what exactly Elkia is currently lacking!"

"...It's...a charismatic...figurehead...to rally, the people..."

"In other words: Our first priority is a national project to *raise the ultimate idol!*"

The two of them shouted out the *second reason* and looked at Holou, who, for her part, was just silently writing more questions on her scroll with a pout.

"Yo, Holou! You hear what we just said?"

She had heard. She just wasn't convinced. Her face said it.

"Your argument cohereth not! What business hath Holou with thy lack of charisma?!"

"You don't have to do anything with it. You just have to use your mad charisma to win us authority."

Yeah, like the Shrine Maiden and the Eastern Union...! Sora smirked. No need to have the actual head of state be trustworthy so long as there was a figurehead to bring the nation together.

"Holou hypothesizes that your true meaning is that Holou should be *like her host.*" But if they just wanted her to be like her host, the Shrine Maiden... "*Holou's host doth neither sing nor dance!* Ye must state the reason for which Holou must become an idol in this inscrutable sense ye describe!"

"This is the nineteenth time you've asked! So I'll answer you as I have all eighteen times before: *Heaven wills it!*"

As far as idols were concerned, there existed no greater talent than the one who stood before them. To *not* make her into an idol would be to desecrate the treasures heaven had bestowed upon them. Sora explained as much and soon felt Steph's icy gaze piercing through him.

"...So basically, this idol thing is just something you personally want to do."

"A cheeky one, you are; really cheeky! This plan is a perfect fusion of my arbitrary desires and actual benefit!!"

As he spoke, Sora thought: *Let's imagine it. A state whose authority is personified in an unmatchable, literally goddess-level babe, the perfect idol...*

Sora knew, as did Shiro: *I'd move there immediately!*

Sora looked far, far into the distance, toward his boundless ideals, as he spoke...

"What overcomes the barriers of race and brings a country together as one? ...*Love.* What is love? Affection, faith—*worship.* One who is worshipped is called a god. Also known as an icon. Otherwise known as an idol. Which can only mean a cute girl. And therefore, Holou! My logic is bulletproof. If you think you can refute it, just try!"

"...Well, yes, it is impossible to argue with specious nonsense."

The bounds Sora's syllogism took between each of its seven steps were quite exhilarating. Steph replied with a skeptical squint as Holou continued to sulk.

"Then instruct me specifically in what ye would define as a 'perfect idol'! I shall recreate it for you!"

Sora and Shiro sighed and shook their heads at Holou.

"*Hff...* You're talking to two who have mastered idol-raising games of every stripe."

"...Building...the perfect...character...is not, that hard..."

A sleazy grin spread across Sora's face as he spoke.

"Look. You just need the right choreography that'll look sexy but, y'know, not *too* sexy! And then you get the costumes, and the songs with phrases like, 'I love you so much'! And you have her cough up lines here and there like, 'I love allll my fans! ♥' And you give them the hope that they might actually have a chance with you, so you get them to line up for a meet and greet, you close the distance, and *bam*! There ya go!"

Besides, just look at Holou's beauty. An Old Deus shouldn't have any problem performing perfectly.

"I'd bet on it. You're gonna bring us a buttload of fans and a truck-load of money."

"...Is it just my imagination, Sora, or do you sound bitter?"

Steph caught the dark trauma behind Sora's eyes, but he went on.

"But remember what we said. We're gonna make you a *star*."

"...Not two-dimensional, not fiction...not even three-dimensional, or plastic...but a *perfect idol*..."

Sora and Shiro paced in no particular direction as they defined just what it meant to be a star, a *perfect idol*!

"What we seek is the unrealistic spirituality of two-dimensionality, combined with real life and the presence of three-dimensionality, to make something that is neither two-point-five-dimensional nor three-point-five-dimensional, nor four-dimensional, nor... Uh...?"

Sora's passionate spiel ground to a halt. He looked to Holou.

"Holou, you said you're 'polygenetic,' right? Like, how many?"

"I-it dependeth on the definition... But we might suppose that Holou's nuclear coordinates lie on 13 + iR variable dimensions—"

"Exactly! Like, over eleven dimensions! Literally an idol from another dimension!"

Sora brazenly plowed right through this report, which flew in the face of his old world's understanding of physics! Then, even more courageously, he bellowed out his lofty ideals!!

"She is the hope that allows us to live! Even if she should have a boyfriend, get married, grow old!! A blessed being who will sob tears of gratitude! *That* is our Avalon, the distant ideal which we envision—the perfect idol..."

Having come to the close of their heated discourse, the young man and his little sister held a brief silence as if to bask in the afterglow.

"...Do you see?"

"I do not."

"Nor do I."

God and human alike rejected the call to their ideals out of hand.

"Well, it's all right if you don't understand! I mean, it's not like we do, either!"

"...Nod, nod."

They'd said all that only to end with "We dunno, either." Cynical stares met their enthusiastic nods.

"Still, I have faith in you, Holou. You'll be the one." Sora smiled wistfully. Maybe she'd even *transcend* his ideal. "I mean, you don't age, and you don't even go to the bathroom! How could anyone question whether or not you're destined to be an idol?"

His eyes agleam, Sora had made his last, but certainly not least point—

"...No... I've had enough... My stomach is full..."

—and Steph choked out a nauseous refusal.

"That's fine! We'll resume Holou's lesson. '(Save Me) Godly Summer ☆,' from the top!"

"...You'd better...prove yourself, today...or tomorrow's gonna be, ugly...Holou."

"H-Holou is not finished! She grasped not the meaning of even half of your statements— Oh! Sora! Shiro!"

Holou protested in vain as Sora and Shiro dragged her off.

Steph sighed to herself. "We could be attacked at any time..."

Sora answered anyway. "Hmm? We're not getting attacked."

He jabbered on. "Didn't I tell you? We closed the castle because there's nothing to do." There was no useful move for Elkia to make. Sora rehashed the first reason. "They can't attack us. No one can do shit about us the way we are now."

"......"

He knew what Steph's silence meant as she peered at him. The Commonwealth of Elkia had domestic issues from its too-rapid expansion. Yeah, that was a pain. But that could be perfectly well cleaned up by the rest of the currently on-break castle. You know, by Steph.

What was important was how Sora and Shiro, the monarch of Immanity, were seen from *outside*. Here, there was a great country that had subdued numerous races, even higher races, and absorbed them into itself to swell with riches. And it wasn't simply overt games—they'd even beaten Elven Gard, the greatest country in the world, indirectly, without even fighting them! They'd swiped their land and thrown the rest of their nation into internal tumult. Now people might think that their own nations were in the process of getting undermined. Becoming a great country? Multiracial commonwealth? Who cared about all that? Here's what Elkia really was, as far as anyone was concerned.

—A conquering empire, ready to take on everything through games.

And its king and queen were some kind of incomprehensible freaks who kept playing and winning, even against gods. If put in terms of a strategy game, they were winning too much. This is where all the other players would start ganking them from all sides. But Sora smirked. It was futile.

"Who's gonna try to play Elkia—I mean, Shiro and me—now?" Sure, they might be owning any and all competition, but that was precisely why no one could challenge them. But, as Sora went on to languidly point out, that was precisely the problem. "Still, it's true we gotta stay on the ball. Since, you know—they're gonna have to play *someone else*."

"...Oh! So...they'll start with the Eastern Union or Oceand?!" How could it be that they could halt the administration of Elkia, now at last the linchpin of a commonwealth, without issue? Steph exclaimed as if now she saw at least one reason.

Indeed. Ordinary administration must be the least of the worries of the other countries of the Commonwealth. There were surely forces spying, slipping in to undermine.

"Yeah... But the Eastern Union's game is still unbeatable... So?" It truly is busy work...figuring out how to squeeze their foes for all they've got.

"Even so, it's not time for us to take the initiative...so there's no move for us to make. And what do you do then?"

"...*Skip a turn*..."

"......"

Okay, then. Their trap was ticking along just fine behind the scenes. Their associated states were utilizing it to its fullest, ordinary administration be damned. Even so, it looked as if Steph wasn't convinced that this was enough of a reason to shut down Elkia's government.

"...Shiro and I aren't even looking for people to trust us." Sora grinned and thought, *That's not who we are, d00d.* Sure, people might call them the monarch or the agent plenipotentiary or whatever, but at the end of the day, they were just gamers. "It's always best to leave things to the experts. So we leave politics to the politicians." Likewise, leave gaming to the gamers. "We stick to what we're good at. We solve problems the way gamers do."

"...*Hff*... All right." Steph couldn't help but chuckle at Sora's positivity. "So I take it you two have something in mind." But she still did not seem entirely satisfied.

Whenever Sora and Shiro did anything, there was always...*something* behind it. By this point in her acquaintance with them, Steph could figure this out. Still, given that they, as ever, showed no interest in sharing it with her, she had to get in at least one jab:

"But, Sora, you've misread many things lately... Is everything okay?"

"Misread?! Me?! When, where, and at what hour and minute of what day of this planet's revolution?!"

In that game they'd played with Holou the other day—the game against Old Deus—Sora had misread a few things. " " had even admitted a *defeat*. Steph baited him with this effectively.

"...Brother, you dork... You're like, a little kid..."

"An actual little kid is telling me this?! Fine, I misread things! I'll never do it again, okay?!"

But he merely shouted back in desperation under Shiro's icy gaze. Their voices sounded as if they were just joking around, but if you looked into their eyes, you could see the resentment bubbling up from within.

It seemed Steph could tell it was no joke to them.

"So! Just how are you planning to exploit me now, to the point of *closing the rest of the administration*?" *That's why you've blockaded the castle, isn't it?* Steph smiled bitterly.

"Oh, Steph, you're getting the picture! Here ya go!"

"...Holou's...costume..."

Sora and Shiro shoved a sheaf of papers at Steph and smiled back.

"By tomorrow, okay? We don't have anyone else who can do the job. You'll make it in time, right?!"

"...Don't worry, Brother... *No*...is for liars..."

These corporate scumbags seemed ripe for a scandal.

Steph gazed into the distance and mumbled:

"...Now that I think of it... You never give me a day off..."

■■■

Outside the Elkia Royal Castle, where about a million flags' worth of foreshadowing was taking place, a group in black was weaving through the din of the merchants on Main Street. Cloaked in robes from head to toe, with hoods pulled low over their eyes, they hid their faces from view. The group silently marched forward in the most inconspicuous way possible.

```
Seher report: Old Deus response con-
firmed. Target coordinates estimated as
Elkia Royal Castle.
```

Prüfer report: Coordinates identified:
Agent   plenipotentiary   of   Immanity.
Inferred name: Sora.

They shared the data from their long-range observation and crowd noise analysis as they walked forward. Forward, ever forward...

—Acknowledged. All units, *prepare to engage target.* Start advance calculations.

In accordance with the destiny of flags to be checked, of foreshadowing to be fulfilled, they marched on, in Sora's direction: forward...

⏻ CHAPTER 1
DEFINITE
HALTING PROBLEM

It was where Sora and Shiro had given their coronation speech. Now, standing on the balcony of the Elkia Royal Castle overlooking the square, was a lone girl. Her clothes flapping in the wind, her inkpot floating in the air, she closed her eyes—and waited. Then came the signal of which Sora and Shiro had spoken, the sound to herald the epic debut of a new idol. The music exploded at a high volume.

"H-Holou is Holou! Though she comprehendeth not, she is an idol? ...So it seems!!"

With this cryptic introduction, she began to move her mouth and body. True to her word, it appeared that she had no idea what was going on, but she didn't let it stop her. She didn't let the line "Introduction/ad lib" in the script she'd been handed just before break her. This divine young girl, Holou, sang and danced, unaware of the hints of tears forming in her eyes.

There were four people who were paying especially close attention. One was Jibril, the Flügel girl sneering from the sky. The other three, watching Jibril's projection of her vision on a magical screen, were Sora and Shiro, pouting on the throne, and Steph, swaying from insomnia beside them.

This would be a good time to describe the incessant mumblings that had emanated from Steph as she spent the night making Holou's costume:

I see. So Sora and Shiro intend to make Holou out to be the villain. But even if she said, "I'm a god. Sora and Shiro owe their success to me. And by the way, I'm an idol." Just who was going to take those ramblings and say, "Oh, I see!!"? And just what kind of morons go and cheer this on like, "Oooohhh!"?

That was why Steph had asked Sora and Shiro any number of times what their *real* purpose was. Now—

"……This can't be……"

—the cheers of "Oooohhh!" echoed from beyond the screen from the thousands who had gathered at the square to see Holou. Thousands might have hardly amounted to a fraction of the population of the Commonwealth, but it had to be said that there the morons were, waving their hands.

"…Perhaps Immanity is done for…"

Come to think of it, there had been cheers at the game with the Eastern Union as well, when the Immanity Piece had been at stake. And those cheers had been for the destruction of bras and panties. She should have learned something about the culture of her people then. Perhaps there was no use worrying about the country's internal affairs.

Steph's smile was a hollow one, out of an optimism founded on resignation. Meanwhile, the two malcontents on the throne grumbled with smiles most dangerous:

"Damn it, this suuucks. Hmph… We won't forgive this."

"…Heh, heh-heh-heh-heh… You've got some…nerve…"

Steph interjected:

"You mean Holou? It's a good song, and she's doing her best given the absurdity you've put her through."

"Yeah… Of *course* the song's good, and Holou's trying hard. That's the thing."

At first, they had planned to use the hit songs on their phones they'd brought from their old world. Until Shiro whispered…

"…*They'll come, you know? JASR*C's gonna get us, even if we're in another world.*"

So they made their own sound using the deft phrases of Laila and the Sirens, the slick progressions of Fiel and the Elves, and the magic of tablet music software. Of course it was good. Making music is easy even when you're in another world…with this tablet!

And no one could deny that Holou was doing her best singing and dancing. Apparently still unable to grasp the concept of expression, her movements were stiff and her voice was devoid of feeling. Yet, even so, the girl who had doubted eternity was trying.

And that was precisely the thing—!!

"It's the stage, the *stage*! The heck's with that crappy set?!"

Sora pointed to Jibril's projected image of the balcony where Holou stood. It was supposed to be a stage decked in lavish effects made possible by the equipment of the Eastern Union. Instead, it was just a balcony. Thus, Sora howled.

"They caved to the agency's pressure and canceled on us at the last minute?! WTF?!"

Elkia did not have an idol industry. This made for the best possible "blue ocean" market space, a potential for monopolization that Sora and Shiro gloated over. However, the Eastern Union had not only an idol industry, but agencies as well—and they appeared to be fairly antagonistic. So they'd told Sora and Shiro they wouldn't give them the equipment for this critical debut concert—*the day of.*

"Way to pick on the little guy! They're totally messing with us!!"

"…What difference does it make? Holou's what's most important, isn't she?" said Steph, completely at sea, in response to Sora's rage—but all it did was fan the flames.

"We've literally got a goddess here!! Look at this crappy stage! How easy do you think it is to get signed with a big label once you've gotten pigeonholed as an underground idol? This is a major strategy issue!!"

"Your words elude me, Sir! But why didn't you just ask someone else?!"

Who else? …Of course. Any one of the other races in the Commonwealth. The Flügel had Jibril, the Old Dei had Holou, the Dhampirs had Plum… These magic-users could be counted on to do more than just special effects. They'd physically change the entire environment. But!

"That's what we *would* have done, if we had *time*! Which is why I'm so pissed they canceled the day of!!"

Effects would require some fiddly rite compilation, which was not Jibril's specialty. It would take her some time.

Holou would first have to comprehend Sora and Shiro's will, which would take even more time.

The Dhampirs' illusion magic would make it easy…if Plum cooperated. Not happening.

And so it came to pass that the production consisted of Shiro playing music from her phone and Holou amplifying her own voice. Sora and Shiro both licked their lips and laughed savagely at this epic half-assery.

"You bastards have got some nerve making an enemy of the state. I like you. I'll kill you *first*."

"…We'll show you…what happens…when you, cross…the government…!"

A major agency, are you? So what? We are Bl4nk Productions, the only agency directly operated by the state! If you think we're the little guys, you picked the wrong fight!!

"Could you not abuse your power so openly?! You're the monarch!!" Steph hollered in a desperate attempt to interrupt their villainous train of thought, but the two didn't seem to hear her, as they kept on deliberating...

"Anyway, Sora? Shirooo...? *Sigh*... Producers?!"

"...Hmph, what? We're gonna smash, all the agencies, in the Eastern Union...and steal...their idols."

"So we're thinking about how we're gonna produce them! Is your business more important than that?!"

"*Any* business is more important than that! So!"

Having slashed straight through Sora and Shiro's deep devices, Steph kept on hollering.

"Do any of those people waving their hands out there really believe that Holou is the culprit?!"

If they did, Immanity was in its last days, Steph lamented. Sora chuckled.

"Well, probably not many. For now."

"...What?"

"I said this before, but there's no need to believe."

Her concept—her ether—was wisdom, conceived of doubt and hope.

"Whether they believe or not—their doubt will power her."

Doubts and desires, rejection and wishing—all would amplify her power. *And this is the most important part*, Sora thought with a sharp glint in his eye.

"It's a cute girl doing her best to sing and dance... Whether you get it or not, who could *not* wave their hands?!"

"I had hoped most everyone..."

Steph gazed into the distance, her eyes full of sincere sorrow for Immanity. Sora laughed and went on.

"Also, if Holou does this legit, no one's gonna be able to attack us."

"...You were saying something like that yesterday. What do you mean?"

—Hmm.

Having adjusted their plans from here on somewhat, Sora and Shiro nodded subtly. Then they slowly looked back at Steph, and in place of an answer—

"Okay, it's time! Steeeph! We've got a quiz for you!!"

"...'What do people think Sora and Shiro are?' ...Ten seconds...!"

"Uh, what?!"

—they responded with a question. Panicking, Steph listed whatever she could think of.

"Y-you're the monarch of Elkia, you're Immanities... Oh, and you're from another world. Also—" She glanced at Sora, blushed as she choked on her words for a second, and continued. "You're twisted and perverse. Your personalities are atrocious, you're frauds—"

"Hey, enough with the 'It's okay to call him bald because he is' theory! Truth hurts, damn it!"

And Sora and Shiro were considerably hurt.

"...Bzzz... Your ten seconds...are up... You're...stupid."

"Pay attention to the question, sacrificial pawn. You're talking about what you *know* we are."

Deftly slipping in his mark of disapproval, Sora pointed out her error.

"We asked what people—most people—*think* we are."

"Um... Uh?"

Steph still seemed befuddled. Sora rose from the throne.

"In Immanity's darkest hour...suddenly arose two *heroes!*"

Sora spoke with passion, his voice projecting far and wide, his movements exaggerated like those of a trained stage performer!

"They beat the Eastern Union's game that not even Elf could beat! They even defeated Oceand's game, which no one had yet been able to! They defeated Flügel; against all odds, they defeated Old Deus! So valiant were our heroes, only the third in history to bring down a god, as they came to make every evil empire shake in its boots! But the truth was...they were *just humans?* Who's gonna believe that?"

He wrapped up with a voice suddenly chilled.

"And not just *any humans*. They were shut-in gamer losers, on the low end even among their species. In the words of a certain princess…they were twisted, perverse, atrocious frauds. How could they do that?"

Steph let out a small groan at Sora's backhanded speech.

…Well. They could, actually. Or rather, they did. But—

"Man, I sure couldn't do that! I mean, I'm an Immanity! You know how Immanities are; they're those disgusting worthless insects who've just barely managed to stay alive, right? What now, what now? What's this? It's like, you know, as if—"

Sora squeezed out the grin that tended to activate one's reflex to punch him—and followed up—

"—they're totally different people!"

"Oh…! Y-you mean like Chlammy in the tournament for the monarchy?"

Sora and Shiro smiled to see that Steph finally got it. Chlammy had thought that Sora and Shiro had seen through Elven magic. And she'd assumed that mere Immanities couldn't possibly.

"Pop quiz: What do people think Sora and Shiro are?"

"…Answer: Agents…of another race…another country… *Spies*…"

That's right. Sora and Shiro had been consistent in what they'd *made* people think they were. As when they had declared war on the entire world at their coronation—*mysterious agents of some unseen power*. And that bluff still held strong—no, stronger. Why?

"Okay, so we've established that little twits like us could never do such a thing. So who could?"

Steph stood silent, unable to think of anyone. But Sora smiled in approval.

No one could. Well…Sora and Shiro could. Other races probably could have. But as a simple matter of fact, to this day, no one had.

"…You know what that means? We're the ones who do what no one can—"

An absurd suspicion, but—

"We're the ones who can win any game—so they suspect we've got some mysterious, unbeatable trump card."

"…Which is…way too dangerous… To take it head-on…would be, suicide…"

—now that they'd defeated even Old Deus, that suspicion began to sound like reality. So then what? Steph finally connected it back to the beginning:

"Oh! S-so they'll come to cut us down from the periphery… Is that what you mean?!"

"Yep. All they can do is poke at us to find out what we are—to reveal our invincible trump card."

"…And they have to…do it fast…before, anyone else…*even at the cost of losing…*"

"…? Even at the cost of losing?"

"We're talking about a trump card that can beat anyone. You gotta do something about that, right? Seal it or own it."

Moderate losses could not be begrudged in this process. By those who little knew that it was all futile.

"But we don't have any such trump card, nor any such secret identity to find. ♪ 'Cos all we are is mere humans who just straight-out won the games—which is exactly what no one's gonna believe! ♪"

"…So…these chumps…are gonna look, for what's not there…lose their stuff…and go home! ♪"

Their devilish grins made Steph take a step back.

"Oh… You know, someone might even get the wrong idea about whose spy we are."

"…? Whose?"

Who could do what no one could and produce a trump card that could beat anyone? Thinking that Sora and Shiro, being from another world, would be good targets for blame. Sora chuckled—and said his name with sympathy.

"Tet's. Like he got bored and decided to troll everyone by making us out to be some cosmic threat. ♪"

After all, there was no doubt that Tet, the One True God, had been the one who summoned them here. It was a far likelier story than that mere humans had beaten higher races.

"Well, I gotta feel sorry for Tet, but it's the final boss's job to stir up animosity."

"...Tet... Stay...strong..."

Lightly trolling Tet, Sora and Shiro put that aside and looked back at the screen with discontent.

"H-how lightly you invoke the name of the One True God..."

They went back to their interrupted thoughts, seeming to have no more interest in Steph's muttering.

Sora and Shiro had already adjusted their plan for what to do about those idol agencies in the Eastern Union. But to actually do it, there was this thing—

"Question is, what will we do about Holou's next concert... right...?"

There was very little problem with the agenda in their task scheduler. Meet and greets, autograph sessions, friendly visits to various companies—all that basic footwork was pretty solid. But watching Holou valiantly sing and dance on that crappy stage made Sora and Shiro grind their teeth.

—*If the next show in five days' time goes down like this, we won't be able to call ourselves producers.*

At the very least, maybe they should just procure the equipment itself from the Eastern Union— No, someone would probably get in their way again.

"We've got no choice, Shiro. Let's have Jibril weave us an effects spell. If we've got five days—"

"...I-is it okay? Somehow...I can only, imagine...something, exploding..."

"I-in the worst case, we'll have Elkian artisans make us a set. But the only one we can count on for effects is Jibril. I mean, we could have her make a virtual space or something... Let's be specific about the image we're looking for."

In other words: *At the very least, let's not kill anyone.* They opened an app on their tablet, not wanting to trust the Ten Covenants too much. The two of them were no artists, but they were trying to draw Holou's stage effects and share them. There they were, discussing it with each other and sliding their fingers over the screen, when—

—*Ding-a-linggg, da-ding-a-ling-la-ling...*

Sora, Shiro, and Steph all gawked at the sudden unfamiliar sound.

"......Brother...phone..."

Shiro remembered now—it was the ringtone Sora had set.

"Ha-ha-ha... My sister, your big brother's phone exists only to play games. I know you know this."

While Sora laughed at himself, he took his phone in hand. An unfamiliar sound, indeed. No wonder. He couldn't remember when he'd last heard it... After all...

"Not to brag, but your brother's friend list is perpetually at zero. Who'd call me?!"

"...You really aren't bragging..."

Cleanly wiping the pity-eyed words of Steph from his memory, Sora expertly flicked the incoming call from a private number to reject it—

"It's either a wrong number or a delivery... But in any case, it's a pain in the ass to get this out—"

—but before he finished the gesture or his sentence, he and Shiro looked at each other. It was so sudden, so incredibly unexpected that it took them so long to notice how freaky this was.

—*Why would his phone ring on Disboard?*

"Hello...? Who's this?"

But not even a second after this realization, a torrent of thoughts went through Sora's head. He immediately decided he had to answer—so he did. While his phone still read *No service*—

"⠮⠂⠶⡏⠩⡏⠹⠂⠱⠒⠱⠌⠻⠏⡯⠨⠹⠯⡯⠻⠹⠱⠹⡏⠹⠈⠾⠒"

—all that came through on speakerphone was just noise.

"...? What is this? It's just noise, correct?"

"...Some, kinda...cursed...phone call?"

"Yeah... I *wish* it was only a cursed phone call..."

While Steph and Shiro seemed dubious, Sora responded with apprehension. A beat later, Shiro, too, clouded with panic as she realized.

As far as they knew, Disboard didn't even *have* the concept of radio waves. This was why Sora, upon asking himself, *Should I ignore it?* immediately answered back, *No*, and picked up the phone. If there was some kind of magnetic field that had been caused by magic—say, some indiscriminate accident—then it wasn't just about whether to pick up; they'd have to shut off both their phones and their tablet right now or risk losing them. On the other hand, if it was *deliberate intervention*, that was an even bigger problem...which they couldn't let stand. And as if to answer his caution and confusion—

"⁝∴⁝. **encryption** ∶⁝.⁝ **principle—analysis** ⁝∶ **complete** ⁝⁝∶˙ **magnetic field** ∶⁝ **control** ⁝.˙⁝ **test**"

"_____?!!"

Sora and Shiro went pale as the creepy noise began to fade into something like a voice.

"...? What is this? What is going on?"

No one answered Steph. Sora and Shiro didn't even know. Even so, they knew well enough this was trouble. After all—

—Someone was meddling with this world's technology. Disboard had neither radio nor base stations, and this phone signal had even implemented scrambling.

No. They shouldn't even know that this device was used for communication. Yet, here the signal was.

An evil phone call? This was a horror far more hair-raising than some stupid curse. And it went on:

"Bidirectional communication established—able to initiate conversation."

In this short time, someone had uncovered, analyzed, and mastered a technology that didn't exist in this world. After the clear intonation that replaced the noise came the echo of a man's voice.

"We request an audience with you, O King of Immanity, O Spieler. We—are Ex Machina."

It was as they had feared: a targeted intervention from someone they couldn't just ignore. They'd have to figure out how much this individual knew about them and their plans.

—*This could overturn their strategy from the very bottom.* Sora replied:

"...Sure thing, bro. Let's meet."

He muffled any emotion in his voice and answered back into the phone. That instant—

There was no sound nor wind, no shock, no vibration, nothing... Let alone any context. But the area that stretched from the front of the Elkia Royal Castle to the throne room suddenly turned into a path of rubble.

"............Come again?"

It took several full seconds for Sora to be able to manage a response. Before him was a group clad in black, leisurely wending down the avenue of destruction. He let out a silent scream.

—*No way. They smashed the castle in only a second? That's not just some bullshit—it's not even* possible!! *The Ten Covenants are supposed to prevent destruction of others' property without consent! So...*what kind of fraud is this?

Sora glared sharply at the strangers before him and was answered by the man who headed the procession.

"...We are unable to shift to coordinates outside our vision and scope of knowledge, you see..."

With each step the group took, the rubble they left behind warped and vanished...until, by the time they stood before Sora and Shiro, it was as if nothing had happened.

"…Therefore, we took it upon ourselves to rewrite space… We beg your indulgence of our indiscretion."

And there they were, all in order before them in a throne room restored to normal. Hmm… It was as if to say, *Apologies for the temporary entrance!*

"…Look, you guys… Don't you think you should knock first, or send someone, or take any one of countless other proper procedures?"

"S-Sora… Th-the castle is closed… All the staff are on holiday!"

"Ohhh, yeah. Anyway, what is that thing you did? That's so useful. Would be perfect for stage—"

"…B-Brother! C-calm down…! Get, a grip…!"

The series of shocking events was starting to throw Sora's thoughts out of alignment. As Shiro shook him in a frantic attempt to fix him, the group in black silently, mechanically doffed their robes.

There were thirteen of them draped in black like the grim reaper. Sorry, correction: not people, but robots. Beneath the skin of their joints lay not flesh, but metal. Drooping on the floor were not their tails, but their cables. Sora and Shiro knew this group. They'd seen them in the Great War simulation game. They were, just as they said—

—Ixseed Rank Ten… *Ex Machina.*

"Soraaa? I can say it now, can't I? There, you've already misread something!"

—*Who was the smart-ass who was just saying that no one could attack them?* Sora was too occupied to answer Steph's squeaky interrogation. The twenty-six artificial lenses of the unhooded Ex Machinas were all focused on him. Their presence was inorganically overbearing, like being inside a server room. Their every movement gave the stifling illusion that every pulse, every nerve signal in Sora's and Shiro's bodies was under scrutiny. Or was it an illusion? Amidst his thoughts jumbled by panic, Sora silently answered Steph.

* * *

—I didn't misread anything... I just don't get this—!!
No one could challenge Sora and Shiro head-on as they were—
that much was an unshakeable fact! At the very least, Sora and
Shiro didn't look like the types to have some sort of ace in the hole.
Regardless, if they were to be challenged, they held the right to
determine the game. And on top of that, Sora and Shiro had nothing motivating them *to agree to a game they were likely to lose!* They
could just propose a game they'd win for sure, or not play at all!!
He said no one would attack them because he was certain everyone
knew this. So why—?

This was a race of people that Sora and Shiro themselves didn't
even know how to find, one they barely understood. Why, of all
things, would a completely unknown race—

—against whom " " might lose in a face-to-face fight show up here?!
Why had they focused on him—?!

"...I apologize that I have no true name. My designation is Einzig."
Disregarding the chaos, one of the thirteen stepped forth and
bowed lightly. He looked perhaps a good decade older than Sora. At
the very least, he appeared male. His face seemed unnaturally—well,
he was a machine, so that's a given—and rather perfectly sculpted,
like that of a doll. His reddish-black hair and pale blue eyes gave the
inescapable sense of something inorganic, artificial.
But.

"As such, I am Ex Machina's... Mmm. Agent plenipotentiary, I
suppose you would say."
As this "Einzig" approached them, there was clearly something
more than mechanical lurking within his voice and eyes: intelli-
gence, and *emotions.* It brought a cold sweat to Sora's and Shiro's
faces.

If they were just machines, it would be no matter. Be it a super-computer, a machine was just a machine. Especially when it came to games, there were plenty of ways to outstrip and transcend machines. But if this was the race that had slain the strongest of the gods, Artosh, and triggered the end of the war— If this was the race that had learned infinitely, adapted repeatedly, and in the end slain the strongest— If this was all true... Then, if the feeling contained in those eyes was a shard of the proof... If their fears from the intervention by Sora's phone were justified... If Sora's and Shiro's true identities, and even their strategy, were leaked...

It would mean that even " " could throw any game at them—
—and still be all but completely unable to win.

Confusion and panic brought Sora's thoughts to a clear state of emergency, but the mechanical man before him froze them in place. Ten Covenants. Can't harm. But still— No, *therefore*, the man stretched out his hand. It went past Sora's cheek and touched the throne as the man spoke:
"I have longed to see you, Spieler. Come, let us build our love."

Shiro turned to stone, while Steph covered her mouth and blushed. (What was she so happy about?) This sudden whisper of devotion caused Sora to make just one wish with all his strength before shutting down his consciousness:
Begone, foul memory...

Sora's consciousness drifted to the surface... It was a feeling he knew well, the feeling of waking up. He sighed in relief.

...That was the worst dream ever. He must have been overexerting himself. Better rest a bit. But now—

".......Brother...... Brother, wake up..."

That's right. See, Shiro was calling him. Time to forget about stupid dreams and answer his little sister's call. Sora smiled gently and slowly opened his eyes—he'd see Shiro, and probably Steph, and...

"Remonstration: This unit will repeat once. Transfer command. Current Einzig lacks aptitude for mission."

"I shall repeat myself as many times as it takes: No. The Spieler's chastity belongs to me alone."

Sora also saw the man who had whispered his love to him bickering with a female Ex Machina.

Ah, how cruel. To think that not only was it not a dream, but that his memory remained intact—

"It belongs to *me* alone!! Wait, did I just announce I'll be a virgin forever?!"

Sora's wholehearted curse shook the castle as he jumped up.

"...Oh... Oh, good... Brother, you're—you're...alive...!"

"Of course I am!! What could be worse than having a heart attack when a guy confesses his feelings to me?! Hey, asshole!!"

Grabbing Shiro, who was crying in relief, Sora pointed to Einzig and bellowed on.

"You're gay, a pretty boy, *and* an android?! That's overkill! D00d, have some self-contr—"

He stopped and took another look around at the Ex Machinas before starting up again.

"*And* you're a *butler*? You're going all out, aren't you? Just who's your target audience here?!"

That analytical, scrutinizing presence was now gone. This was not the macabre, solemn black garb of the ranks of god-killing machines.

...Well, their garb was still solemn, and black...but in the manner of a *tailcoat* and *maid costumes.*

So basically...one butler robot and twelve maid robots.

Plus, they were... How to describe it...? Overall...*slack.* It was their expressions or something that gave off this inescapable whiff of a pile of junk.

Sora wanted to scream, *Give me back my dignity!*

Einzig, the gay butler, answered:

"Hmm... Though perhaps your question was rhetorical, I can only answer that the audience I am targeting is you."

"Oh yeah? Well, you missed by a mile! I don't know what you're here for, but leave your maid robots and go home!!"

Einzig smiled at the belligerent Sora as if to comfort him. As if seeing through his continued roiling to the panic inside, he spoke.

"Fear not, Spieler. We have come to assist you. *We are your allies.*"

......

Einzig's announcement only caused Sora to clutch at his head.

—*I can't take this anymore. I just can't figure it out—why they're here, why they're junk, why they're "allies"! And why, most of all, they've got a gay pretty boy butler and maid robots!!*

Sora lost control and screamed the magic words:

"Jibriemoon!! Help meeeee!!"

Not a moment later:

"Here I am! ♥ From one 'Good morning' to the next, I am Jibril, overseeing the lives of my masters! ♪ Did you call me to serve?! Or to slay?!"

Jibril, the Flügel who had been remotely projecting Holou, appeared from the sky. Full of excitement, a smile spread wide across her face, she took one look at her surroundings, and—

"Oh my! Good heavens... Ex Machinas! I should expect no less from my masters. What luck you have for finding rare items!"

—neither party hesitated.

"You've called me to *slay*! ♥ Wait just four seconds— Oh?"

"Deployment: Irregular Number elimination sequence— Error. Requesting factor identification."

Jibril produced a blade of light, while the Ex Machinas simultaneously deployed their massive weapons—and they all froze, seemingly confused. Apparently, they'd completely forgotten about the Ten Covenants.

"...Look, am I asking for too much? Isn't there any sane person who can explain to us what's going on?" Sora pleaded.

With the next Great War that had been about to start before his very eyes forcibly canceled, Sora gazed into the distance and thought, *Tet. Sorry for trolling you.* He and Shiro offered a prayer of thanks to the One True God for the Ten Covenants.

—*Ahem.* Someone cleared her throat.

"...Ex Machina, the god-killing race that slew the god of war Artosh in the Great War." Jibril smiled as if to assert that she was sane. "They also annihilated half the Flügel. Truly the most saaaavage and barbaric of killing machines! ♥"

Look who's talking. Weren't you the one who was just making a seamless transition into a genocide? All three Immanities looked at Jibril, unconvinced, but she continued on.

"But it seems that the spoils were more than they deserved. Posthaste, they were all but exterminated." Casually, Jibril added, "No new units have been observed since then. It is speculated that they lost their ability to produce new ones."

"...Wait. You mean...the *ability to reproduce*?"

She dropped this critical information on everyone way too casually. Sora furrowed his brow as he checked. Jibril nodded.

"Indeed. Since the Great War, individual units have been seen wandering about on rare occasion, but they've always been units that existed at the end of the War. It's about time they were designated an endangered species, don't you think? ♪"

......

In other words, these were the ones who massacred Jibril's creator and kin. And they were face-to-face with someone who all but annihilated their race. Not to mention, this wasn't a case of their ancestors having fought each other... It was they themselves...

"...Uh, yeah... I guess there's some bad blood there..."

"......"

—*The Great War was a long time ago. It's over. Water under the bridge.*

...It was hard to say that to the very parties who had nearly killed one another off. Sora, Shiro, and Steph screwed up their faces and looked down.

"What? I have never lost to an Ex Machina, nor do I harbor them any resentment," Jibril said blankly.

The three of them stared at her, wide-eyed.

"I am well aware of the *respect* I must pay to such an able foe."

"But weren't you just talking about slaying them?"

Seeing Jibril's smug face, Sora couldn't help but take a shot.

"...We killed them. It is inevitable that they would come to kill us. Why should such natural order demand resentment?"

"But weren't you just talking about eliminating her?!"

Seeing Einzig's similarly smug face, Sora was about to deliver his comeback, but...

"...? Of course. I shall kill them with the utmost of my respect, hospitality, and vigor."

"Fear not. We are now capable of permanently disabling all functions of the Regular Number without killing her."

"What's the difference between permanently disabling all of someone's functions and killing—? Uh, never mind."

—*We're not mad. We're just gonna kill 'em.* The humans gave up on debating this theory and took it with strained smiles.

"In any case, allow me to correct you on one fine detail, Irregular Number. We have not lost the ability to reproduce. We have only been waiting for the right partner," the Ex Machina proudly stated.

It's not that I can't get married; I just haven't found the one. Einzig's assertion felt strangely familiar.

"And that, indeed, is what brought us here..."

Suddenly, he looked at Sora and the others with a totally straight face, in turn causing their expressions to tense.

Ex Machina was on the brink of extinction. And why were they here, right now, in front of them? And what did they mean, "allies"? *Depending on their answer...* Sora, Shiro, and even Jibril seemed cautious.

"Yes, you are *the one*, O Spieler—who now calls himself Sora, as I understand..." Amidst everyone's stares, Einzig took another step toward Sora. "Yes, it is you, Spieler!! Come, let us build our love. Let us reproduce!!"

"Not this agaaaain!! And don't strip! Are you broken or something?!"

At the sight of the stripping sex robot, Sora covered Shiro's eyes and shouted out what he half knew to be true. They were from the Great War—six thousand years ago. Antiques? They were artifacts.

"...Indeed. I have already exceeded my service life by five thousand nine hundred eighty-two years. Though I might utilize sleep mode to the fullest to extend it, functional degradation is inevitable—but fear not, Spieler!" Einzig paused his disrobing and smiled. "My thoughts and my love are still in perfect working order!"

"If your thoughts are designed to lead to this behavior, that's an even bigger problem!!" Sora clutched his head and screamed at Einzig, who had resumed stripping.

"What do you think, Masters? Shall we go ahead and kill him for now?"

"...Jibril, I, permit it...!"

"What good will your permission do?! P-please, let us all calm—"

Jibril and Shiro, spurred to bloodlust, and Steph, struggling to soothe them—

—were interrupted by a whooshing sound followed by a loud crash. The stripper had been thrust into the wall like a stake...

"Vote: Progress stalled. Responsible unit temporarily stripped of command. Command inherited by current unit."

...and stepping forth was the female Ex Machina who had been arguing with Einzig. Like the others, she was clad in a maid costume. She looked like a human girl in her midteens, though she was a machine. She, too, had that perfect doll face. The female Ex Machina lowered her head, capped in ineffably unnatural violet hair, courteously plucked up her skirt and curtsied, and continued.

"Apology: Severe bug observed in subset of population."

"It's severe, all right. Someone's liable to get sued for this—but wait, did you just finish him off...?"

It had happened too fast for him to see, but he presumed she had kicked him into the wall. There the half-naked pervert was, twitching—not a very tasteful wall ornament, but it made Sora wonder.

...Doesn't this infringe on the Covenants? Is this that consent thing?

"Addendum: Ex Machina units are synchronized in cluster, lack individual identity. Self-harm allowed by Covenants. Also, forceful contact of this unit's leg determined to be an unfortunate accident. This unit is absolved of any wrongdoing."

...So it was like how processors in a parallel configuration were counted as one? In any case, the Ex Machinas had an agreement—so it was fine.

The mechanical girl who had eliminated the provocative pervert continued to speak.

"Objective: Requesting cooperation. Purpose: Preventing extinction of Ex Machina."

—Ahhh! The savior of coherent discourse has come! Sora was overjoyed.

"Hmm... By all means, I would hear your tale, but first—may I hear your name?"

"Apology: This unit lacks a name. Apologies."

Sora asked for the name of his savior, but she merely lowered her head.

"Disclosure: Unit identification number Ec001Bf9Ö48a2. Role Alt-Emircluster Befehler 1."

...These guys could stand to be more user-friendly.

"Right... That's too long, so I'm gonna call you Emir-Eins. How's that?"

"................."

...Uh, uhhh... Was that the wrong thing to say? The long silence began to make Sora doubt himself.

"Confirmation: Unit name...'Emir-Eins' applied. This unit looks forward to prolonged mutual acquaintance."

Sora and Shiro looked puzzled as Emir-Eins bowed her head deeply.

"Disclosure: Supplement to explanation provided by Irregular Number. Ex Machina was devastated in Great War."

But Emir-Eins raised her head again and went on coolly.

"Continuation: Final Battle damage report. Four thousand eight hundred seven units impacted by Godly Smite and Union onslaught. Five (including current unit) survived. Four thousand eight hundred two vaporized. Next: Nine thousand one hundred seventy-seven units engaged Artosh camp. Ninety-nine point six nine percent lost. Twenty-eight units avoided irreparable damage. Result: Remaining units exhibited severe cascading faults in memory, records, personality retention. Probable cause: Accumulation of logical errors due to illogical operations in destruction of ether—"

What she described was the price of deicide. It defied imagination. The race that had become strong to a theoretically infinite extent had destroyed half the Flügel and challenged a god with a force of almost fifteen thousand...and only twenty-eight of them survived. The sheer magnitude of it made Sora and the others gulp audibly.

"Conclusion: After aging, current operational unit count thirteen."

Thus, Ex Machina arrived at their current number, she explained.

"Issue: Ex Machina reproductive function available. But said errors placed hardware locks on all units. Reproduction enabled only for authorized user."

—*Right.* Sora mumbled, nodding softly.

"…That sucks."

"Acknowledgment: Condition sucks."

Despite Emir-Eins's echo of acknowledgment, Sora and Shiro looked at each other with relief.

It appeared that the worst-case scenario they had envisioned when the phone rang—that an all-powerful enemy who had seen their hand had appeared—was not the case. Einzig's declaration of "allies" and Emir-Eins's request for "cooperation" stood at face value. The Ex Machinas wanted them to be their allies and cooperate so that Ex Machina could avoid extinction. And of course they, for their own part, didn't want a race to go extinct. That would be creepy, for one thing. But even apart from that, if a Race Piece was lost, their game would become unwinnable. Besides, that "rewriting space" thing they did would make for the best stage equipment ever. With this race as their ally, Sora and Shiro's issues with Holou's concerts would vanish. Why not cooperate? Why not…indeed…

"…………"

But there were still several things weighing on Sora's mind that he couldn't easily shake off, to begin with, the questions he'd had from the beginning: *Why now? Why them?* He didn't get what they were going on about, either: What did they mean by "Spieler"? It sounded like it could mean many things.

"Analogies: Puppy soaked by rain. Candle flickering in wind. Sad. Can Master ignore?"

"—Uh, no, I guess I wouldn't… But…"

Sora considered this with evident caution, but Emir-Eins nodded. "Good." And continued with a placid smile, but without light in her eyes.

"Testimony: This unit will die unless you make babies with her."

"First there's a perverted pretty boy, and now there's a psycho babe? Don't threaten me!!" Sora wailed, feeling betrayed by the one person he'd thought to be an oasis of sense. "And anyway, how am I supposed to make babies with a machine?! I mean, how do you guys reproduce?!" As he hid behind Jibril, Shiro tucked under his arm, Sora let loose the biggest question of all. At the very least, he shouldn't have to "build love"—much less with a gay robot!

Jibril answered him as if she'd just remembered.

"According to the rare descriptions available of Ex Machina, it seems that two dissimilar units connect their 'production mechanisms,' compare data, and produce a unit adapted to the conditions demanded of the next generation... If I remember correctly."

"Then they both have to be Ex Machinas, right?!"

"Denial: Soul observed. Non–Ex Machina data compatible."

...Uh, all right. Must be like how Jibril was saying she could have Sora's baby "virtually." That was how Sirens reproduced, too. But in those cases, they were saying they had to mix souls or something.

"...So how would you *get* the data? Not some mechanical trick?"

Sora seemed worried about being like cattle to an alien, having any manner of bizarre contraptions mounted upon him. Emir-Eins answered with a confident nod to ease his worries.

"Boast: Hole assembled for Master. Conventional sexual intercourse supported."

"Wait, why'd you do *that*?! At least make it a *little* mechanical!"

Why was this world so...y'know...extreme?!

"Reply: Update based on past failures. Performance excellent. Probably."

Sora wondered what these "failures" entailed, but he didn't ask.

"Remarks: Initial plan involved simulation of hole of female Immanity. However, data insufficient. Therefore, real-time feedback model adopted based on responses of Master to stimulation. Internal structure, strength, pressure, viscosity, temperature, virtual pulse, and secretion optimized continuously. Final assembly designed exclusively for maximum pleasure."

......

"Seduction: This unit is brand-new. Would Master care for a demonstration?"

——.

"...Brother...why'd you go, silent...?"

"I—I—I—I didn't go silent! Nor was I subtly tempted!" Sora shouted, growing flustered under Shiro's gaze.

"Unit! You dare to steal the Spieler from me?!"

"'Steal' my ass! I'm not yours!! Get back in the wall, you piece of junk!!"

"Agreement: Master is free to love whom he chooses."

"Didn't you just try to steal my freedom with a threat?! ...Wait. Could it be that this guy—?"

An unpleasant idea crossed Sora's mind.

...This guy, Einzig. Does he...have one, too? A hole?

"Oh, fear not, Spieler. I have no hole. I—"

"Arghhh, shut up!! I didn't ask, and I don't wanna know. Why don't you just go home?!"

So now the situation was as follows: Ex Machina had a hardware lock limiting reproduction to someone called the Spieler. In other words, they'd *only accept Sora.* And the method was, uh...you-know-what. But there was still another question: why—

"Wait—let me say something!" Steph, who to this point had kept silent, now intervened. "So you're saying you'll reproduce by, uh... s-sexual intercourse...right?! *Why with Sora?!*"

"Yeah, Steph! That's it!! That's the line I was waiting for!!"

Yes, the unresolved question. Why now? Why Sora? Couldn't they find anyone else "compatible" in the course of six thousand years as they teetered on the brink of extinction? Meeting eyes with Sora as he thought this, Steph nodded deeply—and howled!!

"Take my word. This man is the worst!! Who in their right mind would want to reproduce with him?!"

"That is *not* the line I was waiting for!!"

"Oh, Dora. To slight my master before me... It seems you are eagerly looking forward to what follows death, aren't you? ♥"

"...Then...maybe you...should stop...grinning, like an idiot... every time, you see him?"

"Wh-whaaaat? Wait, no, I didn't— Hey, when did I grin?!"

If you wanted to know what infighting looked like, this commotion was it, but—

"Reiteration: Said errors placed hardware lock."
"Those errors...are called—our 'heart'..."
Emir-Eins and Einzig spoke softly—
"...Your...'heart'?"
—and the other eleven Ex Machinas—the *machines with hearts*, as they said—were tranquil. Yet, Sora murmured at those words that called back to the beginning, and all listened.
"We originated as machines... We had no 'hearts.'"
"Denial: Strictly not even machines."
"True." Einzig chuckled at Emir-Eins's correction. It was such a human gesture one almost forgot he was a machine. "Machines are tools. Tools are made for a purpose... But we were not."
"Acknowledgment: We adapted to damage. To all threats material and immaterial. Passively. Reactively. Just existing. Nothing more. Like plants. Meaningless. Purposeless. Null..."
......
"Near the end of the War—a unit we call the Preier acquired the 'heart' and shared it with us."
All the other Ex Machinas nodded to confirm Einzig's statement. One couldn't know just what travails had led to this, but—
"—Now, the Preier was *head over heels in love* with one man."
Once more, the Ex Machinas nodded, *Mm-hmm...* And...uh...
...Wait, what?
Einzig proceeded to destroy all the tension left in the scene as he picked up steam.
"And such was the 'heart' she shared with us! In which case, it is self-evident how we should thenceforth behave!"
"...Uh...like, all head over heels in love with the guy?"
Twice more, the Ex Machinas nodded, *Mm-hmm*, a bulwark facing Sora. The tension was gone.
"And so we were locked so as to never accept reproduction with one other than our true love!!"

"Avowal: This unit refuses to make babies except with Master. Cannot conceive. Apologies."

The Ex Machinas nodded *Mm-hmm* a third time. It had already become a farce. *So, in other words—* Steph spoke up for everyone.

"Ex Machina does not *wish* to reproduce with anyone else. And that is why you have not reproduced—am I understanding correctly?"

"And that's why you're on the brink of extinction? That's just stupid!!"

Einzig brought his face uncomfortably close to Sora's. "It is no matter. For, after six thousand years, here we are together once again...O Spieler."

"D00d, I'm *not your guy*! I wasn't even born then; shit, civilization barely was!" Sora shook off Einzig's hand from his chin and whispers of love from his ears and howled on. "Jibril! Is this how Ex Machina are?! Are they blind?!"

"I understood them to be a formidable race that excelled in observation and analysis—that might even pose a match for me individually in combat..." Surprisingly, Jibril seemed to be the most confused of them all. "...Is this the price of deicide...? I would hate to think that *this* is what I struggled with..." Her vacant whisper receded beyond Sora's and Shiro's perception.

"You needn't be bashful. You are the Spieler. Our analysis is infallible."

"Your analysis has already failed at the point of you saying I'm bashful! How do you get that?!"

This android was able to contradict himself in one line. This piece of junk was incredible, in a bad way. "Hmm," he mumbled at Sora's question.

"The evidence is wide-ranging. First, your appearance— Hmm. Unfortunately, it resembles his little. The Spieler was a more comely individual... But the ravages of time cannot touch this unshakable love!"

—Is this bastard looking for a fight? Just ask for one. Sora heaved, but now Emir-Eins— No, likely the entirety of Ex Machina analyzed the input in parallel to produce this report.

"Report: Match between individual 'Sora' and sample data 'Spieler' estimated ninety-six point two three percent."

Sora couldn't help but laugh at their "conclusion." He didn't know what kind of transcendental mathematics they'd used to come up with that result, but probability was just empty theory. When you were just going off *existing data*, however you crunched the numbers, all you could say was "likely." Sora meant to laugh it off with one word, "ludicrous"—

"However, logic only serves as reference data. It amounts to little more than a *ludicrous puzzle game*."

——Wha...what...?

Sora couldn't believe what he'd just heard. A machine—a computer—took these words out of his mouth? And this computer, which had denied logic and mathematics, went on heatedly, illogically:

"Neither zero nor one hundred exists in probability. Though one might operate on the data to infinity, one can only add more nines to ninety-nine point nine nine nine percent! *And all this can be overturned by one unknown datum!* Therefore, we believe logic to be a hopelessly incomplete tool."

"...Uh, yeah... I—I agree. I'm glad we're—"

Shiro was atop Sora's lap looking like she was about to pass out, flapping her lips uselessly as if gasping for air. At least Sora had been able to say something, but—

"In that case, in the end, what can you believe in, Spieler?" His voice clear and impassioned, Einzig showed his unnatural sparkly teeth and put his hand on his chest. **"It is my 'heart' that tells me thus: You are the one we have waited for!!"**

Sora swallowed.

✳   ✳   ✳

…Yeah. That's right.

In a world where nothing was certain, there was just one thing you could still believe in:

What you *wanted to believe.*

Call it faith, or idealism, or sentiment, or will. That's right—all you had to do was follow your *heart.* Some answers could only be found purely by believing that your decision would be right. That a race of machines, an embodiment of logic, could come to such conclusions defied comprehension. Ex Machina truly knew no bounds. Such adaptation and learning ability, enough to inspire awe and fear…

But seriously, they've got the wrong guy.

That was all well and good, but be that as it may, the cold, hard truth was this was all one big mistake. How sad it is that the answers our hearts show us, quite often, are wrong. As Sora gazed into the distance, reflecting on the harshness of reality—

"Query: Master does not currently wish to make babies with this unit? Mind-boggling self-control. Incredible."

—the maid robots gathered behind Emir-Eins.

"No, I'd seriously love to; I mean, I am a guy, and lemme tell you, sexy androids are totally— *Urgh*—"

"…Denied, rejected… Not selected, refused… R-18…!"

Shiro flatly rejected Sora's true feelings with a jab of her elbow. Still, they couldn't just keep up the rejections, or else Ex Machina would perish. And it was hard to say no to the perfect stage equipment for Holou. Sora and Shiro receded into rumination over this problem before them.

"Hmm… You cannot escape your bashfulness, can you, Spieler?"

"Look, you're out of the question! I said go home!!" Sora cried.

"Well, then—" Einzig went on:

"We collectively request a game of you."

—A *game.*

The words made Sora's and Shiro's eyes narrow to a blade's width.

"If we win, you will be *compelled* to select one unit with whom to reproduce."

"…And otherwise?"

"Yes! Then you will be *allowed* to select one unit whom to reproduce!"

"What's the difference?!" Sora yelled.

However, as he exchanged glances with Shiro, he was boldly chuckling to himself.

"Hey, S-Sora! They *are* attacking us, aren't they?!"

"I must say, though by no means do I expect my masters to lose, Ex Machina—"

Steph and Jibril were both asking in their own ways, *Can you win?* But Sora just smiled.

"Sure, why not… But it's gonna be me and Shiro playing you together. We've got something to say about the wagers, too…"

Huh… When you looked at it, it was simple and convenient. All they had to do was make them pledge to unlock their reproduction lock. If it was a lock that came from the "heart," the binding force of the Covenants could undo it, thus preventing their race's extinction. Then, if they also made them pledge to help with Holou's concert production, everything would be settled.

The worst-case scenario was already out of the way.

They didn't know who Sora and Shiro were, let alone the extent of their abilities. Hell, they even got Sora confused for someone else. In that case, however powerful Ex Machina might be, " " just might be able to beat them. But it wouldn't be easy. Sora began thinking carefully about what kind of game to play—

"With my apologies, Spieler—we reject this."

—only to be cut short by Einzig.

"You will play the game individually. Our cluster will play our side *in parallel*."

……*What?*

"Additionally, Ex Machina will determine the game."

Following up on Einzig's words, Emir-Eins gestured forth with her hand and announced the name of the game. It appeared before them as polygons suspended in the air:

"Lösen—Game 001: *Chess*—"

......*Dude.*

Sora forced a smile through his headache and checked with the two Ex Machinas.

"Hey... Let me get this straight. I'm the party being challenged here, right?"

"Indeed. Your assertion is most sound."

"And you guys are close to extinction and in need of my help?"

"Acknowledgment: Problem?"

The Fifth of the Ten Covenants: The party challenged shall have the right to determine the game.

"D00ds, I have the right to determine the game!! Plus! Even if we're playing a game to make babies, you're the ones begging me to do it with you! What's with the haughty attitude?!"

Sora tore at his hair, only to be told:

"Query: Extinction of Ex Machina inconveniences Master. Ex Machina has leverage. Strange?"

Emir-Eins looked at Sora blankly.

"Soraaa? You definitely misread this, didn't you? —In fact, aren't you *trapped*?!"

Steph's falsetto didn't make Sora feel like opening his mouth.

These guys would be a good match even for " ". A transcendent computer cluster, capable even of illogical operations, that would laugh at oracle machines and hypercomputers. And they wanted to take Sora on alone? At *chess*? Their intentions were crystal clear:

Accept *defeat*, or we'll go extinct.

That's right—it was a threat. They were making themselves hostages in order to force him to lose. He never saw this coming, except when he did: Coincidentally, Miss Cowering-in-the-Corner Jibril had just pulled this trick a few days ago. But now, to threaten the extinction of their entire race? Even if you saw it coming, there was nothing you could do about it. It was perfect. They'd got him good. So... C'mon—!!

"You pull such a filthy trick and *that's* your demand?!"

If you're gonna make a person take on someone out of their league, under conditions with no advantage for them, then you could demand whatever! You could make them bet the Immanity Piece, for example! So why would you use that just for this asinine demand that didn't even specify a date or time?!

"Oh, Spieler, I'll not ask your forgiveness... I foresaw that you would be too bashful to accept our entreaties!" The dumbass android was crying manly tears, his fist trembling. "But this is necessary in order for you to face your feelings! For the sake of love, we must be firm!!"

Pissed, Sora tutted to himself. *Whatever.*

"Jibril. Get us a table and chairs. This game—is going down."

She didn't even ask if it was all right. She just drooped her head, vanished, and came back with the furniture, on which Sora proceeded to sit as he continued speaking.

"But I get the first move. And I'm changing my demand for if I win."

It wasn't as if they had any plans for him to win. So:

"If I win, you unlock your 'production mechanisms' immediately. Ditch all that pretentious shit about not making babies with anyone except one specific person and get it on. Plus, you let us use you as concert equipment—cool?"

As if to acknowledge Sora's inference that they'd take whatever, Einzig followed his lead and sat at the table, smiling gently.

"Very well. But then let us add a few demands, if you don't mind."

After Einzig listed them all, he and all the Ex Machinas raised their hands.

"...Brother...?"

Shiro looked up at Sora uneasily, but he grinned savagely and raised his own hand.

"Who do you think I am? ...You'd better not think this is gonna be easy for you, you pile of shit."

And thus the thirteen Ex Machinas and one Immanity spoke:

—Aschente...

Meanwhile, far to the west of Elkia, on the continent of Valar, in what until a few days ago was called the state of Tírnóg in the country of Elven Gard, was an unclaimed territory now rid of its Elven inhabitants due to Sora and Shiro's machinations. Above this empty area, just waiting for a fleet of Elkian pioneers to arrive, floated an enormous landmass—a city in the sky. It was the capital of the Flügel, built on the back of the Phantasma Avant Heim. Somewhere on that pile of countless cubes, which suggested skyscrapers snaking about each other...

"...Av'n'... Will you listen to my recent worries?"

...was a girl with two different-colored eyes and a horn protruding from her jade hair. A broken halo crowned her head. The first Flügel, Azril, was talking to the Phantasma within her.

She was the agent plenipotentiary of the Avant Heim government, the Council of Eighteen Wings. She also held a Phantasma within her and amounted to the representative of that race as well. Deep down in the darkness, where the cubes were piled high, excluding every ray of sunlight—

"I...think everyone hates me. Is it just my imagination?"

—Azril was hiding in the darkness between cubes, crying to herself.

Physical laws such as those of gravity and space meant nothing to the Flügel, and as such, they had no concept of infrastructure. They saw no reason to build roads or stairways in their city. But now,

Azril, who had been compelled to "play life with restrictions" that reduced her to the level of an Immanity as a result of her game with Sora and Shiro... Azril, who had been merrily walking along with a large pile of books...

...had just learned the natural corollary of her unique state that, if she took one wrong step, she would fall to the bottom.

While she was at it, she also learned that it is agonizingly painful to fall from such a high place, as well as that when you fall down a crack it is impossible to get out. Azril's tears at this day of discovery were met by Av'n'—Avant Heim—whose voice boomed back at her from within.

«*I can scarce know the feelings of love and hate.*»

As a Phantasma, he hardly had a sense of self—*But*, he continued— «*I surmise that, if thou dost so doubt, it is most likely so.*»

......Yeah.

"...Yeah, I knew it... Everyone hates me. Still—"

For a moment, she gave a little smile, accepting everything.

"Why won't anyone come and help meeeeeeeeeeee?!"

Then her cry burst with tears from the dark crack.

"I know they hear me! There were even kids who saw me fall! I heard them going 'lol' at me! I'm their big sister; I'm the leader of the Flügel! Someone should help meee!!"

As only silence and the oppression of the walls answered her, suddenly, Azril smiled and thought. Oh—she knew. The Flügel were all busy right now.

—A city once ruled by Elves, which was now the territory of Elkia. More accurately, according to the wording of the covenant that had been exchanged, it was the property of Sora and Shiro. Flügel would drool to see the mountains of books left behind by its displaced Elven inhabitants, but they couldn't plunder them out. Sora and Shiro made use of this principle to offer Flügel this proposal:

"*For every book, you have to give us a copy and a handbook on Elven urban facilities. First come, first served! Privatize 'em for the win!*"

They also set a time limit—until the fleet of Immanity and Were-beast pioneers arrived. Thus, the Flügel were in a mad race back and forth over the land. Flügel would get a massive number of books, Sora and Shiro would get just as many books, and Immanity would get explanations of how to use the Elven facilities they couldn't understand.

"...They even managed to get the kids who weren't cooperative with them to do what they wanted... They're really something."

It was impressive, she admitted. It was no wonder they were busy. But—

"Does it take that much time to help me?! Can't they spare even two seconds for meeee?!"

—Now she was sure. They hated her.

This place deep in her city would be her grave.

"Hmph... There is no hope or salvation in this world. Everyone is alone in the deep darkness of despair."

Waxing poetic, she made up her mind to wither there.

"...I never would have expected you to attempt poetry, my elder. Did you hit your head?"

When she raised her head, there was a light at the end of the darkness. A literal angel, walking to her and speaking.

"Oh, you've hit every place on your body. Well, that's all right. It did take me some time to find you, though."

"J-Jibsy... Y-you came to look for your big sister...?"

"Well, yes, though I'd prefer it weren't necessary. I hope you won't give me too much trouble, but..."

Without any trouble at all, Jibril teleported Azril out of the crack and saved her. Azril took back her words and apologized to the world she had cursed. Not just anyone, but her youngest, dearest sister had come to save her—!!

"Hope and salvation are real! Here they are! The world is full of light, and— Ngyah?!"

Blubbering and leaping at Jibril, Azril instead slammed into a wall with her face.

"I knew it! This is where it was… What a waste of time…"

Having warped out of the way as if it were the obvious thing to do, Jibril sighed, book in hand. That was one of the books Azril had when she fell, wasn't it?

"…………Nyah? Hrh?"

Azril was dazed. *Huh? Huh?* Her thoughts spun in futility.

"…Uhhh… Huh? Jibsy… You came to…look for me?"

"Yes, Elder. I heard that you had this book when you slipped and fell, so I— Oh, I see! Pardon me. I apologize for my misleading phrasing. Let me correct myself." Jibril glowed. Ah…her smile was indeed that of an angel. "I came to look for this *book*. I did not come to look for *you*, and I do not plan on doing so in the future. ♥"

—Darkness fell once more over the world. *Up and down, nya-ha… I knew this world was crap…*

"Well then, my masters are waiting, so I'll be on my way."

"Nyaaah! Waiiit, Jibsy, I beg you! At least carry me up—"

Azril grabbed Jibril tearfully as she caught her getting ready to shift far away. Then.

"……Jibsy. Why were you looking for *that* book?"

Azril cut herself short and narrowed her eyes to ask. It was a copy of an Ancient Dwarven book. Azril, no more designed to forget than any of the other Flügel, knew its contents word for word.

"My masters have been troubled by certain *dolls*. I thought I might give it another read to see if any clues presented themselves."

—Yes. She was looking for *writings about Ex Machina*. And with that, she vanished into thin air.

……

Azril was once more left at the bottom of the city, alone in the dark.

"…Nyaaah? …Those scrap heaps…in Elkiaaa…?

But her voice came from lower than the bottom, and her smile's shadow was deeper than the dark. Avant Heim himself swayed at this very different leader of Flügel. Like an earthquake of the heavens. As if you could hear fathomless malice. A vortex of emotion was swelling into view. With one word—

"————*Gather.*"

—all the other Flügel except Jibril knelt before her that very instant. Azril, the first of the Flügel, the weapon created by a god to slay gods, what boomed from her was neither a plea nor a request. It was an order.

"We'll shift Avant Heim to Elkia. Everyone get ready!"

Warp a landmass far larger than an island in its entirety to the next continent across the sea. What a bullshit order from a bullshit being. But all prepared without objection. Azril alone spoke:

"...Jibsy. Av'n' and I would love to meet those rubbish dolls."

Her murmur with a plastered smile was echoed by the cry of Avant Heim, which should have been as comforting as that of a whale but now brayed so as to make all who heard it shrink.

"I'm thinking we can talk. I figure we can have a *fun* chat."

...Yes. A fun chat would be desirable. Even Azril had finally begun to enjoy things. It wasn't the time she wanted to make enemies of Elkia, Sora, Shiro, or, heaven forbid, Jibril. It would be best to settle things peacefully if possible. Though of course—

"If it's *not* fun...I'll kill them till there's not a speck of dust left. ♥"

—that was just provided it was possible.

CHAPTER 2
RETRODUCTION
INDUCTIVE INFERENCE

It was in the Eastern Union's capital island—its capital city, Kannagari. There lived the Eastern Union's creator, a golden fox whose residence was known as the Shrine. Currently, in this place where Werebeasts came to venerate her much as a living god—

"…You lot… I've been trying my best to keep my mouth shut, but…"

—there was the fox, first of all, whose patience at last wore thin as she finally opened her mouth to speak. She was a woman with a monocle and fox ears, her two large tails covered in lustrous fur. The founder of the Eastern Union and the agent plenipotentiary of Werebeast, the Shrine Maiden, watched—

"Hmm? Oh, we're just makin' ourselves at home. Don't mind us."

"…Keep calm…and carry on…"

"That you would fail to provide us with the grace of tea speaks volumes about the quality of your country, does it not? …Oh. Pardon, now that I think about it, I should scarcely enjoy to be served pet food. I must then commend you on your excellent discernment of your place."

—as the group that had warped into the Shrine out of nowhere, without any proper greeting, had proceeded to lounge on the sofas quite at ease. They were Sora and Shiro, and the smiling Flügel Jibril, who scarcely had the standing to lecture anyone about politeness. One other personage was observing this brazen bunch.

"Holy Shrine Maiden. All you must say is '*Get out*,' and I shall expel these ruffians posthaste."

It was the aging Werebeast Ino Hatsuse, smiling as a blood vessel or two bulged from his face. Meanwhile, warping behind him upside down, Jibril went on smiling back.

"Dear me. It seems a little doggy has announced that he will expel my masters and their humble servant, yours truly. I must be hearing things. Typically, even animals are able to exercise proper judgment in whom they bite. ♥"

"Ha-ha-ha, pardon me; I had imagined that even a birdbrain would understand the Ten Covenants. However, put your mind at ease. Even uncomprehending riffraff such as yourselves will be swiftly removed from the property of the Holy Shrine Maiden upon the retraction of your permission to stay."

—*We still have a long way to go toward racial harmony*, reflected Sora, Shiro, and the Shrine Maiden.

Once Ino had finished exchanging piercing glares with Jibril, he turned to Sora and Shiro.

"I expected that even you hairless monkeys would have perceived that there were more important matters at the current juncture."

This section of the Shrine they had all gathered in was called the Annex. Looking up, they saw five screens of various sizes suspended from the ceiling. On them were five Werebeasts, presumably representing the Eastern Union in games. One of those Werebeasts they knew well.

Fennec fox ears and a big tail. A little girl, now crimson all over. It was Izuna Hatsuse in bloodbreak mode, running around the cyberspace city in heated virtual battle.

"…Dwarf? …Hardenfell? Looks like an ass-handing."

It was the first time Sora had seen them, but, from the physical characteristics, it would appear that the opponent was Ixseed Rank Eight, Dwarf. A high race just below Elf—but against Izuna, they weren't playing around so much as being played with. Other screens showed other opponents, but they were pretty much all getting rekt.

"This I'll thank you for, loves. We've got all our bloodbreakers out in the field, with the exception of us two old ones. And the fish are biting."

The Eastern Union had its full-dive VR games and its best gamers in full operation. They didn't have time to chop all the fish that were coming for their block, looking, presumably, for hints as to Sora and Shiro's true nature. So, as she of course grasped that Sora and Shiro were the ones behind it and acknowledged her indebtedness—

"So? You come knowing that we're busy, and you're in the way… Might I ask what you're after?"

—she first gave a chuckle at Izuna's leaping for joy at victory and then, back in her rhythm, she turned back to Sora and Shiro and asked.

"Sure. Frankly, we're just really uncomfortable at the castle right now. Like, scared. So we came to hide here. You see…"

Sora's voice suddenly dropped an octave. The Shrine Maiden and Ino narrowed their eyes.

"This shit is actually kinda serious. We need your help—especially Gramps'."

"…Mine, you say…?"

—The Shrine Maiden and Ino knew a thing or two about Sora by now. Sora, who always acted so aloof, so comfortable and audacious—was actually just a poseur. He'd never say it himself, and he'd never admit to it. But he knew this all too well, and since he had no mind to belie his true nature, certain others—Shiro, for starters—knew it, too. There had never been a time Sora was comfortable. Not once. He was always serious, always trying hard, searching desperately for ways out, clinging for dear life to Shiro. For this man to be evidently uncomfortable, and, of all things, to ask Ino Hatsuse for help… Anyone could see it was no trifle that Sora was most solemn to introduce.

"—I'm too popular. With maid robots. Save me."
"…………"

I'm too popular. Ah, one of those lines all male-born individuals would like to say at least once. A line that, when actually heard from another, inspires the will to punch him in the face with all one's might. But, ah… At last Sora felt he understood. *I'm too popular. I've got too much money.* Those were the lines—but! When you were actually in a position to say those lines, *it really wasn't awesome at all!!* Those guys *actually had real problems.* Serious problems! Far too grave to be written off with envy and an "I wish…"!!

"King Sora, it sounds as if the situation is in fact quite serious. Allow me, Ino Hatsuse, to provide what little succor I can."

As the agonized Sora wept internally, Ino gallantly nodded and placed his hand on his shoulder. With a warm and trusting smile, he added:

"If I may, Your Majesty… There is not a soul in heaven or on earth who would love you. Please rein yourself in. This is a mere obsessive fantasy, an idle delusion. I suggest that you take a nice, long rest."

Ino's pitying eyes made the subtext clear: *Those babes of yours exist only in your imagination.*

"…Ino Hatsuse. Fetch my private physician…"

"I am at your bidding, O Holy Shrine Maiden, but is this not the ideal opportunity to allow King Sora to pass away?"

"You say the chief of the Commonwealth is delirious? Think of what it could mean for our country. Let's have him die some other—"

Sora would have interposed in the free discourse of the two.

"…*Acquiring Master.* Lösen: *Asura-Apokryphon.*"

However, another person's voice echoed from the void, their presence speaking much louder than words—

"Discovery: Master located at last. Reward: Explain reason for move to these coordinates."

A maid robot stood in the Annex of the Shrine as if she'd been there all along: the violet-haired Ex Machina, Emir-Eins, tilting her head quizzically. In contrast, gaping even more bewilderedly than the Shrine Maiden or Ino—

"Hey, wai— How'd you figure out...? How'd you even get here?!"

—Sora thought better than to answer, *Because I wanted to get away from you guys.*

"Reply: Reopened fissure in space left by Irregular Number. Time elapsed. Apologies for making Master wait."

Emir-Eins apologized for entirely the wrong thing, and Jibril's face appeared strained. Jibril had shifted them someplace Ex Machina wouldn't be able to, as they couldn't see the place and didn't know it. She'd thought they wouldn't even be able to track them, yet they'd reopened her hole in space. It hadn't even taken an hour. One could hardly imagine Jibril's mental state, but—

"...It seems...I have underestimated my opponent once more..."

—given the murderous intent in her voice, it was quite clear that her pride had taken a hit—

"—Wha...? Is it Ex Machina?! How—?!"

—all the while, Ino had recovered from stupor enough to shout, and the Shrine Maiden was now on her guard. But leaving all that in the dust, Emir-Eins— No, the Ex Machina just proceeded indifferently. That is to say:

"Lösen: *Love Success Situation Forme—Checkmartyr— Prototype 0008.*"

This came not from Emir-Eins's mouth, but once again from the void—from several voices. This time, the interior of the Annex of the Shrine was rewritten into a different world. In contrast to the

Shrine Maiden and Ino, who watched aghast, Sora and Shiro watched calmly, sighing:

—*Seriously. These guys could make the perfect stage equipment.*

The events unfolding further confirmed Jibril's records. And just as the echoing voice had said, this was the *eighth time* this space-rewriting shit had gone down. Ninth, if you counted when they first showed up. It was getting old. Per the book's writings, it seemed they added matter to rewrite the scenery *without changing* the matter that was there. Complex lines raced through space, forming polygons, rendering images. Intermittently, chaotically, yet steadily, that which lay above the surfaces of matter—the void—was filled at high speed by the 3-D textures spat out by Ex Machina to build a virtual environment.

…Make no mistake, this was still the Annex of the Shrine. Still matted with tatami. But no one would think it was in this state—not even the Shrine Maiden, who lived here. Time, space, nay, causality itself were transcended to loose a sight to behold—

"………"

First, there was Sora, suddenly clad in a suit.

"…You wanna see my panties? I'll show them to you… ♥ Because I love you, Teacher… ♥"

"Oh, no faaair! Teacher's thing belongs to me! Right, Teacher? ♥ "

"Um, Teacher? When I think about you, I start to feel all funny…down here. I wonder why?"

"Teacher! ♥ I want you to give me another…private health lesson. ♥"

Then there were girls wearing backpacks, spouting out lines that would be difficult to write while sober.

…Altogether, there were eleven schoolgirls as small as Shiro—or even smaller—who we are certainly not saying were elementary school–aged. So here they were, after school in a virtual elementary school. Among the transfigured Ex Machinas was a quiet girl in glasses and a tough little tomboy. But all were in fierce competition for their one true love, Mr. Sora, and a certain "fatal act." Something like that.

...A fearsome power had created an even more fearsome and ridiculous sight. Everyone was dumbfounded. Only the girls in question continued to clamor on.

"Ooooh... We'll never settle this at this rate..."

"Okay, then whoever makes Teacher feel the best gets to keep him!"

"Okaaay!"

"All righhht, I'm not gonna lose, so watch my smooth, flat little—"

"Like hell, it's okay!! Knock it off, you psychos!!"

As their folly approached its inevitable conclusion—*We should all just do it first!*—and the little girls began to pull off their clothes, at last, Sora's mighty roar shook the classroom.

"Hell no, *hell* no! I'm not doing it with any of you! And none of you gets to keep me, okay?!"

At the back of the classroom were Shiro, seated with her hand on her cheek; the Shrine Maiden in a sailor uniform; and Ino, practically busting out of his schoolboy uniform. They were all staring at Sora as if he were dirt, and Sora yelled as if it were capable of chasing this fact from his awareness.

"Why nottt?! Because we're kids?!"

"Don't you know all characters depicted are age eighteen or over?!"

"Shut the hell uuup! That's not even the issue! All the organizations and important people and stuff, they never listen to that kind of logic; if you're gonna do that kind of crap, you gotta gate it at least! You wanna get me locked up?!"

After shouting the little girls down, at last, Sora clutched his head and pleaded:

"...Please. I'm begging ya. Just, get lost for a while... 'Kay? ...Seriously."

As if they'd finally concluded that he meant it, the polygons broke. The sunset classroom turned back into the good old tatami room as if nothing had happened, and the self-described elementary school students of most dubious legality reverted compliantly to their proper forms. Back in the Annex of the Shrine with eleven *non-loli* maid robots, transcendental computers far beyond oracle

machines—scratch that, beyond hypercomputers—used their staggering power for purposes most pointless and analyzed the data without evident emotion. So—

"—Target sexual arousal index curve analyzed. Resistance factor speculated. Initiating adjustment deliberation."

"Sexual arousal confirmed above baseline. Moral conflict speculated. Searching for solution."

—Having freely laid bare Sora's sexual predilections, they calmly began shifting home.

"Hey, don't just slander me and then leave!! King Sora loves boobies, too, y'know?!"

Sora stood in the Annex of the Shrine, screaming at the sky as the veritable shitstorm faded into nothingness, and then there was silence.

…Uh…

"…So. Would you care to explain?"

"Explain what? I told you, I'm just too popular with maid robots!"

The insanity had raged beyond comprehension. The Shrine Maiden was too nonplussed to even be disgusted. Sora tore at his hair.

"They're telling me I gotta make babies with one of 'em! D00d, this is the worst thing ever!!"

—That was the style of their approach. And note this was the eighth time.

It wasn't so bad at first. They'd come on to him doing it wrong in the plebeian way that made you want to tell them off. Like, there'd be eleven childhood friends going, "Let's go to school together! ♥" Eleven childhood friends he'd never seen before. And they wanted to go to school together. They didn't have a clue about childhood friends or Sora's willingness or lack thereof to go to school. Then, boom, there were eleven big sisters, eleven widows…and so on… and so forth… *What next, eleven samurai?* He sneered, and that was that—until…

"…But it doesn't seem you were entirely indifferent, does it, lad?"

"That's why I'm saying it's scary, d00d. Those Ex Machinas, they know no limits… What a fearsome race—!!"

The Shrine Maiden's cool sarcasm was met by Sora with a trembling fist and a puckered expression. Indeed…while their approaches had been so far off the mark each time, with each trial, they grew closer and closer. Using their absurd powers of observation, analysis, computation, and adaptation, the Ex Machinas were able to infer from Sora's reactions what his preferences were, and they steadily adjusted the scenario to hit him where it counted.

The fact that Sora was okay with Loli owed a great deal to the fact that his little sister was *just too beautiful.* The Ex Machina had yet to get a read on that, but their approximations were drawing ever closer—!!

"…Brother, you've got…a nosebleed…"

Even now, here he was, drawing Shiro's squinty condemnation. But Sora blocked her opinion and her gaze with both hands and shook his head melodramatically.

"*NO. That's a big fat NO…* Shiro, my little sister. Mark your elder brother's words."

Out of a hundred healthy young men in the world, probably a hundred would agree with this statement. It was his conviction. No. His faith! Sora, thus, explicated the *truth*—!!

"Even if the lass be one he himself fancies not, he who is born male must, of necessity, experience an unbridled yearning which enjoins him: I wanna be popular with girls!! An ambition? Nay—it is the very driving force of what it means to be a man—!!!!"

If there be any man who might dissent, let him step forth. I will then humbly withdraw my long-cherished belief. Acting as they might be, they were just the sort of luscious ladies he craved. Mistaken as they might be, they were that sort of girl that had fallen in love with him! This being so—!!

"Reckon the seductions I have endured and observe the diamond bulwark of reason with which I have stood out against them! Do you not find it worthy of praise? Yea, and if not praise, certainly no blame—is this not so—?!"

He was getting a little carried away by being popular for the first time in his life. That he wouldn't deny—but! What man in the world could blame him? Sora's impassioned case wound up.

—Clapping. Sighs.

The clapping was from Ino and Jibril, struck to the heart by this fine speech, wiping their tears. The sighs were from the Shrine Maiden and Shiro, unpossessed of any more attractive way to respond than to roll their eyes.

Bathing in a sea of both accolade and censure, Sora still acknowledged it: That his dear diamond of reason had survived every trial unscathed owed entirely to—

"Lösen: *Love Success Situation Forme—Checkmartyr—Prototype 0009.*"

Wait—here once again, out of the blue, the polygons raced through the room and distorted its aspect. Ex Machina's tenth rewriting of space, all told, the sight—indeed, that very sight was that to which Sora owed the soundness of his reason—that being—

"Heh. That girl who was saying she liked me? I feel sorry for her, but I had to decline…"

"…Hey. I didn't ask you anything. What are you babbling about, you pervbot?"

—Einzig.

The sunset streamed in from the small window. This seemed to be the basketball club's room. Clad in uniform, Einzig languidly began dialogue with no context. Sora, finding himself involuntarily in the same costume, answered unenthusiastically, but—

"…Hmm, you ask why I declined?"

"I said I didn't ask anything! Nor do I care— H-hey, get away from me; go away!"

With little regard for his opinions or consent, the kink machine advanced on the frightened Sora with the smile of a true sportsman.

"Don't make me say it... The only one this unit— Excuse me, this *man* loves is—"

"SHUT UUUUUUUP!! GAAAH!! GRAAAH!! STFUUUUU-UUU!!"

The advances of pretty girl robots might have chipped Sora's diamond. However, the advances of the flaming gay robot switched the focus from his reason to his sanity and shriveled him in horror.

"You just try to finish that sentence! I'll run away someplace you can never see me again!"

—*You know, such as the afterlife!* It was enough to make Sora shout. The memories responsible for his horror spun through his brain like the zoetrope of his last moments.

■■■

He wasn't going to let them win that easily. That was the resolve with which Sora had begun his chess match against Ex Machina. But, of course, it ended quite one-sidedly. He must have known it would. Even so...

"..........Shit..."

"...Brother... It's all, right...okay...?"

Shiro hugged and whispered to Sora as he cursed at the board.

—*I knew it. I'm not like Shiro.*

Sora ground his teeth. No ordinary person could see through all the possible states of the chessboard so as to call it tic-tac-toe. His opponent, Ex Machina, had been a transcendent computer—there was no way he could out-read them in perfect play. Even so, he'd lost tens of thousands of times to Shiro. Regardless, he'd concocted countless strategies, countless conventions to beat Shiro, which she'd thereafter beaten. He'd applied those, he'd even tried to exploit the errors common to machines and misdirect them, but it was utterly ineffective. As Einzig said with evident pleasure:

* * *

"…You truly are the Spieler… To force us into a stalemate…"

Yes, it ended in a stalemate—which meant abject failure.

He couldn't win. At some point in the game, Sora had decided as much. So he'd focused on stalemating. The first player to move always has the advantage in chess, and if he's only aiming for a stalemate, all the more.

…He'd played a transcendent computer that never fell for the same tactic twice, always adapted, and he *hadn't lost*. Shiro aside, for Sora, wouldn't you say that that was a phenomenal accomplishment? Might that not be what the clinging Shiro and the watching Jibril and Steph were thinking?

But it was all for naught. One of the appended rules was *A stalemate shall constitute Ex Machina's victory*. Whether he lost or he stalemated, the outcome was the same. Even so, he'd simply insisted on his pride that told him: *Like hell I'm gonna let 'em win*. This could not satisfy him. He gritted his teeth at this travesty, this shame. But Einzig— No, Emir-Eins, too—

"—I could see your *will* in your play. You must be the Spieler."

—all the Ex Machinas grinned strangely at Sora.

……?

No one got it: neither Sora nor Shiro, neither Jibril nor Steph.

"Well then, in any case, it is our victory. Allow us to enforce our demands as per the Covenants."

But apparently having no mind to explain, Einzig stood.

"Gahhhh! Shit! Okay! I lost, fair and square!!"

Sora unleashed an explosion of desperate self-righteousness. He could mope and pout all he wanted, but it wouldn't change a thing. Regrets and countermeasures were for later! The question at hand was *what to do now*?!! Having so deftly transitioned his thinking, Sora pointed at Einzig and crowed.

"But guess what? You bastards—you never said *when* and *with whom*!"

And that was exactly what had been so queer about their demands. Sora watched for a reaction.

These were the guys who had just trapped him so easily. They couldn't have overlooked such a glaring flaw. There was something more. Some ulterior motive. Sora's eyes searched for it. Einzig peered right back.

"Quite naturally. Who would dare to coerce love? It is your choice, Spieler, whom to cherish."

"...Hmmm... I seem to remember someone being awfully coercive recently, but maybe I'm just imagining things... That's the biggest surprise today," Sora quipped.

Einzig smiled in earnest—or at least, as far as Sora could tell. Was it even possible to see through a machine's lies? Wait, was it even possible for machines to *lie*?

Einzig responded, "Yes...and thus, we would that you provide us immediately with only *specific information*."

Sora squinted at him carefully. Despite the vague bullshit, there had been one demand he'd have to comply with immediately. It was among the additions: *Immediately provide us with information about your preferences...*

Sora still couldn't get what their deal was, or the point of such vague demands. Perhaps when he found out just what they wanted, he could figure out their intentions. Did they really mean to be his allies, *or could it be*—? Sora glared as Einzig went on.

"Ex Machina suffers most indecorously from a dearth of information by which we might be loved by you."

......

"You must be more specific! Under what conditions will you love this unit? How must I express this love in order for you to accept it? It is the data by which to unravel these puzzles that we lack!"

The Ex Machina girls nodded in unison at Einzig's speech. Sora was busy groaning and holding his violently throbbing head, so Steph checked for him:

"Umm… So Sora is supposed to do…uh, *you know*, with just one of you?"

They nodded back, *Mm-hmm, mm-hmm.*

"…And…you each…want him…to pick you, alone…?" Shiro asked.

They nodded back, *Mm-hmm, mm-hmm.*

"And thus, you desire to know what you must do for my master to love you," Jibril added.

And they nodded back, *Mm-hmm, mm-hmm.*

Could it be—*this was really all it was*? Still holding his head, Sora looked at Einzig and squeezed out his voice.

"…I can say one thing: I have no data for the likes of you!"

"Wh-what? Why, Spieler?!"

"How do you *expect* me to love a flaming gay robot slinking and twisting right in front of me?! It's *impossible*!"

He pushed back the slinking pervert—quite literally, with a mighty kick that sent him back into the wall.

Emir-Eins took over by making one calm and simple demand.

"Determination: List of required information: Master's porn. End."

"…Prawn? Why has the conversation turned to talk of cuisine?"

"Oh, little Dora, you mustn't be so demure. You know as well as anyone that we speak of my master's masturbatory media. ♥"

Oh! Now she remembered. Jibril continued on as Steph blushed.

"But why his pornography? How could it bear on being loved?"

The befuddled Jibril was answered by Shiro's bemused whisper.

"…Brother's, pornos…could show them, what he likes… Ex Machina, is dangerous… An *enemy*…!"

They could reveal his preferences, allowing the robots to act accordingly—and make him fall in love with them. Now Shiro saw their dire and cunning plot. She shook and bit her nails. Beside her…

"…………"

…Sora, besieged on every side by unbridled sexual harassment, exhaled, looked at the ceiling, and thought. The Ex Machinas had shown up out of nowhere, come after him, again out of nowhere, and beaten him at a game, yet again, out of nowhere. And now this—*What did I do to deserve this?*

"...Well... I guess I lost... Ha-ha, ha... *Sigh...*"

Having shed a solitary tear, he pulled out his tablet. Though he regretted it, just as Emir-Eins had determined, he had porn. Which she'd demanded he surrender. He'd sworn by the Covenants. He couldn't refuse. But then, she could have demanded something really devastating. Perhaps he should be grateful she was satisfied with sexually humiliating him. And so he wiped his hand on his shirt and handed Emir-Eins the tablet.

"——Ecstasy..."

Emir-Eins lowered her head in thanks, and their fingers brushed against one another just for a moment, allowing Sora to confirm: *No static discharge.*

"But I'm *just* showing you my porn. You can't look at any of the other data, and you obviously can't destroy any of it, all right?"

"......Hmm? This— Spieler, is this a storage mechanism for your secret books?"

"Inference: Unknown recording medium. Stores multiple data files... Searching for operation method."

Einzig had returned from the wall. He and Emir-Eins inspected the slab dubiously. Sora interjected.

"It's in there. I opened the folder for you, so...the rest is up to you."

Yes—this was payback, a fine troll indeed. He smirked evilly.

"......? ......?"

Seeing all the Ex Machinas puzzle over how to analyze it, Sora sneered duskily to himself. It was a tablet PC, an electronic device from another world. Sure, they'd messed with his smartphone, but that was because he'd left the radio on. All the data in the tablet was recorded in otherworldly language and otherworldly programming.

And he'd forbidden them to view or destroy the non-pornographic material, so they couldn't use brute force. Moreover, Emir-Eins's nonconductive fingers wouldn't work on the touch screen.

"I gave you what you demanded. Didn't say I'd include support. ♪"

"…This man truly is no pushover…"

Steph had to admit she was impressed that Sora had still been able to flip over his defeat. But Sora was grinning, *That's not all*, which only Shiro on his lap noticed.

"But dear me… The only pornography I can recall in my master's possession is the recordings of little Dora and others in the bath… What use would such information as that serve?"

"—Hey, that's true, isn't it? Why are you dragging me into this?!"

It was unlikely that even Jibril had read everything they had on their tablet. She might have managed to decipher the language of another world, but still, there were many concepts and assumptions that would be unknown to her. Even though Jibril knew from an in-depth survey of the tablet's contents that there was hardly a wealth of porn within it…

"Observation: …Cannot detect lie in Master."

…Emir-Eins merely stared at Sora in response, as if analyzing him. But the outcome was preordained. There was no point in anyone trying to lie to someone assumed to be able to read their biological responses.

"Addendum: Cannot detect lie in Irregular Number or Immanity woman."

Just as he'd said, Sora had handed them his porn folder; he just hadn't explained how to read it. There was no falsehood in that, nor did it violate the Covenant. As Sora's grin carved ever deeper into his face—

"Comparison: However, *cannot detect Master acknowledgment of statements of two.*"

—these next words of Emir-Eins froze him in place.

* * *

"Conclusion: Provided information is camouflage. Presence of more important information speculated. Request to Einzig: Use situational judgment as coordinator. *Aus.*"

——*Wha-wha—wha...wha...whaaaaat?!*

"Einzig to all Seher and Prüfer: Analyze the principle of this medium!"

"—Jawohl."

"Whoaaa! H-heyyy now, can't you wait just a moment?!"

The Ex Machinas calmly began their analysis in spite of Sora's hollering, and before he was even finished, their calculations had culminated into the following report:

> "Analysis complete. Records determined as data for catalytic stimulation. Pattern analysis: Object identified as data processing unit employing binary code by means of combination of conducting and insulating material. No patterns match known data formats. New compatibility layer required. Unknown current unrelated to spirits also detected as method. Loading—extraction of data by voltage load—may damage data or medium."

"A-all right, then you can't! You can only touch the porn—"

While taken aback that they'd figured out that much in an instant, Sora cut them off. But the subsequent merciless blow came from Emir-Eins.

"Instruction: Search for data structures that fulfill sharing conditions. Sort key: None. Target: All."

"Hey, hold on there! I didn't say you could view all the data!"

"Rebuttal: Meaning of data not identified. Therefore, Search All not privacy violation."

—B-bastard—!

```
"Search complete. Records found in deep
archive. Catalyst degradation suggests
heavy access. Data structures meet
sharing conditions: usage frequency,
active time, hidden status. Inferred
to be porno."
```

—*Hey, hey, come on, now*—! They could see through his lie that he wouldn't lie… Under these conditions, we can roll with that. But to see through his rhetoric that *Here's the porn (but I never said all the porn)*—and then to *find* the rest of the porn—come *on*—!

```
"Judged feasible to load and copy
area containing relevant records only
by placing limited spirituelectric
load. If data is then synthesized and
decrypted, porn can be acquired."
```

"—Confirmation: Master, authorize execution."

"Like hell I will! B-besides, can you even prove that it's porn?!"

If they hadn't identified the data's meaning, it could be the wrong data! He'd only given them permission to access the porn, and if this *wasn't* the porn—

As Sora badgered Emir-Eins, Shiro mumbled softly:

```
"…Hidden folder Macroeconomics…eight point two three
gigabytes… Definitely, porn."
```

"Wha—?! How did you know, Ms. Shiro?! Just how much of that do you—?"

```
"Confirmed: Structure size matches spec-
ification. Copying."
```

"Hey, wai— Don't— **N-NOOOOOOOOOOOOOOOOOOOO!!!**"

——……

*   *   *

...And so... In the throne room, where the Ex Machinas, Shiro, Jibril, and Steph all fell silent...

"No, *noooo*... My—my—my precious secret collection...!"

...only one man's grief-stricken lamentations filled the air. The precious porn he had brought from his old world, the reams and reams of erotic manga, had all been lost forever. The data had been corrupted, and no matter how many times he smacked the screen, it told him, Could not load.

"...Brother... I'm, sorry...?"

"It's okay... It's okay, Shiro. It's not your fault... It really isn't..."

Shiro hugged Sora and apologized, but Sora shook his head. It had been Sora's fault for losing. And anyway, protecting the other data and the tablet itself from loss was the top priority. What he should have done was tell them honestly and fully where the data was to keep their losses to a minimum. Shiro hadn't done anything wrong—she'd done exactly what he should have done in the first place. Still... It could never erase the pain of the loss of his precious fap material, gone forever. But what pained him more than its loss, per se—

"...Brother... Porn...is best fresh... You already, used it up..."

Comforting Sora by rubbing his head, Shiro went on gently.

"...You couldn't, get off to it, anymore...could you? Let's find... more porn...together."

"Look, your brother can't help but be distraught that his proclivities had been an open book to his little sister all along! And, I mean, how is it that an eleven-year-old maiden is speaking for the feelings of a man who's just lost his porn folder?!"

The despair was no different from having your porn stash found by your mom. The war criminals responsible: Einzig and Emir-Eins.

"Now we shall promptly proceed with the analysis of the data, Spieler! Please wait."

"Declaration: This unit will dedicate all resources to becoming the ideal wife for Master... Trying."

With that, the eleven Ex Machina girls all bowed deeply in unison.

■ ■ ■

This marked the start of Ex Machina's mad approach based on porno manga. It had only taken a few hours to reach the present time…and this filled Sora with dread. In just a few hours, they had decrypted and *understood* the data from Sora's old world. Even unknown concepts—school, childhood friends, walking to school together, elementary school backpacks. They'd grasped his *culture*. And from cartoons. Based entirely on porno manga. It was only natural that, given their reference material, there would be some strain in their interpretation, some bias in their scenarios. But however conservatively you talked about their speed of understanding and learning—it was prodigious.

—And yet.

Taking all that and skipping all the vile memories, foregoing the synopsis. Eastern Union. Shrine. Annex. Sora brought himself back. And the first thing he said:

"Why are you still stuck on the super-gay route?! Cut it out already!!"

Past the nightmarish memories, before his eyes lay a true nightmare: the pervbot in his basketball uniform. He was closing in on Sora, whose objections were closer to a shriek. And yet, Einzig alone still would not learn, his smile just as cheery as ever:

"Hmm… But you see, it means nothing unless you accept my love for what—"

"I'd rather kill myself! Knock it off with the stupid cosplay!!"

Appearing to finally understand the seriousness of Sora's refusal, Einzig drooped in chagrin. At the same time, the Shrine's tranquil furnishings were restored, causing Sora to breathe a deep sigh of relief. And not just Sora—the Shrine Maiden, Ino, Shiro, and Jibril, too, each in their own ways.

As if all that hadn't been enough—

"...I apologize, Spieler... There was only one record for reference on man-on-man affection... It is so difficult to analyze your preferences for this category... I can only curse my inadequacy in causing you discomfort."

Einzig heaved a sigh of his own, causing Sora to tear at his hair.

"*Inadequacy* doesn't even begin to cut it! I'm not into guys! Will you get it through your head already?!"

"But, Spieler, your tomes did contain a single volume of lurid male-on-male—"

"The cover was a trap! It pisses me off just remembering it!"

The character on the cover was *obviously* a cute girl. Even the art style made it look like it was intended for men. But when Sora bought the book, it turned out to be BL...and some pretty hardcore stuff, at that. Of course, it had been Sora's fault for buying it without checking the contents. But now he had Einzig bringing this up as evidence that he had a chance, and the rage from back then burst back into flame from Sora's mouth.

"Don't you think you picked the wrong reference material in the first place?! D00d, look at this, seriously!!"

Seriously. Look at these porn scenarios they were using. Consider: deciding who should be Teacher's girlfriend by who made him feel the best? That didn't make sense. The girls who didn't get picked would be totally screwed over. In reality, this would lead to one of those "dead ends" where someone ends up getting stabbed. No matter how you looked at it, basing your actions on unrealistic scenarios from porno manga was a mistake.

...Though Sora did admit he was bitter at having his stash nuked.

"What are you saying, Spieler? The information was truly valuable, and not only in determining your preferences." It sounded as if the suggestion came entirely as a shock to Einzig, who turned on his heel. "Your library was truly informative...and that world truly came to astonish us." He had his back to Sora, practically marveling— No, perhaps *actually* marveling. "The education...the physiology, the psychology—it helped us more than we could imagine, indeed, in understanding the 'heart'!"

Sora and Shiro raised their eyebrows at this machine's increasingly heated assertions.

"...Mm? Is...that so...?

The computer that explored the "heart." The world he extolled was one that could only exist with what was, in this place, technology of the distant future. But as Sora considered this, it hit him—*Wait a second.* Ex Machina was imagining their old world based on porno manga. So what was it exactly that was getting Einzig so heated...? But, with no attention to Sora's doubt, the heat of the machine's elocution inflamed further—!!

"Yes... Especially when considering matters of the "heart," everyone—including us—falls into the traps of stereotyping, iconography, association, and bias! Whereupon, we engage in actions which are *entirely meaningless*..."

And finally, his fist shaking in rage at his own folly:

"What madness! To consider the 'heart' by reason?! Is it not evident that the 'heart' is the *very furthest thing from reason*—it is *illogic* itself!! And love is its foremost virtue—but!!!!"

Steadily spreading his arms out wide, he said it loud—he released it from his soul—!!

"—Lösen: *Eros-Apokryphon!!*"

That instant, a massive array of *images* spread out all over the room. Einzig beheld the countless pictures suspended in the air, even stretching space to make room. As his speech raged on, tears formed in his eyes—

"Let us reflect truly! Has any other Ixseed ever shown the 'heart' so clearly?!"

This indeed was love, said the tears of the bellowing Einzig. But.

"What d'you have against me, d00d?! How dare you show everyone my treasures— Oh, I see, you wanna make me cry, do you?!"

Fine, then. Watch me cry!

The next instant, Sora covered Shiro's eyes and cried in a different sense at the—uh, well, the crown jewels, the porno comics. You know…with all the parts moving, and going in, and going out, with all the little hearts and stuff. Countless pages bedecked in art that would classically be described as "Eh-heh-heh-heh." The Shrine Maiden and Ino stared agog, while Jibril drooled.

"So my point is, this is your problem! It's a veritable parade of impossible premises with implausible results!"

Sora aimed to point out the flaws with what Einzig described as the very heart of love. The lazy unreality characteristic of adult manga. However—

"Hmm… Impossible premises with implausible results, you say? Could you be more specific, Spieler?" Einzig looked bemused. "Do you refer to the incoherence? The meaninglessness, or perhaps the absence of motivation leading to the act?"

—*All of them*, Sora wanted to say, but he held his tongue. Einzig made clear that he had an answer to all ready. Now here it was: Einzig powerfully bellowed the answer—!!

"Love *is* incoherent! It is a fallacy to seek logic in the 'heart'! The clashing of souls drawn to each other *is* meaningless! Motivations are ascribed to it only *after the fact*—yes! Just as porno manga teaches us!!"

—Why was this?

"Ah, the civilization that thus clearly demonstrated what love is! The erudition of those who represented this as the natural state of affairs!"

—As Einzig sang the praises of creators who engaged in a speedrun based on how few pages they could spend getting to the hanky-panky, Sora found himself almost agreeing. He clutched his head as several others spoke up. Each had been studying the pages very closely.

"Hmm… King Sora, I am experiencing a renewed respect for you.

It is proper that wolf-girls should have enormous breasts. I commend your taste." Ino was staring at a particular animal-girl hard enough to bore a hole in her as he nodded.

"......Just what are they supposed to be doing in these—? Eh. Well, 'tis no matter to me." The Shrine Maiden, having had zero experience in love, blushed as she feigned composure.

"Master, Master?! Please impart this knowledge unto me!!" Jibril drooled excitedly, begging to get the data back—"Perhaps even experientially. Please, please!!"—or otherwise to receive the most personal instruction possible.

"...Shiro. Your brother's gonna go dig a hole... You wanna get in it with me?"

"...Mm. O-kay..."

—In short, Sora was being publicly humiliated. Sprawled on the tatami with his sister, he gathered the gumption to bury himself. But—

"Yet, even with this glorious knowledge, it seems that my understanding of love is still insufficient for you to love me."

"...Look, before we talk about love, maybe you should understand empathy, or sensitivity..."

The mechanical man who spoke of love without comprehending the scars inflicted on Sora's heart nodded deeply.

"Understood. I shall go do that and return shortly, Spieler! Please look forward to it!"

"I ain't looking forward to shit! Leave and don't come back!!"

After thus cutting into Sora's wails with a firm and friendly smile—*foop*. The prodigious pervert vanished, taking his gallery of obscenity with him.

"...........Phew..."

Peace had been restored to the Shrine. All sighed.

"And when do *you* plan to return?"

Jibril alone thus murmuring, all followed her eyes to nothing:

"...Reply: This unit will return anytime upon request from Master."

As far as Sora and Shiro could tell—no. There probably hadn't even been a hint of spirits—

"Emir-Eins?! Huh? You were there?!"

"Acknowledgment: Always."

Even though the Werebeasts apparently hadn't been able to see the Ex Machina girl who answered Sora's call with a curtsy, she was present. Optical camouflage. As if it were no big deal.

"...Why are you here? Aren't you going back with the others?"

"Boast: Master commanded this unit to get lost. Therefore, this unit got lost."

...Sounds like Sora's usual bullshit. Everyone turned their annoyed gazes on Sora, but something else weighed on his mind.

—*Einzig... Well, he's a perverted little weirdo. Never mind him. But why didn't Emir-Eins act in line with the other Ex Machinas? Apparently she and Einzig were both "Befehler," but— No, wait, the real thing is...*

He'd just realized—Emir-Eins *didn't even actively come after him.*

"Remarks: Master is the master of this unit. Home position of this unit is by Master's side. However, position oscillates at night."

Maid robot. Committed to being a maid, apparently.

"Query: Positions supported tonight: top, bottom. Please specify preference. This unit will make the necessary preparations."

But for being a maid, she was awfully threatening about wanting to make babies with him. It was as if it was already determined that they were going to make love.

"...Let me rephrase. Sorry, but go away for a while— Oh, and one thing first?"

"Concession: Either position equally supported."

"Neither— Wait, what are you talking about...? It's just a question...!" Sora replied, exhausted.

I really don't get what these Ex Machina are up to, he thought. Maybe they had some hidden agenda, but for now, he didn't have enough information to say anything. This was why, so far, he'd had to hold on...and on...and play the straight man:

* * *

"...D00d, what's with the maid costumes?"

Sora managed to get that much out. But—

"Truism: Robots should be maid robots."

"My point is, where the hell did you get that BS?!"

—as the sun rises in the east and sets in the west, so shall robots be maid robots, apparently. Sora couldn't help but groan at this assertion. Did all this information come from his porn...? No, all the Ex Machinas had been in maid costumes since they first showed up.

...Sora preferred to forget that there had been a butler.

"Reply: Since end of Great War, Ex Machina has studied question: What is the meaning of Ex Machina's existence?" asked Emir-Eins softly, yet fluidly.

"Continuation: Hope. Preier transmitted 'heart' to Ex Machina."

She sounded like a recording. A smooth, inorganic playback.

"Recollection: Hope for realization of hope of Spieler—the man she loved."

But as Emir-Eins narrowed her gaze as if staring into a bright light, there was something about her face—her doll-like, vaguely artificial glass eyes, her lips—

"Admiration: Answer was persuasive. Approval granted from all units."

Though they belonged to a machine, a mere doll, there was something within them that shouldn't be there.

"Conclusion: To give all to Master, to serve him, and to be his strength. This is hope; this is will of unit—of Ex Machina."

Her voice had feeling—yes, what she had was hope.

Silence fell in the stillness of the Annex of the Shrine. Sora awkwardly opened his mouth to speak.

"Uhhh... You're really making it hard for me to crack jokes here, but..." He wasn't sure it was appropriate for him to bust the solemn atmosphere she'd created. But not being able to shake a certain doubt, close to a conviction, he mustered up the courage to be a wiseass. "...I mean. That doesn't mean you have to be a maid, does it?"

Even if you took what Emir-Eins was saying seriously, it didn't mean she had to be a maid. Surely there were other roles that would fulfill her will. And in any case, the costume was entirely beside the point.

"Acknowledgment: Eight roles match conclusion. Selection of 'maid'—"

Emir-Eins nodded to affirm Sora's doubt. He was right after all. That was why they didn't act like maids.

"Disclosure: Arbitrary."
—It was arbitrary.

So basically, yeah, they were poseur maids. This made everything make sense to Sora, and everything seem to not matter anymore to everyone else...

"...Interesting! A bit character such as you means to usurp my master?"

...except for one person— Pardon, body. Article? Unit? Hang on, how did you count god-killing weapons anyway? *Well, whatever*, Sora thought, unable to remember.

"And to think that such a throwaway believes that she can upstage me... My, my, this won't do at all." Jibril's halo spun more rapidly as she drew closer to Emir-Eins. "I'm not sure there's room in this story for the two of us. Let me adjust your characteristics to be more unique—even *avant-garde*. ♥"

Jibril's wings turned to surging pillars of light as she muddied the spirits in the air around them. She took a blade of light in hand, proposing to adjust Emir-Eins's character physically—or rather, put her out of character entirely.

"...H-hey, Jibril...!"

Even Sora and Shiro, who could not sense spirits, were able to perceive the spiritual compression and wild gust. Jibril wouldn't be able to put her power into practice—there were the Ten Covenants, after all. She couldn't hurt anyone. Even so, the aura of violence broke through the reason of the Shrine Maiden and Ino and made their fur stand on end.

"Rebuttal: This unit was bound to current Master only recently. True."

Only Emir-Eins stood up to Jibril with a placid exterior. Yet, her emotionless face bore a clear trace of a sneer as she—

"Declaration: This unit had already devoted herself to Master six thousand years ago. Bit character is you. Insolent. Obstructive. Stupid. However, property of Master. Cannot destroy for fear of Master's wrath."

—*provoked* Jibril.

"Allll right! I shouldn't have held you back!! We're done here, right?!"

Sora's panicked squeal was drowned out by the clearly audible rumbling of animosity.

"You have a pretty big mouth, don't you? ♥ Why don't we make it a little bigger and turn it into a gaping hole? ♪"

"Derision: This unit is capable of eliminating Irregular Number alone with current armaments. Easy. Master, please authorize demonstration."

"Listen! Listen to me, okay? I was wrong, so just get out of here! Please!!"

"…Jibril, s-s-sit…"

First, Sora and Shiro's *commands* made Jibril sit down flat on the floor.

Next, per Sora's *request*, Emir-Eins prepared to shift.

"…You scrappy little doll."

"Reply: Hen. Lösen: *Asura-Apokryphon.*"

As the two glared at each other with their parting remarks, Emir-Eins vanished.

Peace had been restored to the Annex of the Shrine—for real this time.

"...You... Just what are you bringing into my house...?" groaned the Shrine Maiden, now grasping the general gist of things.

"It's not my— Okay, I guess it's my fault... Sorry. We'll go."

"...Shrine Maiden...... We're, sorry, okay...?"

Sora objected immediately, then shook his head. He and Shiro both slumped over and apologized. They were the ones who had come to the Shrine. From the Shrine Maiden's point of view, all they'd done was cause trouble. To begin with, they'd come here in order to run from Ex Machina. And now that Ex Machina knew where they were, they'd probably be back in a jiffy... In any case, Sora and Shiro had better skedaddle. They'd better have Jibril shift them somewhere where, this time, they definitely wouldn't find them—

"Ino Hatsuse. You brought them here, did you? Go help."

"At your command, O Holy Shrine Maiden... But we have no duty to help them, have we?"

Just as Ino said, the Shrine Maiden had no duty to help Sora and Shiro. Even when they'd saved her friend—Holou—that was just a matter of using one another. The *trust* of a gamer, and all the more so that of an agent plenipotentiary, was by no means reliance—but—

"We haven't, have we? Still, love, I'd hate to make enemies of those monsters."

That's right—it was because of a command based on a coolheaded "calculation" that Ino sat politely before Sora and Shiro.

"...Hmm. So, King Sora, they have mistaken you for the one they love. This is a most pitiable state of affairs."

"...Uh, yeah... Never would've expected it, but I'm glad you understand..."

At Ino's serious demeanor, Sora felt a seedling of friendship sprout in his heart, and then—

"Indeed... Ex Machina is truly to be pitied... What would anyone have to do to deserve this? Of all possibilities, to fall for a damned monkey like you…!"

Upon the next words Ino spoke, fist trembling, Sora cursed the illusion.

—*Damn you, you old fart.*

Sora almost said it, but instead only incorporated the tone of resentment into his next question.

"Let's be straight, okay…? What can I do to resolve this *peacefully*?"

It really was no laughing matter. He didn't want them to go extinct, and he was glad they said they were his allies, but even that was a mistake. If he slipped up and got on their bad side, in the worst case—so much for his all-powerful concert equipment.

"…A sleazebag like you must've had experience with misunderstandings resulting in stalking a few or maybe a thousand times."

Sora would very much appreciate it if one of those experiences had furthermore resulted in stabbing. Regrettably, though, what with those Ten Covenants and all, the old fart was not dead yet. But if anyone had some idea of how to deal with stalkers, Ino Hatsuse should be the guy—not that Sora's expectations were very high, but he was grasping at straws here.

"…King Sora, what has come over you? I should not expect this."

However—Ino narrowed his eyes keenly.

"It embarrasses me to think how I have been consistently outstripped by one unable to recognize something so simple."

"…………You…what…?"

—*Simple?*

That was Ino's conclusion, his eyes brimming with a vague disappointment. He sighed at Sora, who was still befuddled, before spelling it out.

"Stop being a quivering little virgin and go get laid, you dumb ape."

—*So they've got the wrong guy. So what?*

The man notorious for thinking with his lower half sneered, displaying his fangs as well as his true nature.

"Jibril, let's go. This time, somewhere Emir-Eins and the others can't—"

Sora and Shiro got to their feet and prepared to head home as if to say they'd been mistaken to expect anything for even a second.

"...Sir, could it be that you truly have not realized?"

Still, Ino's voice, sincerely doubtful, deeply surprised, kept them.

"Do you not grasp that the Ex Machinas have a hardware lock that prevents them from reproducing with those other than specified?"

"Exactly! So how's it gonna help for me to agree to make—?"

"In such a case, you may embrace them as you will. If you are not the man they seek, reproduction will be impossible."

...

......

...........?

"—...Huh? Uh, whuhh...?"

Sora took a whole minute to mull over Ino's words and then produced some foolish noises. What would happen if he agreed to make babies with them? He wasn't the guy they were looking for. So the lock would stop him. There you go. Not the guy. Done.

...No, no, no... Wait, wait, wait. Calm down, Sora, virgin, eighteen!! It couldn't be, it couldn't be, how could he have missed that—?!

—*Something was wrong here.* Meanwhile, amidst Sora's confusion, Ino came in and packed it up.

"The mistake, moreover, originates from them alone. Mistaking you for someone from six thousand years ago."

"...Uh, yeah... I guess..."

"You must only answer their demands. Who could possibly blame you?" Ino piled it on. "Once you prove that you are not the man they seek, they will have no choice but to accept that the man has passed. Their only option will be to wager the release of their lock in a game with you and lose. After all, it's that or perish."

...Uh... Huh? I—why did I say no, again...?

An onslaught of perfect logic assailed Sora, when—

"......Brother."

—his little sister's subzero gaze brought him scurrying back to his senses with a yelp.

"Hey! That's the thing! I can't expose Shiro to R-18—"

"Sir... Please consider the matter calmly. First of all, do you not realize that this is your only chance to experience sexual intercourse?"

"—Nice job implying that I'll never have another chance, bastard."

...Not that I'm denying it. Sora groaned, but Ino went on.

"I understand that you have your own issues, Sir. But do they justify allowing Ex Machina to perish?"

"Well, uh... I guess not. But I can't be away from Shiro—"

"You could simply request of Miss Jibril that she block the light and sound, for Queen Shiro's benefit."

Ino kept settling the issues one after another.

"Is this not preferable to the guilt of having allowed an entire race to cease to be?"

And yet, Ino's words made the vague unease within Sora rear its head further and further as if in inverse proportion.

—No. *Something was wrong.*

Ino's assertions made perfect sense. Clear as day. Could it really be that he'd overlooked...something so simple? The way the Ex Machinas acted; the way they'd trapped Sora; the way they came on to him. So many things felt off. For instance—

"One final comment. They demanded that you choose one of them with whom to reproduce, as I understand. If this be so—you could very well do *just as they recently proposed.* I see no reason to refuse."

Sora half listened to Ino's words, brainstorming ideas and putting them in order. He struggled to identify what was wrong—and then, at last, he prostrated himself and came to a solid conclusion.

* * *

"Can you not engage them all in *intercourse* and select one for *reproduction* thereafter?"

"I gotta save the robot girls!! Bye, gotta go! Forgive me, O wise teacher!!"

—He'd just overlooked it!!

How could he have overlooked it? People overlook things!!

"Sorry to impose on you, Shrine Maiden! Jibril, we're going back to Elkia! Time waits for no one!!"

"...You really know how to impose, at that..."

"Yes, Master. Allow me to prepare for a long-distance shift."

As he was bathed in the Shrine Maiden's icy glare and Jibril's sparkles...

"Maaaan! You know how it is! I'm *totally* not looking forward to this, y'know? But what can ya do?! Pretty girls say I have to go save them, I guess I'll go and give the world a good saving! If heaven wills it, I mean!!"

...Sora's head grew cool, cooler, coolest as he lamented. His folly was unfathomable... Why hadn't he used common sense? There were twelve beautiful girls falling over themselves, *begging* him for it as they changed their appearance to suit his taste! Made-to-order maid robots coming on to him! Refuse? Who the hell did he think he was?! Sora, virgin, eighteen! Don't get so full of yourself, cherry boy!

"...But, Brother, you're *not* him... You'd be...deceiving them..."

Shiro pouted sullenly at her brother's fierce self-flagellation. Normally, this would be enough to stop Sora, but today—

"I would... But if it's what it takes to save someone, your brother will lie, cheat, and steal..." Sora answered, his gaze merciful, as if taking on mankind's original sin. "Even if I am hated for it, even if I am blamed forevermore! I shall accept the responsibility...for all."

As Sora spoke of love and benevolence for all things living without reward, his eyes sparkled with the anticipation of a filthy kickback for his base desires.

"Now, let us say adieu to Sora, virgin, eighteen! And sally forth to welcome Sora, *non*-virgin, eighteen!!"

Sora's call to arms toward his future was met with a mumble.

"…Mm? Umm… Sir. I think you may be a bit confused?"

"Is that so, Teacher?! Then guide your foolish apprentice! **Yeah!**"

Sora tapped his foot as Ino pondered.

"Well… Sir, they are machines. Not only that, but presenting themselves on the basis of your pornography…"

"That is so! Have you no objections?!"

While noticing that Jibril seemed to be taking much longer to prepare for a shift than usual, Ino carefully mentioned the hypothesis he'd formed to address this difficult question.

"Might they not be considered…a mere masturbation aid…?"

……

"Well. How do I put this? King Sora, a *non-virgin*? …Ha. Impossible."

……

Then, all of a sudden… All the threads, all the missing pieces—Sora felt them all come together.

"Ah… I see… That's what it was…" He spoke softly, with a smile of an ascetic who had just achieved nirvana. "Jibril… Sorry for the trouble—can we change our destination?"

"—Eh? Ah, yes. Well then…where shall we set our course?"

At last he could see everything, what was behind all those countless weights. The true nature of Ex Machina's words and actions, and most of all—

"Anywhere… Just as long as they can't find us, anywhere…"

In short: *Tee-hee-hee! Wham, bam, thank you, ma'am.* Why hadn't he thought of such a simple solution?

—It wasn't that he hadn't thought of it. Deep down, he knew.

"...*If it sounds too good to be true...* Ha-ha... I knew it..."

Sora, the virgin eighteen-year-old, knew it wouldn't be happening to him any time soon. Shedding a tear for the binding nature of the world—the self-correcting nature of history—Sora and his crew leaped through space.

■ ■ ■

The red moon shone on the island of Kannagari. Sora and Shiro walked a residential area on the outskirts. They were very near the house of a little Werebeast girl they knew, Izuna Hatsuse.

"...This is pretty close to the Shrine... Is Ex Machina really not going to find us here?" Sora had totally thought that they'd be warping to the other side of the world.

"N-no... It's like what they say in your world about being right under one's nose—" Jibril was beaming confidently, but appeared exhausted. "I made a long-distance shift *intentionally to a nearby location*, and I *severed* the crack in space. Even Ex Machina is incapable of reopening severed space, and little could they expect that we used this much power to go three hundred kilometers."

—Not that Sora or Shiro had any idea what she meant by "severing space."

"...To think that even *you* get this worn out shaking off Ex Machina... Damn."

"Well, they may be worn-out ancient rubbish, but they are my acknowledged enemies who slew Artosh, god of war."

Jibril sounded weirdly excited, but Sora thought:

—*Really?*

They were some kind of bullshit, you could say. Rank Ten, my ass—the system's gotta be rigged. According to Jibril's records, it had been because they couldn't use magic—but, d00d. They'd designed virtual spirit junction nerves—those taillike cables—and made equipment to murder spirits like gasoline to produce the same effects as magic. Apparently, it wasn't technically magic. But that brought them neck and neck with Jibril. Such bullshit. And then the Ten Covenants counted Elementals among the "sixteen seeds," so Ex Machina couldn't kill spirits anymore. Magical shit be damned, they shouldn't even have been able to operate after that—but here they were.

—They'd adapted. They'd realized they couldn't use gasoline anymore and adopted renewable energy. Probably in a flash. These guys were so OP it wasn't even funny—but. If Sora had faced these OP hacks—*and they'd really slain Artosh*—

"...By the way, Master, is it really all right? That is, not to return to Elkia?"

Sora, who'd been lost in thought, twitched and stopped.

"Ah— Oh no! Of course, Master, I have no intention of interfering in your decision!"

Seeing this, Jibril hurriedly descended from the air, folded her wings, and knelt—

"It is my sentiment that, considering how preposterous it would be to bequeath your noble chastity to these poor imitators of my service to you, it would be more appropriate for you to use your first slave first, that is, your humble servant—"

"...That's not...the point...! Jibril, freeze..."

Jibril was sliding sideways from an apology to an entreaty, starting to remove her clothes, when Shiro halted her process. But both the frozen Jibril's gaze and that of the Shiro who froze her asked the same question.

—*Why'd you give up on the hanky-panky?*

Meeting their gazes, Sora smirked...*heh.*

"Is it all right, you ask? Ha-ha... **Like hell it's all right! Shit!!**"

The very rude and inconsiderate scream that echoed through the entire neighborhood caused Shiro to swing her hands over her ears.

"To what extent must I be cockblocked?! Just how far does this world intend to test me, huh?!"

The floodgates had been broken, and his rancor could not subside. In tears, Sora thought:

—*Okay, fine, whatever! So there's no sex? Sure, that's cool, too!! I get it, already!! I've got enough culture not to demand hardcore smut out of a cheesecake game!! But, d00d!*

"Why you gotta bait me?! You put in hardcore assets, the characters, the art, the whole damn scene, and then you say *there's no way to trigger it*—you corporate assholes have a bug in your brains!!"

Debug your damn game! Sora was about to scream next—but wait. *The debuggers and programmers aren't to blame*, he corrected himself, shaking his head.

"Yeah. I guess it is possible if you want to. I could go back to Elkia right now and have a harem."

You could trigger the scene. You could play it.

"*But if you do it, you can't win?!* Is this trolling or what?!"

But if you did, you were stuck. No possibility of a do-over. So whose fault was this shitty design? The producer's? The director's? The writer's—?!

"……Brother… Calm *down*…"

"You can't win…? What do you mean?"

His little sister's chilling command and Jibril's consternation were just enough to rein him in. Sighing so deeply as to expel his soul, Sora sat on the road with a thump.

"…What do I mean? Just what I said…"

Ino's story? If they knew he was the wrong guy, Ex Machina would release their lock and reproduce.

Why? Because otherwise they'd perish. It should go without saying.

—But that was wrong.

"Even if they know I'm the wrong guy, they *won't reproduce*—they'll choose to go extinct."

Thus, the cockblock was assured. They looked doubtfully at him.

"…You mean…Ex Machina…*wants* to go extinct…?"

Shiro flopped into Sora's lap as he rested his back against the wall of the alley.

"I dunno about that... If they actively wanted to, they probably would've died out a long time ago..." Sora put his hand on the head of his sister who had taken her comfortable default position. "But I can say, in the worst case, these guys don't *care* if they go extinct."

The other two looked at him for proof. But it was simple; Sora answered.

"If that wasn't the case, they wouldn't *threaten* to go extinct. It wouldn't work."

If you don't do what I want, I'll kill myself! That only worked when they were really ready to kill themselves. Sora couldn't say for sure that he understood the feelings of machines. Still—the Ex Machinas' eyes as they used the threat of their extinction to force him to play chess...were serious. It had been with a foreboding close to conviction that Sora had accepted—and.

That's what was eating at him.

"...Look... Ex Machina was the race that triggered the end of the war, right...?

Then they were the makers of this world where everything was decided by games. Why would *they* be willing to sacrifice their race? Why—

"Why are they so willing to break this game...?!"

He didn't get it. He didn't get why they would mistake him for someone from six thousand years ago. He didn't get any of this.

"...Seriously, are their circuits fried? Are they bugging out?"

That would make things easier to understand... But still, it wouldn't solve anything.

"Then if I may be so impertinent...I have two suggestions."

"Let's hear 'em! 'Kay, go! What's number one?"

Jibril raised her hand, and Sora pointed desperately.

"If you are concerned about the existence of their race, you could store one and kill the—"

"Yeah, that's gonna be a no from me! 'Kay, next! What's number two?"

Drooping with the sadness of having her brilliant idea shot down, Jibril continued.

"Though unpleasant to observe…perhaps we could tolerate their continued existence and misunderstanding."

…Hmm. A more realistic plan. Sora prompted her for more.

"Fortunately, they have not specified a time by which you must fulfill your duty to reproduce with them. If you simply delay it indefinitely—they would constitute one more race that at least claimed to be your ally, which you could add to the Commonwealth of Elkia… Does this not suit your purpose?"

"Yeah… Not a bad idea. I thought of that, too. But there are two problems with that."

Sora smirked, grabbed Shiro in his arm, and stood—

"First! My reason and will are incapable of withstanding this situation!!"

—*Let's have sexxx.* ♥

Could he keep hearing that indefinitely from beautiful girls advancing to seduce him and keep ignoring it…? Only the protagonist of *To L*ve Ru* had that kind of godly fortitude. Sora was merely a man.

"And second! I'll say this as many times it takes: *I'm not their guy!!*"

According to Einzig, they'd gone past their service life by 5,982 years. It would be friggin' ridiculous if they were to just suddenly go extinct one of these days, and here was the kicker—!

"What if they suddenly realized I wasn't their guy one of these days?! What the hell would happen then?!"

"B-but it was they who made the error… They couldn't blame—"

"You want me to count on that kind of logic working on chicks who've been pining over a guy for six thousand years?! If they were that rational, they wouldn't be on the edge of extinction, now would they?! This is heavy shit! Love is some real heavy shit!!"

For starters, the Commonwealth of Elkia hardly had any allies. They were counting on being betrayed by their own. So the issue wasn't making enemies, but rather that they had *no friggin' idea what they'd do.*

"Say Emir-Eins was to grab a kitchen knife and be like, *'User has deceived this unit!* I'm gonna kill you and then kill myself!' —Shit, I can see it! What are you supposed to do then? Huh?!"

A real-live mental case with those crazy powers?

—Worst enemy ever.

If the whole race was willing to suicide-attack them, they'd be screwed. Sora shivered as he imagined that kind of horror in this world.

"Very well, then. I have a third suggestion… Rather, it is a logical extension of your initial demand…" Jibril raised her hand and asked a question. "You proposed releasing their lock with a game… Then if you simply have them wager to fall in love with a pig and you win, will this not settle the matter by pairing them with a partner most suitable for them?"

…Right, the pig stuff aside, this had been Sora's first plan. To use the power of the Covenants to release their hardware lock and bind them to reproduce independently. In other words, force them to forget about the affection they'd cultivated for six thousand years. Jibril's point was, couldn't you just try that again? Sora answered with a question.

"Put yourself in their position, Jibril. Say Ex Machina came to you with a game they were sure they'd win, and they told you if you lost you'd venerate some animal as your master and make babies with him—what would you do?"

"I would pity their severe neural defects and take their heads

to— Oh...." Though she'd begun with a smile, she then drooped apologetically. "Perhaps I am defective... They would surely not accept any such game, would they?"

—Indeed. They'd have no motivation to. It was because they didn't care if they went extinct—because they had nothing to lose—that they'd been able to dupe Sora into a game he couldn't win. It was only because they'd been sure they'd win that Sora had been able to make such demands. If he were to make such demands again—*he'd have to dupe them back.* Specify a game that Sora and Shiro were sure to win and get them to accept it. Get them to accept the demand to forget about their love and reproduce. When they had nothing to lose? *Ex Machina?* —Was that...even possible?

—If he agreed to make babies with them, he was screwed.

If he didn't agree to make babies with them, he was screwed.

And he couldn't think of a single way to trap them—nor was he even sure there was one.

"The hell is with this pain-in-the-ass race?! Give me a break!"

There would have been more options if they'd straight-out come as an enemy. Sora was shouting again, unable to take it, when—

Honk, honk.

"Hngh?! Uh, s-sorry, please excuse me, please..."

"...Eegh... I-I'll, get out...of your way... Nghh..."

The horn made Sora and Shiro, huddled together in the corner of the alley, slide out of the way as naturally as the flowing of a stream.

"...M-Master? ...What's the matter?"

Jibril was befuddled. Sora and Shiro cowered in each other's arms.

"Heh. Jibril... What do you think a loser does when told 'Move'?" Sora was still shivering. Yet, he bellowed with pride: "With the brief remark, 'Oh, sorry,' he *gets the hell out of the way*! This is the true way of the loser!"

"…Just say no…to bugging normal people…"

Ah, our most trusted disciple. Have you forgotten who we are? Regardless of how portentously we may behave, we are by nature naught but awkward, shut-in losers!! Trembling in inexplicable awe before the answer of the two, overwhelming in its majesty, Jibril knelt.

"…N-now I see… Please forgive my foolish question!"

As Sora and Shiro nodded in satisfaction, they were struck by a realization. Albeit a bit late.

……*Hmm.*

"Hey, Shiro… Are there cars in this world? I mean…" The honking white van had passed by them just like that…but… "I mean, not a car… That was, uh, totally a HiA*e…"

The HiA*e. Everyone knew this vehicle, specializing in the transport of light cargo, yet indiscriminating as to its contents. Packages? Refrigerators? You got it. Porn for the con, AK-47s, RPGs, little girls—the flexibility with which it lent itself to all manner of freight was, in a manner of speaking, legendary. So now the question was: What was inside?

"…Lösen: Love Success Situation Forme *Checkmartyr*—Prototype 0010."

As for who was in the driver's seat, at any rate, it was Emir-Eins, naturally.

—It seemed that they had even managed to deploy a motor vehicle from Sora's porn. That was impressive, but not the problem at hand. It had already been pretty well established that Ex Machina was bonkers like that. What Sora really wanted to know was *what it was for*—or maybe he didn't, but—

"H-how…? The crack in space—severed space should be impossible to reopen!"

—to Jibril, on the other hand, even that wasn't the question. She hyperventilated in shock to see how easily they'd tracked them. To be smirked at.

"Acknowledgment: Severed space prohibits tracking. However, fissure clearly excessive for long-distance shift."

"......!"

"Paradox: Destination near. Also, Irregular Number extreme. *Near* implies *on island*. But outside of Ex Machina detection range. List of residential areas that meet parameters: Here. Flügel inferred to lack knowledge of map."

...In short: Jibril's ruse was obvious. Emir-Eins's perfect doll eyes were somehow unmistakably tinged with pity.

"...Knowledge: Irregular Number lacks intellect. Simple-minded. Foolish."

"_____♥"

Jibril's smile dripped with cold malice, swelling instantaneously. Sora and Shiro could swear they saw it with their eyes. The two powder kegs staring each other down were interrupted, not by Sora or Shiro—

"Ah, Spieler, I have made you wait one thousand five hundred three point zero one seven seconds! Now let us go on a journey to first build our friendship!!"

Rrrmmmmmm! Einzig flung open the sliding door and appeared with a smile and a shout.

—Ah, why was it that Sora's premonitions could not be allayed?

"...Crap. You went and used the worst reference possible, did you...?" Sora groaned and clutched his head.

The cargo was that of his fears, that of the vehicle's vile fame. Filmy smoke obscured the rear's dark contents. But in all probability... they were a bunch of cyborg babes, modest in size and undignified in state. Or perhaps they were soon to be...but in any case, this was past the line for past-the-line. In addition—it was *wildly awry*. After a long, deep breath, Sora shrieked:

"Like hell I'm gonna build a beautiful friendship with you! And anyway! I have no interest in being *forced into* anything!!"

—*Did I overestimate you?* he further wondered silently. Up to now, Ex Machina had accurately identified Sora's preferences as they updated their approach. But now this was Sora's very least favorite porn genre: the one where the guy travels across Japan abducting beautiful girls, and a friendship just happens to blossom between them. Sora went so far as to click his tongue at this one-two combo of ultimate creepiness.

"Heh... Fear not, Spieler. We are Ex Machina—we never make the same mistake twice..."

But Einzig answered with a smile, gloating about his race's key feature.

Hrmm... How many times have you made the mistake of humiliating me? Or did you not count that as a mistake?

As Sora started to suspect so seriously, Einzig regaled him further.

"My beloved dislikes nonconsensual acts. Nor does he like to have his sexual preferences made public!!"

—Oh. So he did *count it as a mistake after all.*

Fairly relieved, Sora sighed, but then the next word...

"*—However.*"

...introduced a statement quite contradictory to the preceding. To wit:

"It seems he does not object to <u>un</u>-nonconsensual acts! Furthermore, this vehicle is *private and soundproof*!!"

The fearsome learning abilities of Ex Machina had taught them: *No raep for you. Only reverse raep.*

Sora's reason whispered to him: *Ten Covenants. They can't do that.* But the fear of being kidnapped and having his butt pounded by this sex machine—equivalent to the fear of getting his ass rekt—along with the countless hands that stuck out from the van—was enough to shatter his faith.

"Jibriiiiiiiiiiiiiiiiil! Save me! Heeeeeeeeeelp!!"

"...Brother...! Brother's, getting...ass-jacked!!"
Jibril had to act immediately upon those cries. They warped.

Meanwhile, ignorant of the plaintive wails of Sora and Shiro, Steph ran about the Elkia Royal Castle as if to stomp through the floor, her shoulders high. Sora and Shiro had dumped all the actual work on her—but for once, that wasn't why she was angry.

"What's wrong with them? Cavorting so and then absconding!"

About an hour earlier, Holou's debut concert had finished without a hitch. It had shown sufficient success to disgust Steph. But now Steph was flip-flopping as she saw the flop of the meet and greet after.

...*Meet and greet.* Steph didn't get the concept—hell, Holou probably didn't, either. Sora had said, *Make sure there's security. Some smart-asses will probably attempt some sexual harassment. Also, you should stay out of the castle.* Or something like that. But hell, if there was anyone in the world other than those siblings who had the mettle to sexually harass Holou. Sexual harassment? Look at this. This was normal.

—Seeing the masses cowering, unable even to approach Holou, much less shake her hand, Steph thought, *Yes.* This was the normal reaction. This was as it should be. It should have been. Yet—there sat Holou, next to Steph, in a booth labeled "Meet and Greet Venue"—

"...*O thou... Ste... What is Holou doing here...?*"

The forlorn query of the idol with zero fans at her meet and greet made Steph cry out:

"See how hard she has tried! How can you make this girl look so, without a second glance?!"

Unable to bear it, Steph was running around the Elkia Royal

Castle at full speed. She didn't know what Sora and Shiro were after. But she did know it was miserable to see Holou like this. The people were there. They just wouldn't approach her because they were afraid of an Old Deus. In which case—!

"We just have to show them she's *not scary*—so I'll summon all affiliated with the house of Dola!"

She'd mobilize her family connections—to bring out the shills. Blissfully unconscious of the questionable nature of her use of royal privilege, Steph was scampering about when—

"…Hmm. What was it that displeased the Spieler this time…?"

"Certainty: Einzig intrinsically displeases Spieler. Other issues irrelevant. Immaterial."

"Wh-what…?! Then what would you propose I do?!"

"Suggestions: In descending order of recommendation: Get lost. Self-destruct. Explode. Greatest factor in inability to determine preferences of Master: Einzig."

The very serious voices of the machines could be heard, engaged in a very pointless argument. What had they been doing loitering about the castle all this time? Talking on about how to seduce Sora forever and ever. Each time they tried and failed, they came back here and repeated this—

"—Hey, you there! What did you come here for anyway?!"

It hit Steph that pretty much all her problems right now were their fault.

…No, actually, if you went back, the root of all evil was those two who were making Holou be an idol. At the very least, if Sora and Shiro were here, Holou probably wouldn't be making that face.

"Courtesy: Units imposing. Please excuse."

"Though we burden you, we ourselves are desperate…to discover how we can make the Spieler love us…"

"If you're aware you're imposing, why don't you help? There are thirteen of you, after all!" And thence Steph came to roar out a line most uncharacteristic of her. It was that forlorn look of Holou's, stuck in her head. "If you have the time to think about something so *pointless*, we could be rounding up plenty of shills—"

Then.

"...Command: Disclose grounds for statement of pointlessness. Details of opinion."

"_____!"

The swarm of unnatural eyes gathered upon Steph brought her back, frozen. What had she just said, in the heat of the moment—to these god-killers who had completely outpaced Sora? Steph oozed a cold sweat at the feeling of her insides being probed—but still she asked herself.

—*Did I say something wrong?*

"S-Sora will never be moved...b-by such *falsehoods*...!"

—She answered herself. *I've said nothing wrong!* Such defiance burst forth from Steph, quite against her will as her knees shook. Ex Machina could go on however they wanted about Sora's preferences, but what they were doing—was a *lie*. The Sora Steph knew was not a man who would be deceived by such lies. It was thus—that Steph had said it was pointless. But surprisingly—

"...I...see... Love can never be conveyed by words that come not from the heart... I see!"

Einzig replied dejectedly as he lifted his gaze to the heavens.

"What a fool I have been...to overlook such a self-evident truth! You!"

"Y-yes?!"

"O nameless gentlewoman, I thank you. Now I see the path to producing progeny with the Spieler. All units, prepare to shift!"

"So you really aren't going to help?! And hey, I have a name!!"

Whether they were ignoring Steph or just didn't notice her, the Ex Machinas moved to shift back to Sora, when—

"Forget that path. It's futile."

—a nasal voice echoed forth. And.

*　*　*

A shock raced through without sound and shook the castle—shook all of Elkia. It was beyond Steph's knowledge what had happened. Only the Ex Machinas registered it: The castle had been sealed in severed space, cutting off all external observation and movement.

"It gives me acid reflux just to think that you scrap heaps still exist. I wouldn't let you reproduce on a farm. ♪"

The appearance of the girl, as if from the void, divested Steph of her breath. It was the agent plenipotentiary of Flügel—the first article, Azril. But that itself wasn't what took Steph's breath away. Nor was it the fact that, looking through the window, she could observe that Avant Heim itself had shifted over Elkia like a lid.

"Not everyone is as understanding as Jibsy… Right, you scrap?"

It was that which was loaded in her eyes as she said this: an unthinkable hostility. It was entirely different from that which had been exchanged between Jibril and the Ex Machinas.

"You dingy little dolls who aped the power bestowed by my lord and used your shoddy imitations to trick us and trap us and massacre my cute little sisters and then kill my lord himself—" In apparent good humor, Azril stepped toward Einzig, even clapping. "If you can think of a reason I shouldn't kill you, I'm all ears. ♥"

"…………"

It was enough to show Steph that Jibril and the Ex Machinas had been sincere, as Azril smiled and stroked the cheek of the silent Einzig. It was quite unlike the previous encounter when they claimed to bear no resentment. More mechanical than a machine, devoid of the hesitation characteristic of life—it was pure: It was murder.

"Wait—A-Azril?! Sora and Shiro—Jibril won't—"

That malice convinced Steph, despite the Covenants, that there was about to be slaughter before her eyes. So she raised her voice to interrupt, but—

"*I don't care.* ♥"

—Steph realized she was dead. The smiling glance from Azril

had gouged her heart. Azril continued to smile despite Steph falling apart like a corpse.

"All right, tin men! Let's talk. Here are the rules. ♥" Azril clapped. "I'm gonna ask you a question, very politely, and you heaps of junk are gonna answer, very politely. That's it!" She looked back at the Ex Machinas. "I anticipate a satisfactory answer that tickles us. If not—"

—*Don't make me do this*, she implied.

"Av'n', all the kids in the sky, and I are gonna kill you until there's not a speck of dust left. Getting rid of anything in our way. Elkia, Sora, his sister—even Jibsy. We'll smash the planet if we have to, to exterminate you... So you'd better answer carefully."

It seemed that she was, however, expecting to have to do it.

"Lord Artosh. God of war. Strongest of all the Old Dei—"

After a beat, the first Flügel commanded those who slew her lord to tell her—

"How did you mere dolls manage to kill the strongest deity—?"

What had happened to her lord, the king of all? How was it possible—?

■■■

"Flyyy me to the hmmm, hmm hmm hmm hmmm..."

Sora and Shiro lazily sang a song they only remembered the first stanza of. It was one giant leap for them, one small step for humankind. Suddenly, they found themselves standing on the surface of the moon, leaving behind all of humanity's dreams, struggles, and wisdom back on Disboard. Just like the song, they'd arrived here so casually, carried by Jibril. Viewing the new horizon without a trace of the awe or respect it might have merited, they grumbled.

"...It's not, as blue...as they say...right...?"

"It's not even round. Tet's pieces are all, 'Look at me'!"

They didn't know about Earth, but now they knew about Disboard—seen from the moon, it wasn't blue or round. With those giant chess pieces towering from it, it reminded them of a barrel with swords stuck in it. Would something pop out if they stuck in a few more? ...Maybe Tet? He'd be in a pirate costume, flying through space. As Sora and Shiro daydreamed—

"...Ex Machina, surely won't be able to follow us, all the way *here*. Heh-heh... *Siiiiigh...*"

Jibril mumbled fiercely, looking pretty close to death as she sprawled onto the ground and sneered.

—They didn't have to ask where "here" was. It was the moon, most likely the red moon that Sora and Shiro were always looking up at. Other than the planet, all they could see in any direction was sand, sand, and sand on stone. The heavily cratered surface was windless, and gravity was so weak that you bounced if you took a step. Apart from the sand being red, presumably composed of different materials, even a monkey could see that this was exactly the same as Earth's natural satellite, also known as the moon. Then if you weren't a monkey, there were other questions you had to ask. One being—

"Hey... If I'm remembering right—isn't this someone's place?"

Not that they had any standing to ask after barging into the Shrine and bringing all that commotion...but the Shrine Maiden had given them permission.

—Ixseed Rank Thirteen, Lunamana... It was said that the gods created this red moon as their abode even before the time of the Great War—and this being so, knowledge of what kind of race they were was nonexistent. Sora sure didn't remember making an appointment with them, and he really would rather not have more problems.

"Ah, Master, the Lunamana metropolis is on the opposite side of the moon. This side belongs to no one." Jibril knelt reverently, answering to soothe Sora's unspoken fears. "As you can see, it is a barren wasteland, devoid of air or even spirits. And the races with the power to come here are the very ones for which it holds no value.

However, it is quiet, and the sun will not rise until a good while later in the month."

Indeed, there was no air to propagate sound waves. One would it expect it to be rather quiet here by the standards of the world. Yet, Jibril was saying she'd brought them here for their comfort.

"I also brought with us a globe of severed space sealing in the air in a radius of five hundred meters." She smirked crookedly. "It is not possible to penetrate severed space. In addition, the average distance here is one hundred ninety thousand kilometers. Even Ex Machina would surely find it difficult to achieve such an ultra-long-distance shift. It should also be noted that the red moon has an orbital speed of approximately three kilometers per second. Even if they were to reopen the crack I made in space, they would find themselves lost in space... Ex Machina will not find us here... Heh, heh-heh-heh...!!"

As Jibril cackled, Sora and Shiro wondered: ...*Did you just jinx us?*

...*Ah, whatever.* They wiped the sand off some random rock and sat down, using it as a backrest.

"Hey, why does Lunamana only live on the opposite side of the moon? Why not take it all...?" Sora suddenly asked.

"...Brother, look..." Shiro pointed ahead of them.

There—those countless craters. Finally, Sora saw there was something wrong. If Jibril was talking about a front and a back, that meant that the red moon, too, always had the same side facing the planet. Just like Earth's moon. Then shouldn't the back also be covered in craters—the remains of cosmic bombardment?

"Oh, yes. I misspoke. Let me correct myself, with apologies."

Sora had a suspicion—no, a near-certain hypothesis—which Jibril proceeded to address.

"The back, where lies the metropolis, is of course blessed with air, spirits, and even rich greenery, as I am informed."

Only—she smiled on as she confirmed the hypothesis—

"It seems this side was subject to stray fire during the War. Now it is *dead.* ♥"

…The bombardment wasn't from space—it was from the planet. *So stray fire transformed a lunar surface 190,000 kilometers away into a dead world…?* Sora was beginning to ask seriously why they didn't do it in space— Oh. No spirits…

"Ahhh, whatever! At least now we can think about the most important issue at hand in peace."

Sora took out the tablet. He and Shiro started messing with it. Jibril nodded gravely.

"What to do about Ex Machina… Indeed…"

Sora and Shiro looked at her questioningly.

"Wh-what? Is it a different issue?"

"…Uh, but… *What good will it do, to think about, that one?* …Them…"

"We've got more pressing matters to attend to! Like what to do for stage equipment for Holou's second concert!!"

The task scheduler was already packed. And they'd already had to delegate one important task—the meet and greet—to *Steph.* Any more of this, and they'd totally fail as producers! They had to nail down plans for Jibril to do the effects, as they were envisioning before Ex Machina showed up. And how to accomplish all their other tasks while being chased around by Ex Machina? This by itself was incredibly hard. Sora tore at his hair and groaned.

"…Yeah. It would be ideal to *do something* about Ex Machina and get them to help us. That would solve everything."

Walking, talking stage equipment. Anything was possible.

—Walking was the hard part.

And the talking. And the bugs behind the thoughts they spoke of. And how you couldn't squash or ignore the bugs without breaking the rules. In summary, the problem was that there seemed to be nothing to do about them.

"…Maybe, they'd help…if you just…asked them? …They do, love you…"

"You want me to be in Einzig's debt?! He's gonna ask for my chastity in return!"

"…If it's, between that…and another, girl…I'd rather…have you do it—with a guy…!"

"Hey! *Lil' sis!* Do we have to take things to their logical extremes?!"

Shiro chewed her nails as she laid down her agonized conclusion, while Sora shrieked back.

Even if they got them to help for a bit, in the end, it wouldn't solve anything—he'd still be screwed. *I guess there's no way around it…* Sora folded his hands behind his head, leaned back on the rock, and thought.

"…A trap to make Ex Machina accept a game under any conditions… Let's see…"

Was such a thing possible? Sora and Shiro didn't even know where to start.

"O thou! O thou and thou, O ye!! O Sora and Shiro! What hath brought ye here? Answer me!!"

Out of nowhere, without so much as a sound or flash of light, as naturally and smoothly as if she'd been there from the start—a little girl, Holou, popped out in her idol costume and berated Sora and Shiro.

"—Wha…? Wait—h-how did you know—rather, how did you get here?!"

Jibril must have had pure confidence in that flight and that "severed space" she'd so worn herself out to accomplish. She shrieked to see Holou pass by it as if it were nothing.

"…? I looked up. I chanced to see you here, and so I came to air my complaints!"

"N-no! That's not—it's *severed space*! You couldn't see it—"

—*Just saw you and thought I'd say hi.* Holou's answer, tinged with displeasure, invited further objection from Jibril, but—

"I know not of what thou speakest. Space provideth no severance. Thou must sever the continuity. Thou hidest in an open cylinder."

…No one knew what she was talking about, but it seemed that they were in plain sight as far as a polygenetic entity was concerned.

Thus, a line emerged that one never would have expected to hear from its speaker—in the moment of the century—

"Th-that's...that's...that's bullshit......!"

Jibril shrank away from Sora and Shiro's scrutiny.

"Let us put aside such trivialities, O Sora, O Shiro!" Holou pointed her finger, smoothly slashing through Jibril's deep despair. "Why have ye consigned Holou for *four hours* to hold a meet and greet attended by no one as ye tarry here? Ye must answer!"

Yes, she'd showed up punctually at the time indicated by Sora and Shiro and sat there in her lonely little booth. Apparently the poor, unloved idol had waited out an attendance of zero to the end. It was no wonder she was interrogating them—or rather, appealing to them with teary eyes. Sora and Shiro drooped their heads, unable to provide useful comment.

■■■

"Heh, heh-heh... Unable to escape the Ex Machinas or Holou... What am I good for?"

Thus, Jibril crouched and murmured, scribbling out spirals on the moon's surface. Was it really so depressing to lose in a test of strength to Holou, an Old Deus, albeit a weakened one? This doubt of Sora's did not seem to attract her attention. But all of a sudden, something else did entirely.

"...Oh! Come to think of it, Jibril, against whom are you capable of winning? You've lost to the furry beasts and to your masters... Could it be, Jibril—that you are utterly useless?"

Oh... It seemed she'd seen something that shouldn't be seen. Watching her from behind as she fell ever further into the depths with a smile, Sora and Shiro decided not to say anything.

—*You beat* us, *bitch*, is what they wanted to say, but.

"—Hmm. Ex Machina... Those inorganic humanoid life-forms?"

"Uhhh... I have no idea what you're looking at from the moon when you say *those*, but *the*, yeah, I think."

Having been filled in, Holou was looking with her hand above her eyes as she murmured to draw Sora's bile.

"Wait, don't you know? Ex Machina's supposed to have slain Artosh. They're kind of a big deal."

"H-Holou is a god! She possesseth information! H-however—"

Holou choked on her words for a moment as Sora commented on the unexpected ignorance of a transcendent being able to drive a Flügel to despair.

"Before the current races were created, Holou... Ah... Hngh?! Wh-what dost thou?!"

"Hmm? Oh, I just was thinking your head was at just about the right height to rub, so I did."

"...It's your fault...for having...a rubbable head..."

Holou's objections were met with frivolity by Sora and Shiro, who now understood.

—They realized she didn't want to say *attempted suicide*. They let her off the hook.

...A dizzyingly long time ago, Holou had gouged herself of her own ether and left herself comatose. She'd been awakened only half a century ago by the Shrine Maiden. She probably didn't know anything that had happened in that time... And even after that, she'd been inside the Shrine Maiden... She could only have known what she saw through her. It was just as Holou had said: She had information—knowledge—about Ex Machina, but it was her first time seeing them. Now that she was independent, she could apparently use powers approaching clairvoyance, but she was probably still far from omniscient. Her ability was a far cry from anything that could be considered "all-seeing," because it would impinge on the Covenants. Sora was getting a little sentimental thinking about it when Holou spun back.

"Do it? Sexual intercourse, is it? Why dost thou not then make haste to copulate? To procreate? Thou must abide by thy promise!"

Holou's doe-eyed spamming of the smut button got Sora back on track with the clowning.

—Hmm. Holou, the ultimate being of bullshit, was all about *intellectual concepts* to the point of defying comprehension. Did she have no feelings about the reproductive activity of living things—or could she *just not imagine it*? Sora was sure it was the latter—but first things first—

"How many times do I have to say I'm not their guy…? That's why I've gotta think of a way to make them accept the condition—"

—*of releasing their lock*, he was about to say, when Holou asked:

"How art thou sure thou art not?"

…

——*What?*

"Hey now, hey now, look at this, this supple, silky skin! Do I look like a six-thousand-year-old fossil?!"

"…I am sorry, my master… Though I be but a useless fossil, p-please allow me to stay…"

"Mm? Uh—no, it's not like that! I was talking in human—look, that's not my point! What I'm saying is—!!"

Flustered by the further depression of the voice of the fossil just over six thousand years in age, sinking deep into a corner of the moon, Sora continued.

"*I know who I am!* What, you think I think I'm you, Holou?!"

At Sora's appeal to self-evidence, Holou cocked her head seriously.

"*Holou is capable of error. Art thou not, O Sora?*"

With that, Holou's appearance flipped like a card. It was not even an instant before what stood before Sora was no longer a little girl in costume. It was a young man with black hair, dark eyes, and an "I ♥ PPL" shirt:

"…If now Holou should falsify her memories, she would herself perceive as Sora. Error is trivial."

Sora's face and voice—but not the man himself—asked Sora.

"Ego, time, and fate signify not. I ask on what basis they identify thee as him they call the Spieler, and on what basis thou determinest this perception to be false."

"............"

...Sora responded with silence. No...with a sigh. He knew. Holou didn't mean any harm. She probably didn't know what it meant to mean harm. She was just hoping for an answer to a question, as usual—a draft to slake her curiosity. You could see that now she was getting her brush and scroll out—but *that wasn't the thing.*

—Okay. The question of the definition of the self and its proof... was it? Sure sounded fancy—but it was *total crap*. No matter how you directed your argument, you could only end up at the conclusion that there could be no proof. That was *why* Sora was making Holou be an idol. He couldn't answer her. But then—Holou, having returned to her original little form, sulkily asked him another question.

"What indeed is the basis on which thou definest thyself as thee?"

...

...With that.

—It was as if the one gear that had been missing fell into place. The clockwork that had been disconnected and lifeless suddenly started turning. It was as if he could see Ex Machina's actions, their words, their intent, their will—he could see everything. How could they trap Ex Machina? He felt like an idiot for struggling on that. Sora and Shiro looked at each other and held each other's hand—smirking self-deprecatingly in spite of themselves. These were machines with hearts. What weighed upon those with hearts was always simple—

—and *full of crap!*

"Wh-what is it? Why advance ye forth? Y-ye must answer— Ngyah?!"
They tossed high the god who had shown them the light.

"Damn, d00d! They don't call you a god for nothing! Is this what they call 'revelation'?!"

"...Well played, Holou...! It was worth, giving you the *hollow*, out of our *Blank*..."

"In-indeed?! D-do they call others gods for nothing?!"

Holou wafted up and down in the scarce gravity of the moon as they threw her, unable to grasp the flow of the conversation. She hurried to produce her brush and scroll to record her questions, but they didn't answer them. Putting her back on the ground, Sora and Shiro splendidly turned and spoke forth.

"Jibril! It's been rocky, but let's get back to work—back to Elkia!"

"...Uh, yes... If—if only I could be of service to you... Nghh..."

"—Work? O—O ye—do ye propose to engage in labor?!"

This must have been what the ancient scholars looked like when they first heard about heliocentrism. As Holou was overcome by astonishment and doubt, Sora and Shiro tut-tutted, wagging their index fingers at her.

"Holouuu, what's that faaace? Shiro and I work. What's our job?"

"......It is hypothesized as administration of a monarchy...is it? No evidence has been observed in your actions."

The dearth of clear justification for her hypothesis forced Holou to form it as a question.

"Heyyy, hey, hey... Come on, you future top idol, you!"

"...We have a...job... And it's a...*producer* job...!"

Answering with an exaggerated no, the man who was supposed to be king, at least nominally—Sora—took out his phone. And smashed one more task into his packed schedule.

—*Procure perfect walking stage effect equipment.*

Sora paused from typing, chuckled, and added one more thing.

"Yeah... I guess I gotta do the maintenance while I'm at it... Though whether I can is up to them."

The light left behind by the screen on which he added it was the last trace they left on the moon.

*   *   *

—*Make the wish of the Ex Machinas come true…*

It is time. Take all the rage you have suppressed—and unleash it!!

"NGRAHHH!! How you have seen fit to trouble us, maid robots and Einzig!"

As soon as they shifted to the throne room, Sora's bellowing shook the castle.

"Sorry, but it's our turn now, forever! By the law that all things change, that all is flux, we have come, Einzig!! To announce your return to dust— Hey, is Steph dead?!"

Abruptly, a sight that should not exist in this world, that of a murder scene, turned his bellowing to a shriek.

"—Whatever, that doesn't matter!! Come on, Einzig—"

"Did you just say my *life* doesn't matter?!"

The corpse splayed out on the ground was so incensed by her treatment, she roared back from the fiery pit of hell.

…Well, actually, it had been obvious she was breathing, but…

"Don't you worry— Actually, it doesn't!! But don't you see this is an emergency situation?! Don't you, you know, stress a little?!"

Steph squeaked out a cry of resignation.

"Nah. I mean, it's *Azril*, y'know? We're more like, God, we were smart not to be here."

"…That's why…Brother said…you should…*stay out, of the castle*… Steph."

"My elder is stubborn in normal circumstances. It was self-evident that circumstances involving Ex Machina would get those fools excited."

Sora and Shiro and Jibril demonstrated that they'd grasped the situation at once—or rather, predicted it in advance.

…One should, after all, heed people's warnings. Even Sora's. This was the realization Steph came to as she looked heavenward, and no one cared.

"Oh, Spieler!! At last you have come to us of your own accord!" The old piece of trash wriggled and danced toward Sora and crowed delightedly. "We shall not let you down! For we are not the machines we once were. *All units!*"

"Don't. First—I've got something I wanna ask all you guys." Sora stopped the Ex Machinas as they were about to rewrite the scenery and asked, "You say you're sure I'm your 'Spieler' or whatever. How do you prove that?"

"I already— Ah, yes. I shall say it as many times as I must: My 'heart'—"

"Can you *prove* it? Can you prove that the Spieler and I are the same guy? So that I'm convinced. So that Shiro's convinced. So that you guys are convinced, of course, and so that even third parties like Steph and Jibril are convinced. Conclusively, one hundred percent. Can you?" Sora was serious as he disregarded Einzig.

"Hmm... No, that is impossible. But it is not necessary! For it is *certain*." Einzig himself was sincere—as he wrote it off.

Proof of selfhood was fundamentally impossible, even for someone else. Therefore, Ex Machina could not prove that Sora and the Spieler were the same. Likewise, Sora could not prove that he and the Spieler were not the same.

——Yes. *Normally*, that is.

"You're wrong. Because I can prove conclusively—I'm not."

The hushed gazes of Einzig and all the Ex Machinas—not just their eyes, but all their sensors—focused on Sora. Faced with machines that could uncover any lie, Sora merely sneered: *Perfect*. For there was no lie, no bluff, not even any rhetorical trick in his words. It was just a fact. He could prove it. So that Shiro was convinced. So that Ex Machina was convinced. So that he was convinced, of course, and so that even third parties like Steph and Jibril were convinced. Conclusively, 100 percent. For real.

This was known, and this was why—Sora crookedly chiseled out a smile—it would be enough: Now what he said, whatever he said—

—whatever he *demanded*—they'd have to swallow it.

"Come—let the game begin."

It was back in his hands. Sora flashed them a grin bold and grand. "We decide the game. The rules. The wagers. It's all us." This was what they got. "Shiro and I are one team. All you guys are the other. And by the way, you don't have any choice in the matter." Making no effort to conceal his personal grudge, Sora stuck it to them deliberately. "If we win, you're gonna release your hardware lock! Plus! You're going to abandon your annoyingly faithful wish never to make babies except with so-and-so! You're gonna reproduce independently and not go extinct! That's what you're gonna pledge!!"

"……Hmm. And what do we gain if we win?"
For us to abandon the feelings that have brewed within us for six thousand years—what is the consideration you offer to equate to this? Thus, Einzig's eyes narrowed at Sora, who flashed into a blush and squirmed—
"Well, first, as a bonus…I'll let you take…n-nude photos of me. ♥"
"I see. Very well, we accept. Let us proceed with the game."
"Request: Regarding ownership of bonus. This unit asserts ownership."
"They will accept that?! Then why must this take so long?!"
Steph shrieked at the instantaneous answers of the deplorable scrap heaps. But Sora and Einzig both knew—both *presumed* something else. The nude photos of Sora, just as he said, were just a bonus. He didn't even have to bet them. He didn't even have to put down anything.
"Also, during the game—I'll prove to you, conclusively, that I am not the Spieler."
Because this was the headliner.

"If I can't, or if you refute it, it'll be our loss unconditionally—"

"—and here's the *special prize*: Whoever refutes it first—gets to make babies with me immediately."

——......

"Heh...heh-heh... A test of *who is fit for the Spieler*, is it? A bold challenge laid down by love!"

"Truism: This unit asserts ownership of special prize. All denials rejected. Dismissed."

Seemed the headliner exceeded their expectations...their presumption. Everyone stared aghast as the temperature in the room seemed to rise. But Sora and Shiro alone knew. If Ex Machina lost, they'd lose their love. For them to take on that risk—mere nude photos and determination of a partner for reproduction would never be enough.

If, just as Sora said, it wasn't him and he could prove it, reproduction didn't even matter anymore. It threatened all their hope.

"So, with that, it's time for us to tell you the game."

Steph, Jibril...even Einzig listened up. In what kind of game could one possibly defeat computers that learned and adapted infinitely, that became stronger without bound—that left oracle machines behind?

—What kind of game could defeat these monsters?

While feeling the gazes raining down upon him, Sora named it—blithely.

"—It's chess! ♪ Hey, it's not like you didn't see that coming, right?"

"...Any gamer...knows...if they get you...you gotta, get even..."

...

......?

Sora could see the question marks forming above everyone's heads.

"C'mon, don't look like that. We're not playing just *any old* chess. ♪"

Sora, with Shiro in tow, spun about. He was getting a kick out of all this.

"Game's five days from now, at the *same time* as Holou's second concert! Meanwhile, you get to make and promote the game and set up the stage and equipment!"

"…Work for us…tools… Perfect stage equipment…for the win…!"

Thus, tossing aside the concerns of all, Sora boomed:

"Things are gonna get busy around here! 'Cos this is gonna be the sickest show ever!!"

CHAPTER 3
ORACLE MAKER
DEDUCTIVE DETERMINATION

Five days later, the long-hung placard that read CLOSED FOR BUSI-NESS was finally taken down. Now a new placard was hung from the spire, just as stately as the first:

CONCERT VENUE

"Oh… The throne of the Kingdom of Elkia, steeped in fine tradition. The throne room…"

What Steph saw as she lamented was a magnificent stage beyond compare to that used previously. It was outfitted with countless gadgets and lights, courtesy of Ex Machina, and had perfect acoustics. However, the throne had been removed on the grounds that *This is just the right height for a stage.* Additionally, the walls had been broken down because *We need more capacity.* Not a trace was left of the traditional visage of the throne room that had been passed down for ages. Steph could not help but weep, and rubbing it in—

"…I really want to know! What are all these people doing here?!"

Thousands of people gathered before the trespassing stage, waiting for the show to start. Steph's piteous query was answered from behind.

"Sure, there mighta been some casual passersby when we did it on the balcony, but this is indoors, man."

Steph, who had peeked out from backstage, turned back. Down past the short stairs, there was a table at which a man was seated, on whose lap, in turn, a girl was fixed. It was Sora and Shiro, looking smug as ever.

"...Everyone here *came* here—they're all our cherished true-blue dumbasses, ya know?"

"...I fear for the fate of our country..."

Steph gazed with melancholy at the poor, brainwashed masses. Sighing, she went on down the stairs.

She headed for where the sources of the evil were seated, facing off across the table. On one side, Sora and Shiro, the producers of this travesty, Jibril behind them. On the other side, Einzig, the manufacturer of this travesty, Emir-Eins and eleven other maid robots behind him. With Steph stood a fairly uniform line of victims:

"...O Sora, O Shiro. I ask you once and I ask you again: Why must Holou take part in this inscrutable parade?"

The pouty-faced god waited in costume for her entrance, apparently none too happy about the arbitrary manner in which she had been spun about.

"Hmm... You really hate it that much? I think it looks good on you!"

"...The idol, aura...is bursting...from you...!"

"I lack basis upon which to estimate my wrath! Thus, I beseech you!"

Holou growled at Sora and Shiro, after asking them the same question over and over again, only to get nonanswers each time. But Sora, with a very rare smile—

"Don't worry, Holou... *You'll find the answer within yourself.* Didn't I tell you?"

—one that appeared pure and free of ulterior motives—stroked Holou's head as he told her:

"We dunno what's gonna happen, either. ♪ So it's about time for your entrance. Knock 'em dead!"

"...Holou... Kick ass. Take names... We're rooting...for you!"

"—I comprehend not... I comprehend naught... I know not what it is ye want from Holou..."

Sora and Shiro saw Holou off as she obediently headed for the stairs, albeit grumbling. They got back to the situation at hand, facing Einzig and the Ex Machinas once more.

"All right, then—shall we begin our game as well?"

In other words, they faced the chessboard on the table and confirmed what was about to go down. This game was the answer to everything—why they'd created this stage, why Holou was heading onto it, why everyone was here. A brief word for now.

"Well, ya know—the rules prohibit the use of magic or 'deployments' other than those specified as part of the game," Sora added, reminding Jibril to pay very close attention. "Other than that... Ah, you know the rules, right?"

No one contradicted Sora's smart-assed assertion. Which was all very natural, considering the Ex Machinas and Jibril had built the game together based on the rules specified by Sora and Shiro. Everyone there knew the rules better than anyone. It was basically just chess. *Basically* being the key word.

There was one thing everyone was wondering about, including Jibril and Steph: No matter how you looked at it, this game overwhelmingly disfavored Sora and Shiro. But they themselves did not seem concerned as they apparently took the silence for assent—

＊　＊　＊

"All right, the wagers… Starting with who's ready to pay up…"

"…Ready… Get set… Let's go…!"

Sora and Shiro raised their hands, confirming the wagers and prompting the pledge.

"Acknowledgment: If lose, then: Release hardware lock. Abandon love. Reproduce independently. Avert extinction."

"I vow to emerge victorious with the bonus and the special prize in my hands. You may look forward to it, Spieler."

Emir-Eins, Einzig, and all the Ex Machinas followed their lead.

A tone sounded to indicate that the show was starting, and Holou ran up the stairs onto the stage. There was a moment of silence that felt unnaturally long…and finally, the music blared. Several shouts clamored forth so as not to be drowned out:

"—Aschente—!!"

The music was played back by Shiro's phone and amplified by Ex Machina's speakers. Holou stepped out on the stage amidst the deafening intro to hear—

"Yeahhhhhhhhhhhhhhhhhhhhh!!"

—an explosion of enthusiasm from the darkened seats such as to make it hard to hear the music.

——.

For a moment, Holou's mind went blank. It was a moment by human standards, but more like an eternity of stillness to an Old Deus. Her thoughts were frozen on one word: *Enigma.*

Last time, Holou just followed Sora and Shiro's vague instructions without understanding. But amidst the enthusiasm here, in the *audience*, Holou felt a wish for something more. This hypothesis gave rise to a theory: They expected something from her. It was there that her thoughts stopped.

What did they expect?

She hadn't even determined clearly what expectation was... Truly, what? What was this that made her supposedly insubstantial body shake?

It made her wheeze silently.

Anxiety, fear, tension.

Feelings no god should have swirled within her. Her hands gripped the mic of their own accord and trembled. Her divine eyes swam in search of salvation, not even conscious of it. Then, among the screaming faces in the dark, she saw someone familiar. She saw someone she knew.

——*Host...?*

Those eyes, they did expect something. They were her friend's. Her comrade's. The Shrine Maiden's.

"...H-Holou is Holou! N-now...Holou shall sing and dance, and so forth!"

Holou still didn't know what she was supposed to do. But. Still. Regardless! At the very least, she was almost sure of this!

—*Holou's host desireth not—for Holou to drown in questions!!*

Holou set forth that hypothesis and awkwardly introduced herself. And she moved her mouth and body as she'd been taught.

■■■

While Holou was starting to awkwardly sing and dance, backstage, Sora, Shiro, and Einzig were wildly moving their hands. Einzig was moving two hands, guided by the parallel thought of the entire Ex Machina cluster. Sora and Shiro were moving four hands, their thinking remarkably in tandem. Both were taking their turns at blazing speed as they moved pieces without a moment of confusion.

It was *basically* just chess. With a few special rules. Such as—*not taking turns.*

"...Wh-what is happening...? J-Jibril, who is leading?"

"...I believe my masters are slightly behind... Wait. Now they have— No...a ploy...?"

The moves flashed about on the board so fast, the two squealed in their attempts to follow it. High-speed chess. Average four moves a second. Sora and Shiro played their moves back and forth without having to talk about it. It seemed that the fact that they were competing with Ex Machina like this was enough to astonish Steph and Jibril, but...

...Don't get excited about *this*. There was no special meaning in *that* rule. It's just how it ended up because they wanted to make it like a rhythm game. Whence also—

"...So any moves not in time with the beat are invalid, are they? A mere constraint?"

Just as Einzig suggested, this, too, had no special meaning.

Yes—a rhythm game. A music game.

—Waves of light crashed through the board in sync with the song Holou sang onstage. You had to smack down the pieces in sync with the rhythm, or your move would be invalid—and the piece would go back.

"No shit. You expect us to let you move as fast as sound or light?"

"...But...we, too, were...always perfect...on rhythm...games..."

For " " and Ex Machina alone, this was a mere speed control.

Holou's set list contained thirteen songs, which meant the chess match should have thirteen rounds. No turns. No stalemate. Whoever brought things to a stalemate lost. This made Holou's show and the game sync up. So yeah—that was pretty much all there was to the rules described thus far.

None of that included the special rule. The really special rule was—well, look at *that*. Steph and Jibril nervously looked up at the meter floating in the air.

It was goofy-looking, with an Emir-Eins chibi on it: the Energy Gauge.

It represented the level of excitement, delight, and satisfaction among the audience as measured by the Ex Machina Seher and Prüfer. To put it a bit more bluntly, it showed *how much this concert was rocking*—and it was gradually sliding down at the moment. There'd been no particular effects. It was just Holou awkwardly singing and dancing. This could not be expected to rock.

So let's take stock: Sora and Shiro had *three* win conditions. One, they had to win at least seven rounds of chess. Two, they had to prove that Sora was not the Spieler. And three, they had to make the concert a success—which meant they couldn't let the Energy Gauge run out. The Ex Machinas, on the other hand, would win if they prevented any one of these.

At the very least, they had to beat Ex Machina at *chess*, a *perfect play*. And they had to do it seven times, against a hypercomputer cluster that infinitely grew more powerful as it learned and adapted in less than an instant. That should have been enough to make this game overwhelmingly disadvantageous—no, *infinitely approaching impossible*—for Sora and Shiro. And then they stuck on this Energy Gauge that looked like it would run out anytime now.

As for that final, really special rule…

"…Hmm. I cannot understand it… What is the meaning of *this*…?"
Suddenly, one square on the board flashed in Technicolor. Einzig furrowed his brow at it. This represented the really special rule: At random points in the game, squares would flash, and if you slammed a piece on them, then it was an *effect strike*.

But to spell out *This is where I'm moving*, in a high-speed game of chess with no turns, was like saying, *Come get me*—it was suicidal. And the flashing square was random, which meant that they might

have to make a fatally bad move. Meanwhile, Ex Machina had no reason whatsoever to do that. The Energy Gauge running out was entirely Sora and Shiro's problem. Ex Machina could just ignore the concert and win at chess by a perfect play.

This was what led everyone, including Jibril and Steph, to one conclusion: that this game clearly was overwhelmingly disadvantageous to Sora and Shiro. Even Einzig said doubtfully, "Certainly you could not expect us to hit this, Spieler."

Did he really? But Sora's and Shiro's faces twisted into sneers.

——*Bingo. He really does.*

"I do, actually. I mean—that's the wrong way to put it. 'Cos—we're gonna hit it ourselves, too."

With a wicked leer, Sora took the piece in his hand and spelled out, *This is where I'm moving.* Saying, *Come get me.* It was suicidal, obviously a bad move. He moved *right onto the flashing square* and said:

"But you guys are also gonna hit it. I promise."

Sora glanced at the speechless faces of the Ex Machinas, Steph, and Jibril. They would be speechless. Since they all knew that was the *worst move they possibly could have made.*

But that was the thing!
—That was the *soul of this game*… And so!!

"Looks like you don't get it, pervbot! But you're one thing to us!"
"…All you've…ever been…to us…is stage equipment…!"

In echo to their cry, it came to demonstrate the final rule—the *effect strike.* They'd employed Jibril's *Materialization Shiritori* board to implement it. It launched effects—just as the striker imagined them. It used that space-rewriting trick Ex Machina had always pained their asses with. Now their surroundings were being rebuilt the way Sora wanted. Sora and Shiro crowed.

* * *

"Now—all you Eastern Union idol agencies! Ready to kick and scream?"

"...You'll regret...underestimating...Bl4nk Productions... But you can cry...d00ds."

The Ten Covenants forbade them from harming Holou, other players, or the audience. On the other hand—they could do anything else! In their *shiritori* game with Jibril, they hadn't been allowed to use things that didn't exist. There was no such limit on the *effect strike*—!!

"This show is gonna go down in history!! Ready to scream, Shiro?!"

"...Ohhh, yeahhh...!"

The Ex Machinas hadn't even gotten over the shock of Sora banging out that blunder with no hesitation. Now the scenery shocked Jibril and Steph, too—and prompted Sora and Shiro to yell:

""Repeat after *we*!!""

The throne room had already been rebuilt into a venue. Now Sora and Shiro were rebuilding it again. Light exploded through the stage, the seats, the backstage area—and boom!

""Yack deculturrrrrrrrrre!!!!""

...They weren't even on Disboard anymore. They were in a place no one knew—not even Sora or Shiro, strictly speaking—*somewhere in space*. Amidst the unknown wilderness, all the audience and backstage crew looked at was Holou. Standing on the arm of a robot fighter, a giant screen projecting her to the heavens, Holou sang and danced. Accentuating her performance—or maybe overdoing it a little—were the effects. Missiles traced strange and complex patterns as beams and lasers traced the universe. The silver, spiraling paths of the fighters, the rain of curtain fire, it was all so beautiful, but—

......

This was obviously a war zone, and it threw everyone except Holou and Sora and Shiro into mute amazement.

…Well, it would. Even Sora and Shiro hadn't seen this except in fiction. For those who didn't know it at all, the instinctual associations it aroused had much more to do with running away than rocking out. Sora and Shiro, however, sneered with confidence. When the audience saw the writing on the screen, they immediately exploded into a cheer. It read:

```
Don't worry. It's harmless.
```

"*Howww* can they accept it just like *thaaat*?!"
Steph's shriek at the rebounding Energy Gauge was ignored.

"Ha-haaa! O cherished dumbasses! Have we got a divine set list for you!"

"…It's divine…'cos…she's a god… ♪"

"Galactic idol? Ha!! Small potatoes! She's headed for super-dimensional territory. Make way!"

Sora and Shiro shouted out in glee, not stopping their chess game for so much as an instant. Einzig kept playing smoothly, too, but he and his maids couldn't hide their shock. Meanwhile, without regard for this—

—He'd really played badly just for the sake of a show.
Steph and Jibril squeaked at this eerily familiar behavior of Sora.

"…Oh…! Could it be—?"

"Quite identical…to that time…?!"

—The effect strike projected the image of the one who struck it throughout the venue in ambient sensory effects. Yes, the scene, the shock, the vibration, all extended all the way backstage, around the players. So it was just like that time. That time they'd played *Materialization Shiritori* with Jibril.

They'd risked loss on the first move to check what they could do—and their real aim lay beyond. They'd beaten Jibril by trapping her in a hypernova. Thus, they would beat Ex Machina—by trapping them in effects? Or something.

They weren't the only ones this occurred to.

"You mean to impede our chess...by blinding us with special effects?"

Einzig spoke softly, well up to speed. Steph and Jibril inhaled shortly behind. Emir-Eins paid no mind.

"Negative acknowledgment: Effects damaging players prohibited. Therefore, low impact on Ex Machina. Pointless."

—There was the rub: It wasn't like that time. This was the real world. Which meant that the Ten Covenants prevented injury. The most they could hope to do was distract. And what good would that do against the Ex Machinas? The proof was in their smooth, well-reasoned moves, effectively partitioned from their emotions.

"...Then why could it be that the Spieler would choose loss...?"

The shock of the Ex Machinas was all at Sora's bad move. Even if he cared about the concert, why would he set up the rules to assure his own defeat? Sora and Shiro observed their doubt with another crooked sneer.

—*Wrong. Now you've made a big mistake.*

"Still confused, huh? We'll say it one more time. To us—"

"...All you've...*ever* been...is...stage equipment..."

Sora and Shiro leered and made their move.

——.

"...Einzig to all units: *What just happened? Report...*"

Einzig mumbled this deadpan. The other units choked on errors. Sora gave them his most ironic smile yet.

"Why I'd *choose loss*? I made that move 'cos I wanted effects. Loss can kiss my ass."

Sora decided to answer Einzig's question—silently: *What just happened?* Sora spelled out, *This is where I'm moving.* Saying, *Come get me.* It was suicidal, obviously a bad move. For the effects. It seemed Einzig and the bots were pretty sure they were winning. Sora grinned. Four moves. He and Shiro made four moves, back and forth between each other—and everything changed. And now—

"Well, then! A little smug about managing to get me alone into a draw, are we?"

The Ex Machinas saw how it was. And couldn't believe it. Sora and Shiro bathed in the looks of Einzig, Emir-Eins—all the Ex Machinas. But, as if cracking up, as if guilty, as if so very ironic—

"With Shiro—I've—we've managed to beat Lord Tet at chess."

"…Think of how…the god of play…Tet, would feel…to fall behind, you tools."

Holou's first number reached its end. Right about then…

CHECKMATE. WINNER: " ". ONE VICTORY.

…the chessboard called it. But their victory over Ex Machina, despite making a terrible move, paled before what they'd related. They'd beaten the One True God—the God of Play. The greatest gamer of all. It was a bold claim. It was also a cold, hard fact.

"_____."

The machines knew better than anyone: There was no lie anywhere in their words. Sora and Shiro left Ex Machina's shock behind.

"Time for round two. No time to sit back, Ex Machina!"

The intro to Holou's second song started on the very next beat. The cheers were their signal. Sora and Shiro savagely, boldly, insolently smiled—and spoke.

"*Get used.* That's really all you're playing this game for. ♪"

"…Go for it…perfect equipment… Moar effects…moar… ♪"

To kick all the expectations of the Ex Machinas, Jibril, and Steph to the curb.

"—Sorry, Ex Machina… There's no way—you can beat *us*."
Sora and Shiro, with the start of the second round, calmly got their pieces moving.

■■■

And so Einzig—no, also Emir-Eins and the whole cluster—was forced to provisionally give this unfathomable suspicion the value of fact.

In round two, Einzig barely eked out a victory for Ex Machina.
In round three…now the movement was dizzying.
All units were screaming, *Analysis failed.* They could only take it.
"Pwnd! Okay, Shiro, now it's your turn! Pick your effect!"
"…Ohhh, yeahhh… Wait 'til…you see, this…Brother… ♪"
Sora and Shiro were placing pieces one after the other, without discussion but with plenty of joy. While even straight-up announcing that they were about to do another effect strike. Yes—*another.* Sora and his sister had struck one this round already.
A fatal blunder—that was what it should have been. The parallel processors had spat out the probability of recovery from that effect strike as zero. *And yet*, the two of them were still winning. Einzig and the machines evaluated a new hypothesis: regarding the *true meaning* of the *effect strike*—

> "Einzig to all units: Initiating veri-
> fication. Request supplementary post-
> blunder computation."
>   "—Jawohl."

Einzig instructed the cluster to prepare to clean up as he waited for the chance to verify the hypothesis. Regarding the meaning, the will to be inferred from Sora's words: *You're also gonna hit it. I promise.* The chance came right away.

—A Technicolor square appeared.

Cluster report: The position was fatal. There was a high probability that occupying it would make the round unwinnable. But Einzig moved his piece straight there—and smacked down an effect strike. Because if the hypothesis was correct, it wasn't just a matter of this round—it could spell *defeat in every round.* The need for verification was critical, and so Einzig took the risk and imagined his effect.

—*Bzt.* All light and sound vanished from the venue, as if there had been a power failure. It was the effect of stopping effects. Not having light or sound stopped the concert itself. It wasn't even about the Energy Gauge anymore. For Ex Machina, it was the worst possible move because it would force their loss in this round. On the other hand, it was the best possible move because it would force the end of the concert, and therefore their victory in this game.

"Yeah…you got the picture."

Only the light of the board lit Sora's dark smile. His fiendish voice was followed in a few seconds by another shining square and his sister striking another effect from it.

—*Force this, suckers.*

It was as if the soundless black Einzig had brought was itself part of the effect. The lights flashed, Holou's costume changed, and the music modulated—people cheered. Einzig had thought he was winning by force-quitting the concert and losing by forcing the exploitation of an opening. So much for any of that. Sora grinned.

"We really need you to throw down like that so we can ramp it up, you know? ♪"

"——."

Sora's words set a final value to Einzig's hypothesis: *True*.

Sora and his sister had lost in the second round simply because they'd focused on spamming effect strikes to pump up their Energy Gauge. But then—if they weren't striking any effects—or were striking, say, just one—

"Let's see who can play the *worst*. 'Cos perfect play is boring."

"…Who…wants…to win…at tic-tac-toe…?"

Predators of overwhelming strength—hard to imagine as Immanities—Sora and Shiro smiled savagely. Their self-assured words made it as clear to the Ex Machinas as to anyone what they were saying.

—Beating you is not the issue.

Ex Machina had, in fact, lost the first round. If this had just been a one-shot match, that would have been it.

—The issue is we want to have fun.

Get used. That really was all they'd wanted from Ex Machina.

—Get us our effects. Get this show rocking.

You do that—*and we'll let you pick some effects, too*!

"Screw best response; it's about *worst response*. Can you keep up, O transcendent machinery?"

The smile of Sora, the taunt of a predator letting his prey run, appeared to be an acknowledgment. The hypothesis was confirmed. The meaning of the effect strike was to make the game fun for Sora—*by giving Ex Machina a chance*.

Then—is this to say—
——he plays us—with a handicap——?!

At this verification result, which defied all logic, the cluster thought in parallel. *Is he so powerful that he can far outstrip Ex Machina, or even the god of play himself? Understanding failed.*

No—accept it! Credibility not found. No—at least one part is true! Then analyze it. Interpret it. Learn from it, adapt to it—and, at last, transcend it!! Show the nature of the race. Demonstrate its quintessence—! The style of play conforms to that which Sora—that which the Spieler showed us five days ago. Did he let us win? No. Then where lies the discrepancy—?

"...What's this? Looks like you've finally noticed that my genius sister exists, you junk heap."

"——?!"

Sora had apparently noticed Ex Machina's eyes going to Shiro.

"Honestly, it was really starting to get annoying. We'd really like it if you'd rethink your perspective, you know?"

"...You think...you can...ignore me...? We'll...teach you...!"

The bile and seething sarcasm made Ex Machina think.

—Who...is this girl? No—she is Sora's sister. His family. Her name is Shiro. We recognized this. We did not ignore it. We simply did not assign it high importance. Why? Obviously, because she is an outsider. To play chess in concert with an outsider—what is that? They are not capable of parallel thought, nor do they have time to coordinate. They are only two discrete units operating independently...which meant nothing...we thought...

"...Playing, Brother, alone...or just me...is, one thing..."

"But if you think you can beat Blank, we've got news for you."

Their categorical statement contained not a shred of logical coherence. But why was it that it resonated so deeply within Ex Machina's illogical "heart"—?

CHECKMATE. WINNER: " ". TWO VICTORIES.

The chessboard called it as a sound signaled the end of the third song. Leaning back in his chair and holding Shiro, Sora spoke.

"You'd better etch this into your buggy heads. Blank doesn't—"

Sora stopped. He and Shiro looked up.

"…We did… We did once… We lost… We did…"

"I see, so we can't use that line anymore… I feel depressed now."

"I—I cannot apologize enough, my masters! How I have failed you!"

Something had triggered doom-and-gloom mode. The two sunk deep into their chair, which for some reason prompted Jibril to prostrate herself in a panic. But Ex Machina thought on.

They still couldn't make sense of it. Of what Shiro was to be able to make Sora so powerful, or of the mechanism behind it. But—something did catch Einzig's attention. He gave an instruction to the cluster.

> "All units: Change top analysis pri-
> ority from target path to methods of
> victory other than chess."

If Einzig's suspicions about Shiro were correct, then it could be extremely difficult to reveal the hand of the two in four rounds and overcome it. But extreme difficulty, even impossibility, anything—they were there to adapt to and overcome it all. Who, after all, would have thought that the Spieler would still be present after six thousand years?

"Heh-heh-heh. The Spieler challenges us to overcome him. We accept this challenge laid down by love!"

Einzig's ardent defiance was met by Sora's and Shiro's frigid glares.

■ ■ ■

Backstage, there was only silence. Sora and Shiro sat deep in their chair, resting. The Ex Machinas had paused their communication. After the third round of the game, the third song in the concert, came an intermission. Cheers behind her, Holou came back down the stairs. Jibril watched.

"…Masters. Surely Holou cannot feel fatigue, nor must time pass for her to change her costume?"

Jibril also looked at the Energy Gauge over their heads as it gradually drained.

Ah, the intermission. An important time for rest and costume changes in a normal concert. But in this game, their Energy Gauge was active all the while. Why had they bothered with this needless respite?

"The *audience* is gonna get tired! When you've got a godly set list, you gotta make them wait, even for no reason. You get it?!"

"…You leave, for a while…and get them…worked up…over what's next… Costumes and all!"

Sora and Shiro were straight-faced as they spoke.

—*Are these two even interested in the game with Ex Machina at all?*

Sora felt everyone staring at him thus with wonderment, but he shook it off.

"So! Steph!! Go work 'em. We're counting on you!"

"…………I'm…sorry?" she squeaked. Sora sternly turned to face her.

"D00d, you gotta fill the time! Holou's come off the stage. Who do you expect to keep 'em entertained now?"

"…Steph…have you…forgotten…why you're…here…?"

Steph's eyes swam from the siblings' harsh gazes. After apparently digging through her memory, she nodded a few times and answered, "No, of course not." After all—

"How can I forget something you've *never told me*?!"

Then she started.

"Wait! Why *am* I here?"

Sora and Shiro heaved a long, long sigh.

"…Hey, come on, manager babe. The set list. What's it say after the third song?"

"What, I'm a manager?! …Oh, I think you did call me that once— Wait, it just says, *Intermission: MC, 5 min*! I checked! Where are you saying my name is?!"

What a worker Steph was making herself out to be, having checked the list even though Sora had only once implied that she had a position here, and she didn't even remember.

"Damn it! These schmucks don't have a lick of common sense... Listen up!"

The two of most dubious common sense smacked their heads.

"...Brother...and I...can't go out...in public...!"

"But if we put Jibril up there, there's no telling what will happen!"

"...And Ex Machina...is out, of the question..."

—So. Who with common sense was there left besides Steph? There was only one sensible outcome to this process of elimination, at which Steph looked to the heavens.

"You can introduce the band, you can do a comedy skit; we don't care, just say something entertaining! Just go!"

"There is no band! There is no comedy group! What do you mean, entertaining?"

Steph struggled to resist, but then she saw the Energy Gauge slowly but surely depleting. She shook her head.

"......Oh God! I-it won't be my fault if it gets worse, all right?!"

Steph ran up the stairs desperately.

"...Master, is this safe? If the Energy Gauge were to run out..." Jibril asked as she eyed Holou's replacement skeptically.

"It's fine. She'll get them pumping somehow... She's got charm."

But Sora answered her, not an ounce of worry on his face, and they all looked to the stage.

"...She doesn't realize that she has what no one can possibly duplicate—talent."

On the stage, Steph was shaking from her fingers to her toes. Her eyes darted back and forth wildly. But on her face was a smile free of malice that captured the hearts of all. It could be assumed that Steph wouldn't say anything significant. Clever jokes and witty anecdotes weren't her forte. Yet, there Steph was, standing in the middle of the stage, looking for the best words she could find to bring out her heart. Or perhaps something other than words.

She struggled so hard, she tripped over nothing. Her momentum threw her precipitously off balance, and she sailed toward a piece of equipment that rested on the stage. As straightforward as she was known to be...she smacked her face straight into it. Her face slid over it, she fell, and her skirt flipped up to put her undergarments in plain view. It looked like this:

_O/|_

The crowd was highly amused by her ability to pass out in the shape of ASCII art—they roared with laughter.
"...Yes...that marvelous...talent...for comic relief..."
As soon as Shiro had called out the name of the talent, the Energy Gauge slammed full. All anyone could do was nod at the ineffable force of her argument, while—
"...How is this? Doth this constitute the 'perfect idol' ye seek?"
—having shuffled into her costume, Holou muttered.
This was the best she could do; the youthful god around hundreds of millions of years old pouted, clad in a flashy school uniform.
"Oh, c'mon! You can barely get Idol Rank A with that! You need to *express* yourself!"
"...Anything below S, is a fail... We want, to win... We can't feel, your heart!"
"Never were ye to feel Holou's heart! Holou herself hath not succeeded in defining it!!"
Cute little Holou argued tearfully with her hard-ass producers.
—Then someone mumbled.

"......It is *will*."
It was Einzig, who had been silent up until now, facing across

from Sora and Shiro. An unexpected participant in the conversation. Holou frowned, but Einzig continued.

"You inquired as to the definition of the 'heart.' I shall respond. The 'heart'—is *will*."

"...Will... What proof be there that Holou hath will?"

"The proof is in your query. The proof is in your search for an answer. You wish..." The machine defined the heart, the will, the wish, life itself, conclusively. "The wish, the will, life. They are indivisible and synonymous. A god with life...must have a wish, must have a will, must have a heart."

A machine born without one, who therefore cherished his more than those born with one. A machine who elucidated its meaning more humanly than a human. Einzig smiled gently. "Therefore," he continued.

"If I share a wish, share a will with the Spieler, it is clear that I am bound to share a life with him!"

"Hey, machine! Computers shouldn't be spouting bullshit. What kind of sophistry is that?!"

Oil barons wear turbans. Oil barons are rich. Therefore, all rich people with turbans are oil barons. Einzig's fallacy was pretty much on that level.

"......"

Seemed Holou still didn't get it. But perhaps she felt something. She looked at Einzig, Emir-Eins, and the Ex Machinas collectively, one after another, quizzically. Then the sound said it was time.

"...P-please...never make me do this again..."

"Sorry, but according to the set list, you're up two more times. G'luck. ♪"

Steph had spent the five minutes passed out, then twitching. Then grabbing the mic upside down. She didn't just make the audience laugh, she got laughed half to death. As Steph came back down, Holou went back up and waited in the wing for her fourth song.

Sora and Shiro waited for their fourth round.

*   *   *

"So! It's about time, huh? We've had our little break, so shall we?"

"...It's time...for...your...effect strike...Brother. ♥"

As Sora and Shiro beamed giddily, Einzig, too, gave a little smile. He spoke what sounded like the conclusion he'd reached after thinking all through the break.

"Yes, Spieler, why don't you go ahead and use us, for a while..."

—*And then.* He was resolute. Audacious. Ready for chess, and for effects.

"We are Ex Machina. We will adapt to anything that exists...and surpass it."

—With his conviction that after trials, they would overcome—

The fourth song started, and six hands started the fourth round.

■■■

And so the concert and the game went on to the seventh stage. Now, as the players were trading relentless attacks and counters on the board—they were flying free.

Scratch that. Free, yes. But technically not flying.

"This is *madness*!! Excuse me, poseurs, doesn't this concern you?!"

"Heh, of course it concerns us. But such are the rules."

"...Steph...you're such a...n00b..."

Sora and Shiro had their best cool faces on while engaged in what was most correctly termed a free *fall*, as Steph shrieked. Well, it wasn't only Sora and Shiro who were so engaged. Steph was, too, as were the audience, and as was, for instance, Jibril, who by the rules of the game could not use magic.

From Machu Picchu to the Death Star, to places Sora and Shiro didn't even recognize. Sora and Shiro and Einzig had traded effect strikes to take everything everywhere. This particular effect strike of Einzig's had erased the ground, leaving them falling through the endless sky.

*   *   *

...So, yeah... Might as well make the most of it.

"H-how can you concentrate on a game at a time like thiiiis?!"

"Heh. How many times you think we've had to go skydiving in this world? We're so over it."

Same old cool face. They'd always wanted to try a game like this if they could get themselves out of the house. Finally, Sora and Shiro were enjoying extreme chess.

What is extreme chess, you ask? It is a form of chess that is played in the air, on a cliff, underwater, on a thrill ride... Anyway, someplace dangerous. That's it. Doesn't matter if you win or lose. That's it, except for one sacred, inviolable rule!

Always the cool face! That is all!

"I-indeed, my masters are noble... Oh...but something must be said for the audience as well..."

"It certainly must!! How—are they *excited*?! Have they truly been brainwashed to this degree?!"

Even Jibril exclaimed, and Steph doubted her sanity, as the Energy Gauge hit its maximum. Just as it indicated, the audience was going crazy, enjoying the free fall as they did Holou's song and dance routine. *But of course they did.* Sora smirked inside, while keeping his hands going.

Ex Machina *didn't know what would kill the joy of the audience*! It could clearly be seen from their advances on Sora as well that they lacked understanding of the *human heart*!

...Well, especially when the conversation was about humans, even Steph couldn't understand. So—Ex Machina just had to repeat the cycle of trial and error, adjusting based on reactions. This trial of erasing the ground was probably aimed to simultaneously obstruct Sora and Shiro and scare the audience. But Sora had already scared the audience out of their wits with his first effect. Now you could pull the ground out from under them or you could drop the sky on them, and they'd just trust it was all part of the effects.

While thus Einzig had released an epic barrage of fail, again his hand went to the shining square.

"What have we here? What kind of epic fail are you gonna accomplish with this terrible move?"

Sora was trolling him as hard as he could.

"Spieler... I have never made light of your prowess. Your power remains ever beyond the realm of my comprehension."

Einzig was smiling back...gently.

"I wonder if you might also give our prowess the favor of your respect. As we made clear, our offer was only to let you use us *for a while*."

Einzig's smile was enough to send a cold sweat down Sora's and Shiro's backs.

"—We are Ex Machina. We will adapt to anything in existence."

As he made his statement, Einzig—no, the transcendent parallel computing unit—slammed down the piece.

"Without boundary. Without limit—without end. And we shall surpass it."

The world was rebuilt according to their image. Heaven and earth were reborn in the venue. Sora thought:

—*There's no problem... Ex Machina has the* wrong guy.

As long as they didn't catch on to that mistake, it didn't matter if their operation speed exceeded expectations. It didn't matter if it exceeded infinity! Ex Machina could never defeat *Sora and Shiro*. But Einzig's increasingly self-assured smile did send a trace of unease through Sora—

And that was when—!

...*Rrrrrripppshhh.*

"......Urp?"

It was the plain old venue again, with the plain old stage, on which Holou's costume ripped with an unnatural sound that was anything but plain.

....
"Heh. Heh-heh-heh... Have you no words? Of course, O Spieler!"

Einzig, presumably taking their silence for amazement, cackled and roared. This was a move that applied all of Ex Machina's unfathomable power in computing and information processing, estimated to exceed infinity, along with the admittedly biased collection of data Ex Machina had gleaned from Sora's porn stash. Sora had to hand it to them.

"...Yeah, that's something. Pretty sharp. Not a bad move..."

He gave his sincere praise as his hands slid across the chessboard without rest. But as Sora was about to continue, *That's still not enough—*

"Whoaaaaaaaaaaaaaaaaaaaaaaaaaaaaaaaaaaa!!"

—a thunderstorm of cheers, along with the glowing Energy Gauge smashing through its max capacity, spoke for him.

"H-how can this be? The theory was unassailable— It couldn't—"

The answer of Einzig—no, probably the result of all of Ex Machina operating in parallel—had proven fruitless. All units, even Emir-Eins, wheezed in bewilderment as—

"Heh-heh... Heh-huh-huh-huh... Ahhh-ha-ha-haaa! Your astonishment is as clear as day!" Sora gave a laugh befitting an evil overlord. "You damage her wardrobe, and if she keeps dancing, people are gonna see her nude! That's the end of her life as an idol!" Sora ignored Steph's cynical look and continued his banter. "*So she's gotta stop dancing.* And that stops the show! So much for that Energy Gauge— But." Sora smiled at Einzig cruelly. "*That's not it.* You're waiting for what *lies beyond*—what happens when she keeps dancing anyway, amirite?"

Sora had seen everything. It rendered Einzig speechless, heaving in consternation. This heated match of wits between Sora and

Ex Machina, between human and machine, brought a twinkle to Jibril's eyes!! Steph's frigid glare was now in the negative Kelvins!! And Sora ignored them all!

"Let's say Holou, true to her status as an Old Deus, knows no shame! Then if she goes ahead and dances buck naked, in any case, the audience is gonna get creeped out and the Energy Gauge is gonna plunge—that's what you thought, ain't it?! A fine attempt. I'll hand it to you, that's a nice double bind you were going for, ya perverted pretty-boy BL-bot!"

If she stopped dancing, the audience would be dissatisfied, and if she kept dancing, the audience would be turned off. Well, now Ex Machina's understanding had progressed further than expected. You couldn't let your guard down with these guys.

"But you got a long way to go, you philosophizing contraptions... Could you possibly assume that the producers would not anticipate such happenings?!"

At that, Einzig and all the Ex Machinas looked over at the stage.

Where Holou's costume was unnaturally torn and rent...and *under it!* There was an itty-bitty bikini charged with spite, just barely covering her important parts as she sang and danced... That had to be far more embarrassing than having her clothes ripped. Seeing Holou reach desperately for the shards of her erstwhile costume, struggling to hide her new one as she danced—

"...Heh. I'll give you one thing. Under normal circumstances, Holou might've gone ahead and danced naked..."

—Sora wrapped it all up by revealing the deep, dark inner workings of his plan. That's right!

"That's why we planted *something even more embarrassing than nudity,* something that would even make Holou fluster with unconscious shame! And *that* is what brings a show *energy*! **Do you understand?!**"

The machines slouched in silence, but Sora and Shiro nonetheless were sure the Ex Machina heard them.

* * *

—*That is deep. So deep.*
Is it truly possible for us to attain knowledge so profound...?
The confidence of the limitlessly growing machines seemed shaken— But just then...

"...! Heh-heh-heh, I should expect no less from the Spieler... But allow me to correct you!"

Einzig popped up from the abyss of despair.

"This move is no mere double bind... It is a triple bind!"

Yes—though only subtly—the Energy Gauge had decreased. That fearsome hypercomputer recognized the meaning of this, at which Sora could not help but swallow.

Yes—they'd *given the audience too much fanservice*!!

Nudity—it was as thrilling as a *happening*! As a glimpse of panties was precious for its very transience! As panties on full display were nothing more than a buzzkill! The machines grasped this deep and penetrating truth—whereupon Sora and Shiro recognized: They would have to strike. An effect strike, to restore Holou's clothes. A blunder, right in the endgame. A move that would put them at a hopeless disadvantage! And then, as if it had been waiting for them to get there, one square flashed psychedelically. That square. That position. Sora and Shiro looked at each other. They knew.

—It was death.

If they moved there, they would inevitably be placed in check, and however they struggled, all that was left was a stalemate—their loss. The double bind had been extended into a triple bind that worked them in a whole new way. Sora commended, Sora respected this adaptation, this development, most worthy of awe.

"...Yeah. Looks like we're losing this round no matter what." Admitting it, he brought the piece to the shining square. "So let's *compromise on winning the next one*—you ready, Shiro?"

Sora's meaningful utterance was answered by Shiro with an utter disregard for the skeptical looks of all.

"...Mm... Didn't, I say...we would find...more porn...together?"

"Oh man! I've got such a good sister! Your brother's so happy!"

Shiro nodded with a smile, and Sora choked with tears as the piece approached the board. For the effect strike that spelled their defeat in this round.

—That same moment.

Sora and Shiro's initial velocity as they launched out of the chair surpassed the speed of light. Or so it seemed to everyone, their act that meant abandoning the game giving no one time to process it. Before Sora's image could even be reflected in the environment. So fast. Faster than anything! Holou's clothes were repaired—no, changed to her costume for her next song—and!!

Rrriiiiipppshhhhrrr.

The unnatural sound Holou's clothes had made as they ripped was echoed by a factor of ten to the forty-fifth power.

""""............Huh?""""

The clothes of the twelve maid robots, including Emir-Eins, and of both Steph and Jibril—in other words, every girl but Shiro—were shredded to smithereens, except for the important articles such as their socks and garters. A moment after their modesty was compromised, each of the maids individually witnessed a gross spectacle—

"—Fear: ...Eek!"

—a writhing bundle of meat in a loincloth swaying without wind, who was admiring her bare body intently. Yes...the abomination vulgarly known as Ino Hatsuse had come for each of them. Twelve of him in total—the effect nightmarish enough to make them squeal—by which time Sora had his smartphone and Shiro had the tablet—and they were sliding under Emir-Eins's legs! The myriad of images yielded by burst mode in storage, they dashed on to their next target…!

—*All right, that's crossing the line,* you may think. *Uncensored low-angle close-ups? That's straight from the red card to suspension from F*FA.* And yet! —Nay. I say nay! No red card will be presented here. No ref's whistle will blow! Why, you ask?!

"M-Masters?! Th-this *mysterious light*—what composes it?!"

"I don't even know where to start, but—why am I naked?!"

Yes. Jibril had inquired about (and Steph had ignored) the light drifting about the girls—the light that just barely concealed their privates from every angle! *Mysterious Light*, with its ever-so-dependable non-euclidean geometry, decided to grace us with their presence! Conversely, this likely wouldn't make the cut using *Pixelation*. But with our friend Mysterious Light, we're in the clear for broadcast! Therefore, this content is definitively *safe* and *wholesome*!! QED!!

…Thus, here lay Sora and Shiro's challenge: There were at least 3.2 seconds until the end of the seventh round, which they would inevitably lose, and another 8 seconds until the start of the eighth round, for a total of 11.2 seconds! They had this very limited span of time to determine the angles and compositions that wouldn't include Ino in the frame! And they had to capture at least one bust shot of each of these fourteen individuals, all before returning to their seat…

Could they do it? Sora and Shiro looked at each other. What a silly question! Could they thread their camera shutters through the eyes of an endlessly towering series of needles and reach the elusory porno beyond? Let's see what happens. " " will get it done!!

……

"A-all right… Now for round eight. We totally got this, but still, let's get…goinggg… *Hff…*"

"…I-it's their…first move… And an…effect strike, too… Egh, fff…"

...Exactly 11.2 seconds. Sora and Shiro were back at the table, panting, faces full of accomplishment. Still, their hands were getting right to that eighth round as they declared victory.

"—Command: Effect strike, top priority. Execute."

"Wha...? My good unit, what are you saying—?!"

The bureaucratic voice of Emir-Eins gave Einzig no time to question Sora and Shiro. Rather, all the Ex Machinas except Einzig glared at him with overbearing pressure.

"Spieler... Is this what you meant when you spoke of a *compromise on winning the next round*?"

Sora merely grinned at Einzig's belated realization.

Indeed—why had they chosen this effect? Well, yeah... For the porno, duh. But there's nothing like making your hobbies useful, is there? Even if it means you need to raise the difficulty a little. Even if it means you need to bring out *Ino*—look how useful it is.

"Vote: Consensus of twelve units. Effect strike, top priority. Eliminate undesirable observation subject X permanently. Destroy. Kill."

"Attention, all units! This is a trap! There is *no need* to counter this effect! We shall only—"

"Warning: Viewing of this unit's body by an agent other than Master deemed unacceptable. If Einzig views this unit's body, then unit will destroy sensors of Einzig. Consensus of twelve units. Final advisory: Effect strike, top priority. Command. Now."

Einzig's reasoned arguments did not reach the maids. While Emir-Eins's tone remained bureaucratic, her words were clearly lacking any calm— Okay, she was pissed.

To stoke the shame of the maid robots and cause them to make the first blunder—Sora had considered this quite the gamble. I mean, first, you had to wonder whether Ex Machinas even had shame. But to be stared at lovingly by those crude hunks of sinew that would chase you down anywhere, those twelve loinclothed apparitions making poses, with a special emphasis on the boobs. Even if you were a machine, as long as you had a heart… No, even if you didn't have a heart! The providence that even flowers wilt and fall—would have to make them think thus, he assumed. Yes.

—*No matter what, this must be eliminated!!*

But…it seemed it wasn't such a gamble after all. It seemed they clearly had shame, and what's more, they even denied Einzig permission to view their bodies, even when redacted by our friend Mysterious Light. And so they placidly went on:

"Vote: Unanimous. Einzig will be stripped of authority. This unit will assume temporary authority. "

It was the collective opinion—no, the determination—of the Ex Machinas who moved to eject the muscle installation rejected by the will of the universe.

"Noooooooo! Attention, all units! You must cease this at once! Exercise sound judgment! Nooooo!!"

Einzig's protestations were futile as his hand took the piece unhesitatingly to the first square that shone. Then—effects took effect as the female Ex Machinas imagined them, which meant… uh…

…Well…yeah… The twelve images of Ino had been murdered, literally, in ways that it would not be pleasant to describe. Sora was just barely able to get Shiro to focus on the board so that she wouldn't see it. Emir-Eins murmured:

"Witticism: Don't worry. It's harmless."

Her nude body was drenched in blood—or rather, something closely resembling it. Definitely not *real* blood. After a moment's delay, our friend Mysterious Light was relieved of duty by the return of the maid costumes. Einzig started.

"All units! Are your thoughts functioning normally?! Would you trade our victory for something so *insignificant* as your nude forms?!"

Sora and Shiro, honestly pretty freaked out, were secretly grateful for Einzig's cry, but—

"Directive: All units to Einzig. Self-destruct. Explode. Dummy. Jerk... *Aus*."

Even if they were machines, it was a grave sin to refer to the bare bodies of maidens as *insignificant*, for which Emir-Eins, speaking on behalf of them all, advised him politely to fuck off and die. But, ah...the sinners know not their sin...

"But why?! All may behold my nude body as much as they—"

As Einzig began to strip, he suddenly disappeared from Sora's and Shiro's vision.

"Eulogy: Player Einzig failed unexpectedly. Regrettable. This unit will inherit current game. No impact on continuity."

Emir-Eins replaced Einzig in the seat as if she'd been there all along.

...W-well. The opponent was, after all, Ex Machina—the whole cluster. It didn't matter which unit was moving the pieces. It didn't impinge on the rules... But anyway. Again, it had eluded their vision, but presumably, Einzig had been kicked by Emir-Eins again. It appeared this time he had not been stuck into the wall so much as smashed into it to form a crater. Sora and Shiro worried about him for a moment—

"...All u-units... W-would you, accept defeat...?!"

But Einzig's voice, full of static, came as a relief to them.

"Equanimity: Master provides nude photos. This unit will acquire. Ex Machina will win."

"It's cool that you're determined and all, but what the hell is that motive?!"

Emir-Eins faced Sora as resolute as a soldier sworn to defend, and at that, Sora couldn't help but squeak. But her next words made him a little more wary.

"Inference: Effective impediment to Master calculated. Victory in this round feasible."

"......That so?"

It was, once more, a *declaration* of an effect strike. They'd already done one, and things were looking grim enough for them for it, yet they were up for another. This could mean one of two things: Either they had a plan they believed in completely, or they were ready to resign themselves to defeat. Regardless, if it was Emir-Eins talking, that worried both Sora and Shiro.

—Emir-Eins. Among Ex Machina, who were in general hard to grasp, she was the one unit Sora still had not managed to read. She didn't advance on Sora, nor did she withdraw from him. She seemed consistently neutral or, perhaps, an observer. Her peculiarity combined with this trait made her feel alien even among these eerily foreign machines. A smile formed on her perfect doll face. Her voice echoed out like the strings of a harp:

"Fact: Master is a virgin."

"Yeah, that's right! What, you got a problem?!"

She relieved Sora and made him shout in surrender. And followed up—with words that resonated deep within his core.

"Corollaries: Master is terrified of females. But his interest levels are very high. Verified by severe agitation upon approach. Also, preferences of Master in appearance and attributes identified with high precision."

With every word she spoke, he thought, *Shit.*

And with every additional word: *Shit, shit.*

As the blood drained from his face: *Shit. Shit, shit, shit!*

His face taut, Sora thought, *I underestimated them! Are they really gonna pull the worst move?!*

He repressed his anxiety and kept his hands moving.

But Emir-Eins moved her piece like the flow of a river as soon as she saw the square glow. And struck her effect strike while elucidating the evident and ineluctable truth—namely.

"Conclusion: Application of numerous hotties will result in Master's defeat…by rendering him unable to continue."

Can't game when you're getting sexed up by mad chicks, can you?!

* * *

………*Say what?*

That's what everyone but Emir-Eins and Sora would have liked to ask as they stared, dumbfounded. Sora confirmed that outlines resembling those of numerous animal-girls were forming around him.

"Damn, they got me!! Shiro, you'll have to hold out alone until you can erase this with the next effect strike!!" Sora wailed piteously.

"…B-Brother…! Is that really…enough…to KO you…?!"

Shiro interjected, seeming to speak for everyone.

You call yourself one half of the greatest gamer in the world? And you're okay with this?!

Everyone's stares asked him as much, but he retaliated internally— *How can you blame me?! Oh, I see how it is. You're gonna fault me for being a virgin? Is it that grave of a sin?! If there were a man who could observe Zhuang Zhou's exhortation to be "clear mirror, still water" in the presence of sexy ladies, he'd already be in nirvana! There is no way for me to continue through this!*

As Sora dedicated himself to the next stratagem, surrounding him…

"Mr. Producerrr! ♪ You worked soooo hard today! ♥"
"Excuse me, I, uh! I just came out of the showerrr… ♥"
"I want you to train me more! **Drill it in**…please. ♥"

…the effects Emir-Eins imagined took form.

"Certainty: Desire of idol producer. Interference from requests for 'midnight lessons.' Delay. Very effective."

There were now forty-eight animal girls almost fighting one another to get it on with Sora. Ambitious idols.

——.

……Hmph…

"Ahhh, what garbage. I shouldn't have let you get me worked up… Damn, though, you really scared me there. Shiro, back to the game."

"…Mm… Yeah… I guess, that's how it is…"

Sora snickered before turning his attention to the game again. Everyone but Shiro raised their voices in alarm.

"M-Master?! D-do you feel ill? D-do you need a rest?!"

"You—you cannot possibly be Sora…! Who are you—?!"

"You'd chew me out either way, wouldn't you?! What d'you want me to do?!"

Jibril's voice quavered as Steph's doubt crystallized. Sora howled.

Yeah, that's right. You got the right idea. But the wrong scenario. This shit is disgusting as all hell!

"I am a dedicated master of idol production. You're proposing that I give 'midnight lessons'? You believe that I will lay a hand on the idols I raise?"

Yes—Emir-Eins had struck precisely the wrong nerve. Sora fixed his eyes on this wench who had affronted his pride as he bellowed with indignation—

"You take me for the scum of the earth who will stoop to such base perversions? **Think again, Ex Machina!!**"

—seeming to rile the very air into a divine storm that would blow them all away. They squeaked.

Sure, they were just playing at being producers. But that's just how Sora and Shiro were when it came to playing at anything.

—*They took it more seriously than the real thing!*

Now that everyone had recalled that, or learned it, Sora clenched his piece and balled up his fist—

"No need to sleep with me! I'll produce the hell out of each and every one of you! Come get some!"

—and he slammed it down onto the shining square. The crash of the effect strike resounded throughout the backstage area with the maids' bewilderment. And—

"Hey, everyoooone! Are you having a good tiiiiiime?!"

—the cheers of the forty-eight animal-idols crashed over the stage.

With colorful explosive smoke, the forty-eight Werebeast idols had been shifted out. The whole audience—no, even Holou—froze for a moment at their abrupt appearance. But they segued right into a dance routine behind Holou. *They were the backup dancers.* The crowd roared as they realized they had just been visited by the crème de la crème of beautiful idols en masse—

"Excuse me! Um, that just now! You could have used that to restore my clothes, couldn't you? Couldn't you?!"

—and Steph roared as she was reminded that our friend Mysterious Light was working overtime while she and Jibril were still naked. No one cared. In spite of her nudity, Jibril was watching Sora and Shiro play. But as it should happen, Emir-Eins, who faced them, was showing quite the same feelings on her face.

—Shock. Distress. Doubt. Ever deeper.

"Perhaps you wonder why we bothered to take the idols you brought and make them backup dancers."

Sora explicated her feelings in her stead, his hands never pausing all the while. The Energy Gauge had already maxed out with all that had followed Holou's wardrobe destruction. Plus, Emir-Eins's two bad moves had by this point all but assured Sora and Shiro's victory in this round. So why? Why had they returned a bad move when they'd had no need to so disadvantage themselves? And also—

"And *how can you still lose*? You just can't get that, is what your face is telling me... Am I right?"

"Acknowledgment: ...Failure to comprehend...!"

The randomly positioned effect strikes—bad moves—by the nature of the game grew more fatal the closer it came to the endgame. Sora's blunder was enough to compensate for both bad moves Emir-Eins had made and put him on the losing end. But—in a flash, the momentum of the game shifted back to Sora and Shiro. Yes—even after that bad move.

* * *

Emir-Eins groaned with perplexity. Sora and Shiro had *surpassed Ex Machina*.

—Chess. The textbook example of a finite, zero-sum, two-player game with perfect information. But the introduction of the *randomly* flashing squares made this a game with *imperfect* information. This made the complexity of the calculation recede to the limit—of perfectly imperfect play.

When could you strike? You couldn't tell that much exactly.

Where should you strike? You couldn't say the risk until the square actually flashed.

When would you strike? The risk of having the squares you would strike known was no small matter.

Would you really strike? Or would you make them think so and use it against them?

And so the 10^{120} possible games of chess came to approach infinity. But the real problem *sure as hell wasn't that*. Sora smirked.

"So far we've played eight rounds, over seven hundred moves. And you still can't successfully analyze the patterns of our play... or rather!"

How far had he managed to read into the *psychology of machines*? He spoke to mark the heart-pounding challenge he'd set for himself, as a gamer and as a person—thus.

"*The more you analyze us, the more powerful we get...* That's what you don't understand, and that's the real problem, right?"

...For an instant, less than a moment, tantamount to nothingness—Emir-Eins's hand perceptibly...stopped. It proved that all the units, even Einzig in the wall, had frozen. It proved that Sora had met the challenge—and he went on imagining what they were thinking.

Right. So the indeterminate nature of this game makes it maximally difficult to calculate. But in that case... Given that Sora and Shiro were under the same conditions, they were *just as screwed* in trying to calculate it. When a race was capable of analyzing and adapting to anything—growing infinitely—how could it be—? How could they keep losing round after round and have their every adaptation foiled?!

That's what they were thinking, right? Sora snapped his piece down.

"It's 'cos *that's the kind of race Ex Machina is.* And we're *not under the same conditions.*"

Yes, he went ahead and said those words that made Emir-Eins and all the maids stare together. He *said* them. He was *able* to say them. He knew they'd analyze his joy, but he *didn't care.* Inside his heart—Sora yelled, *Pwned!* and gestured obnoxiously with his fists. Later he would brag to Shiro. He would keep bragging even if she told him to shut up already. Shiro, perhaps having already inferred Sora's determination, given her unenthusiastic expression—

"…'We are Ex Machina. We will adapt to anything in existence'…"

—repeated Einzig's statement, word for word. And then they both stopped their hands and thought: They were speaking the truth. Ex Machina had been an opponent they weren't even sure " " could beat. But then they found in this fearsome race an opening to exploit—a flaw. A critical defect they couldn't have counted on under normal conditions.

CHECKMATE. WINNER: " ". THREE VICTORIES.

The chessboard called the game, and Sora told them:

"…You can't adapt to something that *doesn't* exist, can you…?"

The sound of the end of Holou's eighth song echoed as they waited for the next to start. A brief interim. Ex Machina's silence seemed to ask what Sora meant, to which he and Shiro replied:

"Well, seeee, if you guys lived up to your reputation, we figured even we together would have trouble beating you."

"………….But nooo… Ex Machina…you guys, are *too strong…*"

They went slack as if melting, so as to get what rest they could.

"—If you'd managed to kill the great Artosh, there's no way you'd draw against just me."

Yes, the same misgiving had been hounding Sora ever since that first battle he'd undergone alone. Now that his suspicions had been confirmed, he spelled it out for everyone, his tone and expression equally languid.

—The words, however, bewildered Jibril more than anyone.

"You can't do it, Ex Machina. You weren't the ones who killed Artosh—*someone else did*, right?"

CHAPTER 4
THE GAME OF LIFE
WISHFUL OBSERVATION

Five days prior, in the Elkia Royal Castle's throne room, Azril inquired as to how they had managed to kill her lord. The strongest of the gods. The god of war.

"Unknown— No. Correction… We *probably* did not kill Artosh." Unperturbed by the swelling malice of the first Flügel, Einzig answered…and went on. "Let me correct myself. It would be a theoretical impossibility for Artosh to be slain—for his being to be destroyed."

Thus, Einzig laid out the hypothesis from over six thousand years ago. The hypothesis formulated by Ex Machina in the face of the god of war. Addressing the question: What is a god? What is ether? A concept that has gained an identity. A law with will. Something that could not exist; something that should not exist. So they had verified this absurdity as the concept of strength. And the conclusion of their hypothesis—was this.

* * *

—*A god is a god for that they are a god.* This tautology defined the god. It defined ether. And thus, before the very concept of strength—*magnitudes* of strength were of no bearing at all. Ex Machina adapted infinitely, grew stronger limitlessly...so that at last they could become the *relative* strongest. Even so, it was a theoretical impossibility for them to transcend strength itself...to surpass the *absolute* strongest.

"For this reason, while it was quite a feat...we destroyed *only* that ether which existed physically. However—" By that they could suspend the manifestation of the concept, temporarily deactivate it, they inferred. "—It is *unknown* even how we were able to achieve that... We should never have been able to overpower strength itself."

Then how had they destroyed the ether of the god of war? Unfortunately, such records had been effectively lost.

—Against the strongest, who changed causation, law, and nature every second, 701 machines had applied an algorithm to combat the unknown and simply adapted in desperation. They had operated on the unknown, which even they could not envisage, much less understand—leaving it unknown. As the logical errors stacked sky-high, they let them stack and operated in the abstract. Incorporating even *illogical operations*, they had adapted faster and faster, approaching units of one-infinitieth of a second...

Thus, twenty-eight units, including Einzig, had managed to escape with *mere critical damage*. Their memories and thoughts were broken; the meaning of it all had been lost; even the timeline itself wasn't clear. However...observing the reformation of the world...they just managed to infer...it appeared they had succeeded in destroying the ether... *And so*—Einzig looked straight at Azril and answered.

"I cannot answer how we defeated him. But if you ask how we

destroyed him, that I will answer: *We have not destroyed him. An entity that does not exist can never truly be destroyed.*"

Concepts did not exist. They only changed, expanded, and shifted in definition...or grew stale. As long as the fantasy of ultimate strength remained, the concept would never die.

"...Therefore, this is what I speculate."

If the concept—the idea, the sentiment, the life ever remained—

"Thus, if the Spieler revisits us, could it not be that Artosh will, too?"

Azril's objection was that the One True God and the Suniaster invited no new gods. The ether of the god of war could never reactivate. But.

"I do not mean that Artosh himself will resurge. The Spieler himself is now Sora."

Einzig was strangely...sure of this. Somewhere in his broken memories, in those of the end of the god of war, the evidence for this must be there—

"...'The strongest' will return under a different name, in a different guise... That is what I mean."

■■■

The air backstage creaked with the extreme concentration, punctuated by the pitter-patter of pieces and filled with the rising tide of the show's climax. There was the music and the cheers leading to the close of the eleventh song...and then:

CHECKMATE. WINNER: " ". FIVE VICTORIES.

"Pwned! That makes us 5–6! Two more and we'll hand it to you!"

"...B-Brother... Please... Let me, rest... I-I'm so, tired..."

The chessboard called the match, and Sora and Shiro celebrated, their voices smudged darkly with fatigue. Thirteen songs. Thirteen rounds. It meant they'd have to win *both* the rounds remaining. Ex Machina used all its sensors to analyze their voices and found that they were absolutely confident.

......

"All right, Steph! Here's the final intermission. Go kill it, okay?"

"...The Energy Gauge has been full for a while. Five minutes—"

"D00d, these last two songs are gonna be a nonstop climax straight to the end, y'know?!"

"...If, anything...you should be, killing it...even harder than... before..."

"That's easy for you to say, isn't it?! Just what sort of humiliation do you—*hwnk*?!"

"I take it that you set out this thick, angular costume in the effect strike in preparation for this moment! ♥"

"*Yes*, Jibril! Go, Mazingo Steeeph!!"

"...It's like...how we say 'Zeeed'...but it's like...how we say, *ze*... for emphasis."

"What am I supposed to—? Hey, that's heavy! It's so heavy! What is this, iron?!"

"Mm? Guess I imagined it a little too vividly... Well, don't worry about it. Go, Steeeeeph!!"

This racket quite aside, Einzig and the rest were thinking silently. Sora had said—*You can't adapt to something that doesn't exist.* Those two were abnormally strong. It reminded them of what they had said to Azril that day. Something that doesn't exist... A concept. A god that they didn't know how they had defeated. That Sora had said they hadn't even themselves defeated. An absolute strength that would go over their heads no matter how relatively stronger they adapted to be. They'd expected it to revisit, under a different name, in a different guise. What if it was " "?

—What if the confluence of the Spieler and the mysterious girl constituted that very strength—?

"...It may be as the Spieler said... We cannot prevail..."

Whether it be at chess or in the concert. But—*what of it*? The statements that Sora was the Spieler and that Sora had become the strongest were entirely compatible! Sora would lose if he could not prove that he was not the Spieler, and was it not impossible to prove one's selfhood—?

"*That cannot be the case!* Am I not right? O Spieler—!"

—It was possible, though the method was unknown. Perhaps it was by sophistry, or traps, or by leading Ex Machina into a paradox from which they could not escape—but! In any case, the proposition that Sora had designed an unwinnable game, above all else, was patently false! It was a challenge laid down by love—could they answer, *Try to beat me*, with, *Sorry, we can't*?

"—I ask all units! Could such a one deserve to lay his love before the Spieler?!"
"""Negative! Negative! Negative acknowledgment!!"""

The roar of Einzig's soul was met fiercely by the shared thoughts of all the units!

"I command all units: Reveal the path to victory! Eliminate all obstacles! Use any means necessary! Execute the task!!"

And just as processes flew through the cluster at time-stopping speed...

* * *

"...Acknowledgment... Motivation low. However, choices limited. Executing task."

...Emir-Eins grumbled and walked onto the stage.

The unit who, while remaining connected to the cluster, did not share her thoughts. Whose purposes for that reason were a mystery even to Ex Machina. Emir-Eins stopped, next to the woman who stood utterly immobilized by her iron costume, *hrmmm*-ing in agony—or rather—

"Report: This unit will take MC role. Master...*join*."

—Emir-Eins stopped and spoke as if she was unaware of anyone except Sora.

"Confirmation: No rule prohibits any player, including this unit, from coming onstage. No violation."

...*True*, thought Einzig. Sora and Shiro narrowed their eyes. But what would come of it? No—in the first place—

"Us? Onstage? Ha-haaa! Are you trying to murder us from the astral plane?! **Rejecteeed!!**"

"...Crowd... Eyes... Many, people? ...*Chatter, chatter, shiver, shiver...!*"

Indeed, it was preposterous to suggest that Sora and Shiro could join her. They'd already started shivering just imagining it.

"Notification: Essentially, victory is required. Simple. Victory itself is simple. Can bring into effect at any time. All too easy."

——What?

Everyone—Einzig and the other units, Sora and Shiro—stared hard at Emir-Eins, trying to figure out what she really meant. But she merely continued on, her words reluctant and therefore very convincing.

"Choice: Membership rejected. Acceptable. *Then unit will win. Outcome equivalent.*"

■■■

Even Sora couldn't read what Emir-Eins was after. For that reason, he assumed the worst—and decided he should be where he could stop her. He accepted as long as he could be with Shiro, but he worried about his own judgment. The one who had first requested that he join—was Emir-Eins.

…*Could* he stop her? No. Before that…

""*Vvvvvvvvvvvv……*""

Amidst the countless gazes of the bustling crowd, drenched in the spotlight, Sora and Shiro vibrated like civilized people's phones in the middle of the stage, worrying about the first problem.

…Could they…even move at all…?!

As the frequency of their oscillation approached the kilohertz range, they racked their brains—and then froze. Something had appeared on the stage with a loud *thump*. Sora and Shiro, and everyone in the venue, found their eyes and breath stolen…as quiet as if they had forgotten time.

It was a girl as beautiful as a narcissus, that "flower amid snow." Her dress layered as elaborately as a white rose…iris eyes peeking from beneath her veil. Her modestly lowered face like porcelain, she walked slowly to the sound of a music box— Or rather…it was Emir-Eins, for some reason all decked out in a wedding dress. Anyway, the audience was enchanted and Sora and Shiro were pretty freaked out as she sidled up to him. After a deep obeisance, she spoke her first words:

"Manifest: This unit is Emir-Eins. Wife of Master—Sora."

…

……*Pardon?*

After the silence of the venue adopted the qualities of a freaked-out silence, these were her second words:

"Apology: This unit regrets enforcing attendance at farce to *mark infidelity of Master.*"

…

……*WTF?*

All members of the audience of the admitted farce froze.

Then—*creaaak*. All eyes turned toward Sora, automatically confirmed as husband by his self-proclaimed wife. Their stares were practically stabbing him to death as they seemed to ask, *The hell is this?* Sora could only weep and answer in his heart, *I'm sorry, I have no idea.* The alleged husband, looking as if he would pass out were it not for the hand of Shiro barely holding him on this plane of being, did not seem to notice the mysterious images moving on the back of the stage. Emir-Eins placidly produced something like a letter and began to read it out loud.

"Reading: It started so fast. Master fainted upon dramatic meeting with unit. Unit astonished."

—Yeah, it started fast, all right. Fast enough to say, *Slow the hell down.* The phone rang out of nowhere, and then the castle got destroyed... Whoever heard of a start like that? But Sora had fainted upon the whispers of love from Assbot Einzig, and it wasn't *dramatic*—more like *dire*.

...Thus, Sora thought...dreamily, as if his consciousness would fade away at any moment. Paying no particular attention to Emir-Eins's long, long spiel, he gazed at the video in the back, feeling somehow that it *reminded him of something*...

What it showed...appeared to be when Sora had woken up. It had been trimmed to show him and Emir-Eins gazing into each other's eyes—with Shiro cut out of the frame. Next would come the footage of Sora applying the nickname "Emir-Eins." A mass of effects gave a somewhat convincing impression that they were lovers laughing together—with Shiro cut out of the frame. Next... the time he handed her the tablet and checked for static...it probably was? The effects and decorations got even thicker to the point that it looked totally as if they were holding hands and he wasn't even sure anymore. But anyway, indeed—Shiro was out at the corner of the frame, out of focus. Meanwhile, as for Emir-Eins's reading—

"Reading: Master took the ring finger of this unit and swore undying love. This unit accepted."
—was starting to get a little threatening.

"Reading: Bride and groom status established. This unit currently recognizes herself as standing at pinnacle of happiness. Report."
And so they had been bound, as it was reported to Sora.

Meanwhile, Sora...was finally starting to get what was going on. Ah, the machete editing of those scam trailers that make a shitty movie look kind of like something decent. Such peripheral complaints aside, he had consistently had the feeling that this video reminded him of something, and he'd finally figured out what it was. It was this video he'd bumped into on a video sharing site uploaded by some goddamn normies who forgot to set it to private. Yes. The utterly banal data of a newlywed couple...on how they met. In light of this, it was plain to see what was going on as Emir-Eins read from a sheet in a wedding dress.

"Reading: Mother and father...not present..."
But the question was *why* it was going on—
"Declaration: But this unit...will be—happy...!"
Apparently overcome with emotion then, Emir-Eins put away her paper. As a pall of silence descended on the venue, Sora stirred up the courage of a lifetime and asked:

"Hey...isn't the reception supposed to come after the ceremony? Not that I would know..."
Sora hadn't been married, nor had he had a girlfriend, nor did he have any friends who would invite him to their weddings. But from

what he knew in theory—this seemed to be a wedding reception, and it seemed to be happening awfully fast.

"...? Conflict: Ceremony complete."

Emir-Eins looked at him vacantly, cocking her head to the side.

This video was her doing. It wasn't even on the level of a scam trailer. This was a straight-up hoax. Now it was showing Sora and Emir-Eins happily exchanging rings someplace he'd never seen. Shiro wasn't even there anymore. This didn't even vaguely remind him of anything that had happened. But.

"Admission: To win in this way was a last resort. This unit failed to live up to Master's challenge."

Remorsefully, Emir-Eins went on. *Still.* Fluttering her dress, turning her head.

"Inevitability: Still, Master will lose with this move. *This unit will win.*"

Her smiling *victory declaration...*

...burned Sora now, too late, with panic, and he howled inside. *He'd blown it*—what the hell had he been doing, standing there slack-jawed, letting all this crazy shit mess with his head?! There was no way Ex Machina—least of all, this chick—would do something for no reason! He was done lolling about. His brain was going into overdrive.

Emir-Eins didn't care. She went on placidly with a little smile.

"Premise: If Ex Machina proves that Master is Spieler, then Ex Machina wins."

...Yeah...that was true. Technically, what they'd said was that Ex Machina would win if they could refute Sora's proof...but on the other hand! Even if they didn't refute it—if they provided a proof that Sora couldn't refute, it would be the same thing! That shouldn't be possible...but was it, actually? Did this series of events bear on it?! Sora shivered as Emir-Eins smiled and announced...her unshakable proof—

"Fact: Master—selected this unit for his wife."

......

...Wha...?

——What...the hell?!!

"Logic: Reproduction possible only with Spieler. Selection of this unit as Master's wife is equivalent to self-recognition as Spieler. Master defined self as Spieler. Irrefutable argument. *Was zu beweisen war.*"

With that, Emir-Eins took Sora's breath away with one final statement.

"Triumph: Pwnd."

Uh...true. If Sora had chosen Emir-Eins as his wife, that would essentially mean that *he'd admitted it*. How could he refute that?!

——How had he overlooked this? No, he knew! It was—!!!!

......I— Huh? Did I choose Emir-Eins as my wife? I mean...did I ever even have a girlfriend?

Yeah, I probably would overlook that. I don't even have any memory of the premise of the argument!

"Sentimentality: This unit was able to win at any time."

Regardless, Emir-Eins spoke with confidence, and Sora began to seriously doubt his own memories.

"Analysis: Master requested the unlocking of production mechanism, independent reproduction. Target of independent reproduction not specified. Therefore, goal was to avoid selecting one unit with whom to make babies and instead make babies with all units. Master is incredible."

——Uh...no, that's...not right, right?

"Admiration: Master's unbound libido. Master's unquenchable prurience. This unit loves it all."

Sora looked to Shiro for confirmation of his memories, but she was still frozen, apparently not recovered from her shock. Emir-Eins continued her elucidation of what could not be conclusively stated to be a mistaken interpretation.

"Apology: This unit was challenged to prove eligibility for the role of Master's wife, or else tolerate mistresses. This unit failed that test. Apologies. However, this unit will dedicate resources to equal twelve units in performance. This unit will try her best."

Emir-Eins's lowered head slowly rose, and there on the stage—in front of the audience—

"Declaration: Ex Machina wins. Reward is immediate reproduction with unit that emerged victorious. Waiting room before ceremony is preferred environment for wedding dress sex. However, scenario revised to wedding night—"

"Wait, wait, waiit! A-at least give me a chance to check my memories!"

—Emir-Eins straddled Sora—*And so we attend to our marriage bed*—prompting him finally to object aloud.

"Rebuttal: Childmaster requested *seven thousand* children. Urgent task. Select clothed or un—"

"I did *not*! That much I'm sure of!!"

Let's say, for the sake of argument, that he'd lost his memory. Even so, Sora would never utter a value of that magnitude; that much he knew. So he grabbed Shiro's hand and started running—

—and was able to *resist*.

That meant there was *no binding force*. What a relief. He hadn't lost! His memories weren't jacked!

"Hey, Einzig! The hell is this? That broad's got *made-up memories*!" Sora hollered as he tumbled backstage at full speed, entirely confident in his words.

So many things about Emir-Eins had felt off to him. The way she didn't approach him, the way she neutrally observed, so self-assured. It all came together now. The thing was that she, Emir-Eins alone—

"…Referencing memory. It seems that, in her memory…you are already married."

Einzig's apologetic remark verified it.

This entire time, only Emir-Eins had been thinking of a different world, a different dimension. Sora should have known. After all, even back when they were at the Shrine, she hadn't spoken of *whom* he'd take—only "tonight," only "anytime"—only *when* he'd take *her*! No. Even back when she'd ripped the porn from the tablet, she'd said, *This unit will dedicate all resources to becoming the ideal wife for Master.* It had already been her assumption that she was his wife!

"…When? Since when?! Since when have you been talking about being my wife?!"

The wedding dress seemed to get in Emir-Eins's way. It took her a second, and then she caught up with him, but regardless looked at him curiously, still decked out as a bride.

"Reply: Master assigned nickname to this unit."

"Well, yeah! Am I supposed to call you Alt-Emircluster Befehler 1? Or Ec001Bf9Ö48a2? Give me a break!"

"…B-Brother…how did, you…remember that…?!"

"Examination: Nickname also known as term of endearment. Master holds this unit in high regard."

Emir-Eins proceeded as if Sora and Shiro's banter didn't register with her. But, as she drew her face close, she did answer Sora's question: *Since when?*

"Conclusion: This unit holds Master dear. Therefore, Master and this unit are man and wife. Couple. Pair."

—*Since first sight.*

Her face drew even closer. Their eyes locked; their lips gradually neared.

…

……BOOM! *And IIIII…will always—*

"Like *hell*! What, so you just assumed we were in love from the very beginning?!" Sora screamed.

He took a step back and cut the background music. *That scared the crap outta me!*

Sora was unnerved by the glimpse into the mind of a true-blue crazed stalker.

"Rebuttal: Assumed? …Negative acknowledgment. Fact."

"…Honored unit… I command you to check your records and memories for consistency with those of the cluster."

Einzig dealt a second blow to the bot with more than a few screws loose, but she kept coming.

"Rejection: Cannot accept necessity. Will not share love of—"

"The vote is done. Twelve units agree. Honored unit, I command you to compare your memory now."

——.

Emir-Eins seemed reluctant, but she was unable to oppose the vote of the cluster. After a few seconds, she sighed and shook her head.

"Report: Memory errors confirmed in all units except self. All abnormal. Weird. Crazy."

You always knew the crazy ones by how they called everyone else crazy. Sora and Shiro, Jibril, Steph, and even all the Ex Machinas looked at Emir-Eins with great skepticism. Regardless, Emir-Eins shook her head and smiled.

"…Hypothesis: Only as examination of hypothesis, which is negligible in probability and assumed false—"

Her facial expression seemed to say, *Ah-ha-ha, no way, no way. Ha-ha, that's impossible.* With mannerisms all too human, with a smile so strained you could almost see the sweat going down her cheeks, the mechanical girl examined the hypothesis, as if assessing the possibility that the planet was triangular—

"…Edge case: Umm… Could it be, Master has not…married unit?"

"I have not."

Sora sent right back the conclusion that the planet was triangular.

Appearing dizzied by a flood of errors, the mechanical girl tottered, and yet, she queried on.

"...Confirmation: ...Master plans to marry unit."

"I don't."

"Reconfirmation: Master plans to build ideal happy and loving family with—"

"—Me? Over my dead body. Lady, I don't even remember dating you, nor do I plan to do that!"

Like a pious believer to whom it has just been proven that God does not exist, Emir-Eins at last asked the final question. Her mechanical face was somehow corroded with despair as she spoke.

"......Hypothesis: Unit was wrong...all along?"

"...Yes...!"

"That would seem to be the case! ♥"

"Well... It seems so."

"...Yeah... Basically, just yeah... *Hff...*"

Shiro's face was angry, Jibril's scornful, Steph's sympathetic, and Sora's convoluted.

......

"Choice: Membership rejected. Acceptable. *Then unit will win. Outcome equivalent.*"

Emir-Eins headed for the stage.

"Einzig to all units: Autonomous memory deletion detected. Upload backup."

"—Jawohl."

Emir-Eins wanted to pretend it never happened. Einzig did not have the kindness to approve her request.

"Hey, wait, never mind that!! Shit, look at the Energy Gauge!!"

"...B-Brother...! W-we've, gotta...get on, to the next song!"

The audience's outcry alerted Sora and Shiro to the precipitous drop in their Energy Gauge, at which they squealed. It should come as no surprise. They'd brought up a girl literally as beautiful as a doll in a wedding dress, enchanted the audience, and then, of all things, *announced she was married.* What's more, they told the crowd the whole show was a farce involving her husband's infidelity, and then damn near *did the deed itself onstage,* only for Sora to reject it and run. This was more than a mere fail. If he'd been in their shoes, Sora would've likely been pissed enough to start a riot or something!

"H-Holou! Hurry, get back onstage! We'll push you up a minute!"

They hadn't a second to lose before the next song, or their Energy would drain completely.

"Report: As calculated. Conformant with original target. Based on…high-level calculations… Eegh…"

Emir-Eins straightened her expression and posture and tried to play cool…and failed.

"Sob: Unit rejected. Unit severely hurt. Requesting permission to self-destruct—rejected. Why…?"

Einzig affected a cool demeanor. He flashed a half smile and whispered:

"This is no time to self-destruct. For now—we have a chance."

■■■

And so the twelfth round began. For the first time, things on the board unfolded the way Einzig and his comrades had calculated. Before all else, Sora and Shiro had to replenish their Energy Gauge so as not to lose on the spot. Which meant they needed an effect strike ASAP—they needed to rush to make the first *bad move.* In the opening, and just once, it shouldn't be much of a problem for them to commit a blunder… However.

Light glittered onstage, and the sound warped to dramatic effect. It brought up their Energy Gauge. That it did, but—

"Whaaaaaat?! This only brings us to *half*?! Get outta here!"

—as Sora screamed, the gauge didn't go up by very much, while the drain rate remained high. Sora, knowing full well that this was the natural order of things, nevertheless shouted on, pleading.

"I get it! I know how you feel! I *totally* get it! But c'mon, guys, let's put it behind us!"

Even the Ex Machinas could recognize that it would not be easy to get the crowd going again once cooled. One or two effect strikes amounted to a drop in the ocean now.

"…B-Brother…! Let me…do the next…effect…strike…"

So, per their words as they flung pieces around dizzyingly, they'd have to spam that shit. Yes—spam shit moves. Three of them, four of them…

"Ngaaah! We're serious here!! That face of yours pisses me off!!"

"Hmm…? This is our full output, to answer your challenge of love."

"Then why do you have to keep giving me those flirty homoerotic looks?! Tag out, already!!"

"…B-Brother…we've got to…concentrate—!"

As Sora lashed out despite the caution of Shiro, Einzig was sitting pretty. He didn't have to strike any effects. He could just pounce upon their every blunder. Ex Machina had returned from a contest of worst response to their true calling of best response. And thus, they dominated—waiting intently for their chance. One chance. Ex Machina's ultimate chance. When it came—it would be Sora and Shiro's fatal and hopeless peril.

—A single effect strike to end it all.

```
"On behalf of all the units, I thank
you. Your madness has given us the
opportunity to answer the challenge of
love."
   "Command: Shut up. Explode. Request-
ing permission to run away—denied…
Plea: Hilfe."
```

Emir-Eins pushed away the gratitude of all the units and asked for the help of some unknown entity. Even rejecting the synchronization of her thoughts, she partitioned herself off, crouching in a corner backstage. But her sacrifice was nothing before this opportunity—this situation that put Sora and Shiro at an overwhelming disadvantage.

They'd been waiting for their chance. Ironically, it was just as the twelfth song reached its peak.

—It came.

"O Spieler. It is an honor…to answer your challenge of love."

Einzig spoke from the "heart" as he took the piece to the shining square. All of Ex Machina, excepting the isolated resources of Emir-Eins, had worked synchronously to glimpse this opening. A square that fulfilled all the requirements and conditions, from which Sora and Shiro could never recover.

"With this, we have earned the bonus prize, those precious nude photos of you, Spieler."

Einzig struck the effect. It was just—

Bzt.

—the same as their first: the effect of no effects, whereby all light and sound was stolen away.

Amidst the soundless silence echoed only the crowd's murmurs.

All that shone in the pitch-black darkness was the board's dim glow.

Illuminated by that dim glow were only Sora and Shiro—

"Next, let us earn the special prize: Let us hear your proof that you are not the Spieler, so that we may refute it."

—and the Ex Machinas, including Einzig, who thus queried *uncertainly* of his determined victory.

"I see… We have to strike an effect to turn things back, or we'll lose at the concert."

"…But, if we…strike an effect…it's *determined*…we'll lose…"

"Hmm. If Shiro says it's determined, it's determined. No way to wind that back. You've got us there."

Einzig acknowledged this inwardly: *Of course.* They'd run the calculations $Rayo(3 \uparrow \uparrow 3) = Rayo(7625597484987) < Rayo(10^{100})$ times. This had yielded them this one perfect chance, whereby the expected values fell into place for every last situational variable. There were 24.2 seconds left in the twelfth song. Even Ex Machina could not pin down how many times squares would flash for Sora and Shiro, or which squares would. But they could estimate the number of times from the trends established over twelve rounds: three going by the mean, two by the median. It was the endgame. Their options were, by nature, very limited, and then to commit a blunder when they were already on the ropes—it would be suicide… Though Sora and Shiro might be the most powerful of gamers, as long as the rules for how the pieces moved stayed the same, they could not escape their fate. If Shiro said it was *determined*—

"If we strike, we're out in the chess game, and if we don't strike, we're dead in the show… Another double bind, huh?"

Sora's summation made not only Einzig, but all the Ex Machinas think:

—So this is the best we could do even with such an overwhelming handicap… The Spieler, wielding power overwhelming, well on his way to equaling strength itself, tested us to see if we were suitable for him. We have with difficulty overcome this test—but we have yet to refute his proof of self, which is what we need to earn the right to make babies with him. Sora…must be the Spieler. And it is impossible that he could prove conclusively otherwise.

Despite all that, there was a feeling none of the units could shake. A misgiving.

The reason they played this game in which they stood to lose all. A fear.

In other words: *What if he really isn't the Spieler?*

They repressed this fear to seek the proof. As for what came next, however:

"But this time…I ain't got no 'nice' to hand you guys…"

—What...?

"I mean, this isn't even really a double bind. Look—"

"...D00ds...we just, have to...do...this."

Sora and Shiro grinned. And, as though it were obvious—like the flowing of the current—they slid a piece through the air. And made their move.

It was just—inevitable.

It was just—invincible.

*They pounced right upon the blunder Ex Machina had made—*to turn it all around—to put Ex Machina on the ropes.

"A blunder in the endgame is fatal. And not just for us."

"...We're...done...making, effect strikes..."

Sora and Shiro smiled, and Einzig gave a slight grin back.

—I see. Now he has us at an overwhelming disadvantage—no, all but cornered in this round. But that will only give them six victories... still short of ultimate victory as the failure of the concert brings them to a loss. A loss he cannot avoid. So he chooses to lose winning at chess, surpassing our calculations. Truly, he is the Spieler... Not one to go down easily...

Then Sora interrupted Einzig's thoughts.

"Okay, fine, there's one way we can give you a 'nice.'"

The siblings sneered as they said in unison:

"" ...Nice try, n00bs... ♪""

Simultaneously, as if on cue, a voice sang out, and Einzig opened his eyes wide as he directed his gaze to the stage.

■■■

Suddenly, in the muted darkness that enveloped the venue, on the stage wreathed in shadow, Holou stood idle, staring at the audience. The restless audience... No. In her divine eyes, which saw that which could not be seen, was only one spectator: the golden fox, the Werebeast. Her host. The Shrine Maiden. Holou's friend.

The beast's eyes, too, saw through the darkness, and they looked to the stage. To her. To Holou, who didn't know what to do. Those eyes stared at her; that face Holou knew—the one she knew so well.

That unease. That worry. That face, the face of one who cursed her own lack of power—that face, for the first time in the eons Holou had seen, caused her to articulate this feeling clearly: The pained expression upon the face of her dear friend...*was one she'd never wanted to see again—*

——She wanted it not——!!

That instant, in the venue enveloped in muted darkness, a little light and a faint voice started. There was no accompaniment, no effects, only the delicate torch Holou lit herself and the voice with which she sang.

...It was terribly amateurish. It was shaky, awkward. But she sang on, dedicated, reaching and swaying and groping for something. There was something about it...something that bled right into you, something that filled you... Everyone listened intently.

It was merely a wish...for her host, the Shrine Maiden, her friend...to *smile*. That's all it was, the humblest of songs... And yet. For this god of doubt, this little god who had doubted her own quintessence, who had conceived of hope and doubt together, it was the first tiny, tiny movement she had taken in hundreds of millions of years. Of certain *will*, she gave her *heart*, to show her *life*...

■■■

"...Holou, one heptalogue props... You, smashed the ceiling...of Idol Rank S..."

"Yeah. You are a goddess. You rule more than eleven dimensions."

Sora and Shiro were still playing backstage while they smiled as if satisfied from their hearts. Holou's song made Steph weep...and even made Jibril shut her eyes in rapture.

"The climax of the endgame. A technical glitch…leading to a solo a cappella."

"…Now, I can see…what the ultimate…effect's, gotta be… ♪"

Sora and Shiro's snark told of the state they had brought upon the board—one of *determined victory* for them. Not to mention the Energy Gauge, which stayed maxed out without depleting even a single pixel. These things spoke to one truth.

—*They'd read everything.*

"…Absurd… How could such nonsense be? …Aargh!!"

Anything could be. Einzig knew that as well as anyone, but still he cried out.

—*They read our effect strike? No, that wasn't the half of it!*

They'd have no choice but to strike an effect: *They'd read that this was what Ex Machina would read!*

Which would turn out the best for the show: *They'd read that such was the effect that Ex Machina would choose!*

And so they could exploit a blunder and pwn: *They'd read that this was when Ex Machina would strike!*

They'd read everything. Literally, everything!! Every accursed thing!!

It was preposterous. Even if they were gods, even if they were strength itself, this was a *game*!! A game of prediction based on clear rules mixed with uncertainty! It should not be possible even for an Old Deus to read the convergence of all possible worlds—to determine the indeterminate! It could not be possible unless one knew in advance everything—

—everything…that…would—

—happen…?

"Ahhh, shit. Looks like they're onto us, Miss Shiro."

"…Mmng… And we, still…have one round, left… Mnng."

The twenty-six visual sensors of the parallel processors all turned to the clowning Sora and Shiro at once. Sora smiled to see how they were putting everything together at this late hour. The game and its rules were so disadvantageous to the two of them. By sheer strength, they'd taken on this overwhelming handicap and yet run far, far beyond Ex Machina's reach. They defined strength, these two who grew more powerful the more Ex Machina adapted—

—or so they'd fooled Ex Machina into thinking all along—!!!!

"Mmm. That's right. This game is overwhelmingly disadvantageous—to a certain party who's not us."

Sora stuck out his tongue like a child apologizing for pulling a prank. Glib as he kept playing, without the faintest sign of remorse, he filled them in.

"There's an unreasonable handicap—on you! ♪ But don't be mad, 'kay?"

"…It's, your fault…for being fooled… An…ancient…truth…"

So basically: Einzig, Emir-Eins, and all the rest of the Ex Machina had, for twelve rounds and 1,047 moves, meant to calculate the incalculable…

…only to have followed directions…

"B-but what do you mean, Master? A handicap on Ex Machina?"

"Huh? I meant what I said. We can see right through 'em with these rules."

—Yes, it is as he says. They left us hardly a chance to win at chess to begin with, and then if we committed blunders—why, we would have lost even without them. Given this, if we were to intentionally commit blunders in order to win, it would follow that we would do so—

"See, these guys only struck effects when relatively safe squares flashed!"

"…And they…always assumed, we'd exploit…those moves… N00bs…"

"All they did was best response to their own blunders, ya know? We had 'em dancing on the palms of our hands. ♪"

We presumed that the conditions of uncertainty were mutual. Yet, in the eighth round, the Spieler uttered meaningfully: "We're not under the same conditions." Is this it...? Is this the true meaning of those words—?!

No!!

Certainly, our strategy was predicated on best response—it was defensive. But that was because of our fundamental premise that our chances in chess were slim! Because they had such overwhelming strength, strength that completely transcended our level of adaptation, which approached the infinite!! Because there was no falsehood in their statement, their conviction of assured victory!!!

But this—*this strategy. To manipulate that to which we adapted, that which we read, and how we would adapt...? Who would stoop to such methods? Some—but not the strong—!! Then how was it? How did they deceive us—?!*

"—Sorry, Ex Machina... There's no way you can beat *us*."

As if reading Einzig's thoughts—no, now Einzig was beginning to believe that he really was—Sora repeated the words he'd said upon winning the first round, word for word.

"*Us*, I said. That's right—you can't beat *us*."

Still no falsehood could be detected in Sora's words. All that could be detected was a response as if this was too obvious to spell out.

"I mean, duh. After all, you're not even playing us."

"...Your, misunderstanding...was probably...our lifeline..."

—*Misunderstanding...? Does he refer to our perception of them as the second coming of the concept of strength? No—that is not it! His words came before that! Then what could it be? To what misunderstanding of ours could he refer?*

Then at Sora's next words—

"You think weak-ass little ladybugs like us would handicap ourselves playing broken, overpowered bots like you? Ha, you make me laugh."

—*Zshh.*

"You know nothing—of the *abject weakness* that makes us stoop to this method to win."

—*Zshh...* Through Ex Machina's memories, supposed to have been corrupted irrecoverably, and through their thoughts, a noisy signal ran.

"...The only thing that can beat the strongest is its opposite—the weakest."

Sora's definition of himself and his companion as the weakest...

—*Zshh, zshh.*

...took the focus of Ex Machina amidst continued noise.

"I mean, bullshit beyond understanding like you can't be beaten head-on."

Yes—they had not been able to overcome the god of war, the concept of strength, with force.

"You don't realize that. You didn't even kill Artosh. So I knew we'd get you."

Yes—the god of war, of strength, had been lauded as a natural enemy—not by Ex Machina. But by...the Spieler......*and*—

CHECKMATE. WINNER: "   ". SIX VICTORIES.

"Hey, you goddamn perverted pretty-boy junk-heap assbot! What do you think an idol is?" With a rather long-winded epithet, Sora inquired of those lost in their muddled memories. "Some two-bit hack-ass producer might say some shit like it's a perfect doll that plays out customers' ideals. But!"

"...Howeverrr...we are...bomb-ass producers... So, no!" Shiro, with Sora, looked at the stage, as if unconcerned with Ex Machina's answer.

"...Holou's...gonna, *be what she wants to be...* That's all..."

"That's hope. That's the aspiration not of customers, but *people*."

While floating amidst swirling memories, the Ex Machinas

looked upon the two. The *two*, whom the strongest had praised as a natural enemy, who boasted of their weakness.

"So. You were asking for the proof that I'm not the Spieler, right?"

"…It's…simple… You…know it…yourselves."

The Ex Machinas listened, still amidst a mental maelstrom.

"…*I* decide who I am. I'm Sora—this is Shiro. We're two in one."

"…Together, we are Blank… Other peoples' definitions…can eat shit."

The Ex Machinas listened to the two who told them that it didn't matter how they might analyze Sora and come up with their own definitions. No, not two. *One* gamer. Who then told them:

"It doesn't matter how much I resemble him, or even if we have the same memories and the same love. *I'm not him.* You wanna refute that? Then first—"

"…Why, don't any…of you, claim to be…*the one…he loved*…?"

…*Ah*… The Ex Machinas closed their eyes.

"That's why you didn't bind me to love you or do it with you by the Covenants…right?"

Einzig, Emir-Eins, and all the Ex Machina units finally reached that understanding…and without thinking, hung their heads and smirked.

"I see… So all along, our eyes were only following ghosts…"

—*So it is… We can never beat them. There is no way we can adapt to them…for they do not exist. We were not playing against these two…but a phantasm of our own. We were chasing our tails, boxing with shadows… How comical we must have appeared.*

Then came the sound to mark the start of the thirteenth and final round. The intro, the first line of the thirteenth, the final number. Music filled the air as Einzig murmured to himself…

But then…what……are we……?

■■■

The thirteenth song. The final number. One move of Sora and Shiro's had restored light and sound to the stage—but that was all they needed. Holou's song no longer seemed to require Ex Machina equipment to intoxicate everyone. Sora and Shiro had thrust two more people onstage with the words "Go have fun"—rude, but they seemed to be enjoying themselves. Steph could dance, believe it or not, and Jibril was bouncing about the air scattering nonlethal light. While the venue came together for a big, happy finale, backstage, things were as quiet as the bottom of the sea.

The thirteenth round. The final contest. With glib smiles, Sora and Shiro had revealed to Ex Machina the way they'd been leading them by the nose. Yet, all this time, not for one round, not for one move had things been easy for them. They determined what Ex Machina should suppose, how Ex Machina should adapt, without letting them know, and exploited the moves they created. They took advantage of the lies the Ex Machinas were telling themselves, the biases of those who rejected a reality without the Spieler. These provided openings, fatal defects—and yet, it was a backbreaker of a challenge. To read, bit for bit, the "heart" of a transcendent machine and lead it on. There should be no need to ask why they would take on such a ne plus ultra. Because they literally couldn't go any further. Even " " couldn't beat Ex Machina head-on.

Yet, now they'd let the cat out of the bag. Now Ex Machina had corrected its analysis of the last twelve rounds and 1,082 moves for the true identity of those two before them—to adapt to Sora and Shiro. Now the brother and sister duo were to lock themselves in a straight battle of calculation with a hypercomputer—to go *further than they possibly could.* Odds were that Sora and Shiro would lose the seventh round. They'd lose the match. They'd lose the game.

—*This is where it gets real.* Sora and Shiro steeled themselves. But…

* * *

"…Hmm. You've stopped moving in the middle of the game… May I ask why?"

Backstage. At the start of the thirteenth round, pieces had been making noise, albeit relatively subdued. But then Ex Machina had stopped even that, stopped their hands. It was at this that Sora's voice echoed. The quiet was heavy, oppressive…yet cold and resigned—it was a quiet Sora and Shiro knew well.

—It was the quiet of despair.

"…Allow me to return your query. There are no turns… Why do you not move?"

"Well, good question… I guess because, like, what's the point of beating a failure of a gamer who gives up in the middle of a game?"

"…Allow me to return your query once more. What *would* be the point…of our victory?"

Einzig smiled, but his usual bravado was nowhere to be found. Now he was truly—just a machine. Just a puppet—no. It wasn't just Einzig. The other Ex Machinas matched his tone.

"You are not the Spieler. What do we stand to gain by winning?"

…*Yeah, I knew that*, Sora said to himself, grinding his teeth. He'd known that proving it would be enough for them to choose destruction.

"We would gain nothing. We would only perish. In which case—it is you who should win."

He'd known what would happen if he proved he wasn't the Spieler. He'd known it would be like this—a literally desperate problem.

"You two should win. No—*you* should—*Nachfolger*. Then the Ex Machina Piece will not cease to be."

He'd also known that Ex Machina would then refuse this game! It was knowing all this that Sora trapped them——*so!*

"You must have known this and trapped us to force us to reproduce and abandon love. We forced a hard choice upon you. You were right to decide that this would be our salvation. We believe that you can use us—"

——*WHONK.*

Sora slammed a piece down so hard it seemed he was trying to destroy the chessboard, interrupting Einzig.

—So!! *This is where it gets* real—*!!*

"...Hey, pervbot. Why you gotta *pose* like that?"

A square had flashed, and Sora's effect strike modulated the music and blazed forth a vortex of light. The big-happy-family ending was giving way to a badass climax. Cheers from the crowd set the house on fire. Sora and Shiro looked at the interrupted board, now tilted in their favor, and informed Einzig:

"Stop babbling and give us your best shot. You don't gotta stop."

"...We're gonna...win...and you're gonna...lose anyway. ♥"

—*Heh.* Einzig smiled as if he'd given up on everything. The parallel thoughts of all units of Ex Machina forced his hand—and moved a piece according to a convention unknown to Sora and Shiro. It was a transcendentally appropriate, unreasonably perfect convention that would send the two astray to their dooms.

—Yes. *Was.* Until about two seconds ago. But now it was a matter for the past tense. The momentary event made Einzig scowl slightly. Sora and Shiro saw this and told him.

"D00ds, is your memory okay? Infinite learning, my ass!"

"...False advertising... J*RO's gonna...sue you... We, told you."

Ex Machina moved with incomparable precision, tracing every convention as if straight on to the future. Sora and Shiro predicted each convention as if breathing in and overturned it with an invention as if breathing out. Ex Machina adapted to each invention in an instant and overturned each with a new invention. Then Sora and Shiro crushed each new invention in one move as if to say it was no invention at all, bringing them right back on top.

It seemed Einzig and the Ex Machinas finally got it. Sora and Shiro told them again with haggard smiles that said, *Come on, realize how tough this has been for us.*

* * *

"If you…think, you can beat…Blank… ♥"

"Extra, extra! We've got news for you. ♪"

She and the Spieler—Sora—had maintained the same style while acting tough. For twelve rounds, wherein Ex Machina had continued to adapt to and learn from it.

Thirteen rounds. This was the last. And here it was, Sora and Shiro's—that is, " "'s—*real style*. They'd known they might have only one chance against these adapters to kick their asses *for real*.

It had all been *to hide it*. That had been their greatest struggle.

"Go ahead and try beating us as we are. 'Cos you'll fail anyway."

"…Give us…all you, got… We'll, humor you!"

Surrender? Like hell they were gonna accept a boring-ass ending like that. They would only accept an overwhelming victory. Nothing else could be tolerated.

—*Bring it on, Ex Machina. Fight us, not your phantasm. And watch us stomp you into the ground.* So spoke Sora's and Shiro's beastly grins…and in turn, they saw a fire begin to burn in the eyes of the Ex Machinas——

——……

"…This 'Spieler' you thought I was—let me guess who he was."

As the hands crisscrossing over the board finally approached their original speed, Sora laid out his reasoning, as if chatting, as if thinking on two parallel threads.

"He was the guy who ended the War… The super ultra-über-cool gamer, right?"

"…………"

Taking Einzig's silence as a yes, Sora nodded. "That would explain it." Jibril had said that Immanity used Ex Machina to end the Great War. It was a mystery how the hell that was possible, but basically—

"Ex Machina wasn't used. You just *helped* the man you loved."

Sora had no way of knowing the details of the exchange. But an Ex Machina called the Preier had loved an Immanity called the Spieler. Which love—which wish, which will had been shared with all the units, passed down. Emir-Eins had alluded to it as the Preier's hope.

The hope for the realization of the hope of the one she loved... Yes—for the *end of the War.*

"But the man died...*just as the War ended...* You let him die."

"...There are no words to express this shock... How do you know all this...?"

The Ex Machinas were perplexed by his divine insight, but Sora bashfully continued.

"Ah, it's nothing really... It's just that Emir-Eins said she was, uh, a new model... A virgin..."

Reproduction enabled only for the Spieler. Hardware-locked...?

"If he survived, he'd use her, right?! At least once!! I mean, even I, uh, never mind, don't worry about it."

Shiro's glare stopped Sora—but he could guess what happened. The War had ended suddenly, thanks to one man. But that man was not the One True God. He died at the end, so then it must have been his partner that let him— No. Sora realized he was being rude and altered the course of his thinking. His partner had *failed to protect* the man she loved... That had to be it.

"Moreover...you betrayed and deceived the man you loved."

——.

Einzig's hands—those of all of Ex Machina—stopped for an instant. Sora talked on unperturbed, his own hands still moving wildly.

"The man wanted to end the Great War without a single sacrifice. You defied his will... You killed many. Over half the Flügel. Probably others, too. Including, of all people—yourselves."

Ex Machina played on silently, but with trembling hands, wandering eyes. Showing clear emotion—confusion mixed with agitation. At Sora's words? Or at their inability to dominate him and Shiro?

"As for what went through your head when the War ended... It's beyond my imagination."

Anyway, it's so...ironic, Sora and Shiro both thought. The hearts of humans were so illogical that they formed logic to invent mathematics. The cores of these machines were so logical that they marveled at illogic to invent the "heart." A race of machines, of transcendent computers that would laugh at oracle machines, and where they ended up—was the same as humans. So, yes...it was crap. The will of Ex Machina, which Sora and Shiro had realized on the moon. The meaning of the machines with hearts... The trouble that kept them waiting desperately for their unrequited love for six thousand years, on till the brink of their demise... What weighed upon those with hearts was always simple and full of crap—

—Sincere. And sacred, and full of crap... Yes...

"...Regret? Guilt? Frustration?"

Probably all of them, and probably none of them, Sora thought. These were troubles from the "heart"...which meant that they would be illogical, indivisible, and abstract. If, despite this, he were to sum them up in one phrase, it would surely be this:

"...I guess you *just wanted to see him one more time.*"

Then, they appeared before Sora. When he'd vanquished Holou—an Old Deus—*without killing her.*

"So you thought, *next time.* When you find the one with whom you can do what you couldn't then."

Then, probably, they must have...

"You waited, thinking, *next time*, when there's a man who can defeat a god without killing, it must be him."

Sora's conjecture mixed with speculation was confirmed by the wavering in their eyes.

Even if they knew the man was dead, and that no matter how much another man might resemble him, he wasn't the same person. Even if they knew that Sora was not the Spieler the Preier loved... Even if they knew that they themselves were not the Preier the Spieler loved—and even if they knew it was not they who loved the Spieler... Still...

These machines with "hearts," who were capable of telling lies... They were something to be reckoned with, Sora thought. That they would *lie even to themselves*... Did they really need to resemble people that much...?

Sora put a stop to that train of thought.

—*That was why...he had to push them away.*

"And then? Those machines with their lovesick brains on full throttle? What did they say then?"

He suppressed his aching heart into silence and laid down the law.

"Like, *thank you* for trapping us and forcing us to reproduce; *merci* for averting the extinction of our race and the checkmate of the world; *thx* for caring about our broken hearts; go ahead and use us as you see fit?"

—He had to push them away——!!

"Why you gotta *pose* and cover your 'heart' like that?! What kind of way to act is that for fully automated alternative sexualities on legs such as yourselves?!"

Yes—after sneering to the boundary of the sneer zone, Sora gave a good *Ha!* and yelled.

"D00ds! Let me know—*what's in Ex Machina's 'heart'?!*"

It was an obvious provocation, a ruse—everyone could see that. But whether they'd judged that it was impossible to lay bare all of " "'s hand in this round, or whether they'd judged that they held the upper hand when it came to processing speed in *worst response*—

—No…

"Very well… Let us inform you… Let us answer your query, Nachfolger—!!"

Such rational reasons, such logic…were surely not what they had in mind. Eyes seething with rage, Einzig slammed down an effect strike and roared to the "Successor" as their environment transformed to match his words…

"We gouged Artosh of his ether and ended the War—and what was left—?!"

—*Nothing!* The venue provided this answer by becoming hollow—white as a sheet. As if to say that neither heaven nor earth, nor any law could signify aught. The audience, Sora and Shiro, everyone floated in space as the song echoed on.

"…There were the Ten Covenants. And the Ixseeds. And—your will."

—*This world was left.* With a peaceful smile, Sora returned an effect strike that painted the blank canvas psychedelically. Pieces towered over the hazy distant horizon as sixteen seeds flew this way and that over this world. While they looked down upon the expanse, floating, the crowd cheered on.

"Yes, there was still the world that had trampled our will!! And divested us of our love—!!"

That itself was the symbol of their penitence. Their feelings, their love had been lent to them only to be taken back, wailed the move of the machines, which erased all sixteen seeds that traversed the psychedelic planet, all the pieces on the horizon.

"That's why you said, *next time, next time*, and made those feelings into a will to surpass to your successors."

From person to person, and across races, Sora's move brought back the vanished seeds and Immanity. They came together, formed nations, and covered the world. It was as if the War had just ended and the world that lay spread out beneath them was reforming.

"And we remained, a comical heap of scrap, having betrayed that will, deceiving ourselves and sleeping, with dreams never to be realized…!"

Neither their feelings nor their will had succeeded them. Their eyes asked what they signified, holders of a love not theirs, sleepers waiting for one who did not love them. Translucent gazes, countless in that back room, reflecting those they had killed or let die.

"Grk! Sh-Shiro! I can't refute that they're comical! Just look at this creep!"

"…Don't give up, don't give up…! If you, lose an argument… we're, done for…"

None of this stopped Sora and Shiro from clowning around.

The scene changed dizzyingly. The effects blazed atrociously. They read each other too deeply to lead the other on. It had become a game of who could read further and respond faster—exactly the preferred field of Ex Machina. Yet, Ex Machina… Actually, Sora and Shiro themselves were blown away even more: The two of them were neck and neck— No, even slightly *ahead* of Ex Machina.

Sora trusted his intuition and played off guesses even he didn't understand. Shiro accelerated her calculation and worked in conventions that rationalized his inventions.

A synthesis of deduction and induction. A fusion of feeling and reason. No trick would work on Ex Machina twice. They uncovered every first time. It was their indeterminateness that gave them that ever-so-slight edge over Ex Machina's processing power. Ex Machina reeled.

"…But anyway!! That's just 'cos you're trash!! What sort of man blames external factors for his own failures?!"

"…A-and, uh…! How do you know, they're…'never to be realized,' huh…?!"

Sora and Shiro's follow-up banter as they oozed cold sweat made Ex Machina's processes slow down.

"Do you mean they may be? Ah… Then let us realize them…!!"

The scene kept changing, as the Ex Machina wished. They wished for the Spieler, ideally. But they showed their feelings for which they had lied to themselves that they could meet him again.

"Do you mean that all the workings of our 'heart' had meaning—*that we may be redeemed*—?!"

Yes… In sum, that was all it was. Such crap… So sacred, this wish. They'd refused reproduction, accepted extinction, advanced on Sora. To ask Sora—that is, the Spieler—would he accept them…? They'd deceived him, betrayed him, played him for a fool, killed and been killed and finally let die. Could they still live in this world? Could he forgive them? It had nothing to do with logic.

They were just…drowning in remorse. It was the wish of machines who no longer knew what to do— No, of their hearts: *Show us the way.*

And that was why Sora pushed them away with a smile. It wasn't something to ask him. *It wasn't even something to ask the Spieler.*

"Hell if I know… That's a question you have to answer, isn't it?"

Sora looked, and the Ex Machinas did, too…at what their furor of effects had produced. It was what they…the machines with hearts themselves…had created—this very world. This world where everything was decided by games—*Disboard* lay beneath them. On the stage, an Old Deus was singing and dancing. A Flügel was flitting through the sky as an Immanity danced gracefully. Amidst a flashing flurry, a multiracial audience went wild over idols of various races. All their faces had the same…smile.

"Did it have meaning? …You've gotta find it, right?"

"…Are you, redeemed…? You've gotta…redeem, yourself…"

Even Sora and Shiro as they spoke, even the Ex Machinas reflected in their eyes had the same face. The Ex Machinas realized that, at some point, the two with whom they burned in competition had made them glow.

—Yes. In this world…you could laugh it off.

"All you can do is be what you want, become what you want."

"…We're, hopeful…for your…hope. ♪"

—'Cos you couldn't *change*. You had to compromise and walk.

"So. Hey. Just for your reference…our personal opinion is—"

"…*It's not a bad world…* That's…what…we think…at least."

These were the very ones who had made such massive sacrifices in order to create this world. And the man probably hadn't died at peace. He must have gone with plenty of regret and frustration. Sora and Shiro had no place to say anything to him or those who were crushed with guilt after him. But they could only tell Ex Machina what they'd first thought when they landed in this world. With gratitude. Indeed:

"*Next* time. *This* time. We're gonna win. That's what this world makes us think."

The chessboard, after announcing Sora and Shiro's seventh victory, halted as if broken. And upon the triumphant stage poured an afterglow of hot applause…

"So! That's what we think, but, Ex Machina—what about you?"

Having given everything, Sora and Shiro basked in the same afterglow with tired smiles. The extreme concentration had fried their brains, and their bodies were heavy as if rusted through…but even aside from that.

…If there were a fourteenth round…they wouldn't win. Of this they were sure. *And for that reason*, the depth of the enjoyment in Sora's and Shiro's smiles only furthered.

—*Next time, you could beat us...don't you think?*
Their faces seemed to say as much, causing Einzig and the Ex Machinas to close their eyes and laugh...out loud...

ONE-TURN END

Elkia Royal Castle: the throne room. It had been a quick ten days since it was warped into a concert venue. But now it was as if it had all been a dream—its former state had been restored as good as new. The throne was back to what, according to Steph, was its proper position, steeped in fine tradition. Also in their proper positions—

"Hmm… You think the turn's about over yet?"

"…Soon… Maybe…three more, days…?"

—fiddling with their tablet, sat the king and queen of Elkia, Sora and Shiro, who both groaned.

…The turn should be wrapping up… The other players should be about done. They thought back to the turn they'd skipped, which could hardly be called a break…

They'd had nothing to do. They'd dedicated the turn to producing Holou. And yet, things got even crazier than expected due to an astonishing guest: Ex Machina. But as soon as the game had ended… Ex Machina had gone away somewhere without a word. Of course. It wasn't as if they'd made them pledge to be their allies. They'd made them pledge to abandon their love, and reproduce so they would not perish. That was all. They could go where they wanted. They could come back as an enemy if they wanted. They were free.

—*But that's kinda cool, too.* Sora and Shiro smiled to themselves. If Ex Machina were to come back of their own will and challenge " " properly...they'd welcome them.

Still, they were left here with fine fruits of Ex Machina's power.

"...Soraaa... Shirooo... The merch is about to sell out..."

A tired-looking freight girl arrived in the throne room— *Ahem.* Steph in working clothes. Sora looked her in the eye as he responded promptly.

"Heh, fear not. The eighteenth printing should be here soon! Sell those suckers!"

That's right—Holou's show had been such a legendary success, merch was flying off the shelves. Though it did have to be said—

"...All we have are block prints and books of block prints of Holou... Can we not do more?" Steph lamented.

Elkia didn't currently have the technology to create anything impressive. In fact, they'd gone to rather unreasonable lengths just to make these pinups and albums. Specifically, they'd photographed Holou with their phones, had Jibril make blocks with magic, and began mass-producing the printed prototypes they'd had the Academy research, which artists then colored... In other words, this shit was the culmination of otherworldly technology, magic, and abuse of state power. Steph was appalled by this senseless commercialization of untold artifice and labor, but even so, she had to wonder:

"I would love to hear Holou's songs more... Won't you sell them?"

Yes... Steph, who had fallen deeply for Holou's song, wanted— rather, everyone wanted more than anything else—to hear her sing again. Elkia was already gaga over the picture albums. Not that Elkia had audio recording technology or media. But surely Jibril could help out the *Kingdom* of Elkia—

"Mmm... You think so, huh? Everyone thinks so. I think so."

Surely the *Commonwealth* of Elkia could do it. Sora nodded to Steph's suggestion.

*   *   *

"Of course we'll sell them. If just for the chance to *crush the idol agencies of the Eastern Union.* ♪"

"...P-pardon...?"

Sora's inordinately evil smile made Steph take a step back, but he and Shiro stood from the throne and raved on.

"The Shrine Maiden attended the performance. Surely you don't think that was by chance?"

"...We invited, lots of big shots, from the Eastern Union... Especially...those involved...with the idol industry..."

"? For what purpose?" Steph asked the siblings as they wandered aimlessly. And then...

"Heh, heh-heh-heh, don't you see? Very well—we shall tell you!"

Sora and Shiro clicked their heels and revealed their scheme—!

"Holou's concert drew an audience of thousands. But! Her reputation has spread throughout the Commonwealth!!"

"...Words, spread like lightning... Picture albums...sell like hotcakes...!"

"But *guess what*! No one's got the video or audio! I mean, *we don't know how to manufacture them*!"

No true business professional would miss a chance to grab some cash. So—!

"All the businesses in Eastern Union who refused to give us equipment will come pounding on the door to pick up the audio!"

"Oh! So then you'll make good with those who—"

"But we'll say *no*!! Buzz off! Get lost! We'll humbly decline and slam the door in their faces—!!"

"...We'll tell them, come back yesterday...and belly laugh...and sneer...and point!"

Steph thought she had it figured out, until Sora and Shiro filled the castle with their screams of how wrong she was. Sora carried on theatrically, frivolously, leaving Steph in a daze.

"Whaaat? I mean, like, think about it, trying to suck up to the big guys; Bl4nk Productions is, like, *sooo* out of their league! You guys totally shafted Holou, and now she's *ours*! ♥ And then when you see she's hit the big time, you act all nice and stuff? *Oh my God!!* That's *suuuper bitchy*! You're, like, *sooo* pathetic, y'know?? ♥"

Nothing could be more pathetic than Sora's rendition of a stereotypical teen's vernacular. Shiro and Steph had the impulse to inform him of this, but instead they waited for his conclusion. He sat back down on the throne, crossed his legs, and arrogantly divulged his conclusion.

"I mean…if you signed an exclusivity contract with Bl4nk Productions, we might consider it."

"…But would anyone really accept such conditions?"

No matter how much revenue it might rake in, it couldn't be worth cutting off all their other contracts just for Holou, Steph argued, but Sora declared:

"Sure they will. 'Cos Bl4nk Productions is gonna be the biggest idol agency in the Commonwealth."

The song of the Sirens, the craft of the Elves, the technology of another world: a whole new kind of music! Under the powerful hand of " ", the unifiers of the races and Holou's producers!! At least some of the industry big shots they invited would have to think this. And frankly, they only cared about some of them. That is to say—! O producers in whose souls ambition reigns supreme! If you be a producer whose soul burns to raise your idols to greater heights—

—*you must switch your allegiance to Bl4nk Productions!!*

"Assemble, comrades, under the banner of Bl4nk Productions, with your animal-girls!!"

Sora looked to the sky, opened his arms, and called out for his compatriots, the heroes, to join him.

"…All the Eastern Union's…idols…suits…and producers…are ours…!"

And with a *huff*, Shiro took her place—on his lap—to hammer the point home.

They were going to gobble up the Eastern Union's agencies. Their talent. Their market. *They were going to devour it all.* Tariffs? Cancel that shit! Tax breaks, special exemptions up the wazoo! You'll see what happens when you cross Bl4nk Productions. Your body will remember the price you paid for opposing the government!

"...Your deviousness is so reliable, it makes my head hurt..."

"But!! That is only the beginning...!"

Sora boldly ignored Steph to lay out his grand aspiration, his endless end!

"Before long, we shall install relay devices not only throughout Elkia and Eastern Union, but throughout the entire Commonwealth!!"

Like TV or radio. They'd make Holou's song boom over every realm!

"Even the assembled technology of the Commonwealth of Elkia is not yet able to achieve this... But—"

Sora's eyes burned with the ambition to make it happen—

"Ohhh! Ahhh... Dear one... Why are you so cold...?"

—and suddenly reflected an unpleasant piece of junk that appeared before him, nose to nose, finger lifting Sora's chin, teeth sparkling.

"You desire such a device... Heh, such a challenge is nothing before my power of love."

"Don't we have any other power source?! Hey, why are you even still here?!"

—I mentioned that Ex Machina had gone somewhere. Sorry, I lied. Most regrettably, there was one unit still here, for some reason, and it was Einzig.

But then...when you thought about it, it would be a waste for Ex Machina to leave. After all, their power was enough to take care of everything, for they were the perfect stage equipment. In fact, there had been plans to bring them properly into the Commonwealth fold in the future—

"Why? Hmm… What is there to wonder about a man desiring to stay by the side of the one he loves?!"

"How many times do I have to tell you, *I'm—not—your—guy*! I thought I bound you by the Covenants to abandon—"

"No. I understand now. You are not the Spieler… You are Sora." Einzig smiled as if sentimentally accepting everything. "Set your mind at ease. For my love is pure and proper—I am in love with *you*!!"

"That does *not* put my mind at ease!"

—Why? Why did it have to be *him*? The *trope* was that the *girls* were still there. At the very least, that wasn't the kind of line you'd hear from a guy!! Sora cursed this world that betrayed every sacred expectation geek culture had given him.

"…I must apologize. I will impose on you but one last time, of reluctance to part. It would honor me if you could overlook it." Einzig's tone had turned wistful. Yet, he concluded with an even brighter smile. "…I shall follow the other units—back to our base." Turning on his heel, Einzig went on with a brisk voice. "Reproduction must now be my top priority…to produce the new Einzig, who will succeed this one who has long since passed his limits. Therefore, this is the time to set your mind at ease…for this will surely be our last meeting."

"……"

Einzig walked off with his back to them. "It is true… My dearest, you are not the Spieler. But—" Still, he spoke loud and clear. "You are the Nachfolger. And we will never go back on our word again."

—*We have come to assist you. We are your allies.*

The weight of his words brought to mind what he told them when they first met.

"Ex Machina will always be your ally. When you rise again to topple the world, we shall run to your aid," Einzig declared, still walking.

"…It might not be I. But whoever we are, we will bring you victory."
Yes: "*Next time. This time*, we will not go back on our word."

"…We can't make you wait that long."
The machine that had chased one hope 5,982 years past the end of his service life now departed without turning. No—the *man*, who now meant to say good-bye.
"You hung in there for 5,982 years. Just hang in a little longer… See ya."
"…*Bye-bye*… Let's…play again…sometime, 'kay…?"
Still, their amiable words did not turn him back. Gallant and attractive, the only reply was a slight chuckle. Sora decided not to notice the trace of tears…

——……

"Man, like, those guys were pretty hardcore. I mean, they were annoying and awkward, but…"
As Einzig's form receded from view, Sora thought back on the machines with hearts and came to a conclusion. They'd embraced paradox and become like people—just as awkward.
—But perhaps more pure. They had persisted in an unfulfilled love for one they knew was gone…for thousands of years.
"…I guess I can see how the epic gamer who ended the war could've fallen in love with them."
Sora so candidly summed things up, and Shiro and Steph chuckled and nodded softly—
—when.

"Hypothesis: If love specified for abandonment in previous game limited to Spieler…"
Gah!
A monotone voice echoed from behind the throne, practically making everyone scream.
"Corollary: …Then Master intended loophole to allow love of this unit for Master. Inescapable conclusion."

That optical camouflage shit again? The maid robot materialized, her violet hair and skirt fluttering. Yes…it was the heretic of the heathens, Emir-Eins, carefully aiming her finger-gun at Sora's heart.

"Determination and Confirmation: Master is in love with this unit. Bang."

Her deadpan wink worked surprisingly well as she expressed the firing of hearts or something from her finger. But Sora, the word *miss* rising from his head as the poorly aimed shot passed him by, replied:

"Emir-Eins? Huh? You're here, too?!"

"Acknowledgment: Always."

"Even Einzig left! What are you doing here?!"

"Rejoinder: This unit is Master's wife."

"*I'm—not—your—guy.* How many times do we have to go through this? Did you delete and rewrite your memory again?!"

As Sora clutched his head and groaned at her hopeless persistence, she grew flustered— No.

"Panic: Misunderstanding inferred. Previous statement was not fact, but rather, the desire of this unit."

"Oh, so you *do* get it…"

Expressing panic only verbally, Emir-Eins corrected herself placidly.

"Summary: Ex Machina lost. Unit re…rejected by Master… Fatal misunderstanding… Chassis temperature elevated: Shame detected. Erasing memory—failed. Already disconnected; how… *Hilfe*."

Despite her calm tone, the contents of her summary grew more and more distraught, to the point that smoke began to rise from her. After finally begging for help, she dropped her head limp like a puppet with a broken string, like a person tortured by the recollection of her humiliating past—but she didn't leave Sora and Shiro time to worry.

"Defiance: Still. This world provides option 'try again.' So. Therefore. This unit."

She raised her head again and looked straight at Sora with those glass eyes. While her hands shook, clenched together at her chest—did she notice?

"Wish: Again. This unit will express feelings to Master. Attempt *this time*...... Okay?"

Emir-Eins was begging, pleading for a rematch. As a gamer, how could he shut her down?

"...Ah, fine. But just one more time. And if you still get pwnd, let's play a different game."

To begin with, she'd just thought he was some other guy and fallen for him as an extension of that. If they were going to play again, Sora wanted her to play *them*, he implied. Emir-Eins plucked up her skirt, took a deep curtsy, and hummed:

"Lösen—Org. *n*—Checkmartyr—"

Then she took a deep breath. No—Ex Machinas don't need to breathe. In that case...it looked to Sora as if she was steeling herself, shaking off her uncertainty and unease. Then, as had happened so many times before, everything around them was rewritten, and everyone braced themselves.

—However.

"Hesitation: Master... No. Contingency judged to require name correction—"

Emir-Eins just stepped, stepped toward him hesitantly. Nothing, not the scenery, not the time, *nothing had changed*. Not her appearance, not her voice, and not her dress—as she approached him. Not the Spieler. Not her Master. Him.

"Identification: Unique and singular target, name: Sora..."

Yes—she called his name. She gingerly extended her trembling hands toward his torso and hesitantly squeezed as she buried her face in his chest. Rubbing it this way and that...as if to feel his heartbeat with every fiber of her being—

—she said only this:

"—Confession: This unit loves Sora."

......

............Uh. This was not good. Sora's arms almost reflexively hugged her back, but he just managed to stop them. He applied his gaping, cracked diamond of reason as he looked upon the transcender who had at last reached truth. Truth. Yes. Like Holou. You could write out the most eloquent poetry of love in the finest calligraphy; you could present a thousand bouquets in front of a full orchestra. You could decorate your words with the most perfect grasp of preferences, conditions, and tastes...and still.

—They could never compare to this inexpert, artless, and desperately brief outpouring of desire from a single girl. They could never compare—to this truth—

The self-evident truth, that is, that this shit was like a hammer upon the diamond rationalization of his pathetic virginity that threatened to smash it to pieces—!! Damn...he'd never had anyone straight-up tell him they liked him before... Sora imprinted on her and was about to say, "I've always loved you, too"—

"Reiteration: This unit loves Sora. This unit is in love with Sora..."

—when his diamond was saved from certain destruction—only to be struck again—that is...

"Effervescence: This unit loves you. This unit loves you. This unit loves Master. This unit loves Sora. This unit loves you. This unit loves everything about you. This unit loves the way you are. This unit loves your eyes, your thoughts. This unit proposes hypothesis that unit wishes to be one with Master. This unit is capable of fusion by neutralization of spiritual boundaries—this unit is amazing. This unit congratulates self. Request to Zeichner. Oh. Unit was disconnected—"

"D00d, d00d, *d00d*, you're freaking me out— Shit, you're hot! Ow, I mean, literally, you're literally burning me!"

His diamond was struck by a machine that was clearly out of

control. It was enough to make him get those cracks in his reason patched up as he cried out. At length, his shriek managed to return Emir-Eins to her senses, if we are to judge from her gasp—

"Examination: Not yet able to control these feelings. Unfortunate accident. No one is at fault."

She backed off and frantically collected herself—or rather.

"Correction: Master responsible for being warm. Master should think long and hard. However, unit delighted. Yay."

"D00d, you actually haven't changed at all, have you?! You're just as married-to-me-in-your-head as you were when we first met!!"

The maid robot showed a perfect example of how to pass the blame, at which Sora squealed.

"Negative acknowledgment: This unit has not won. Yet. But *this unit will try again*. Indefinitely. This unit will do her best."

They'd play a different game if he pwned her... But...*he hadn't pwned her*. Emir-Eins made that clear—with a tiny, tiny smile. At which, abruptly, a murderous aura rose from beside Sora.

"...Where...did you learn...that, tactic...?!" Shiro growled like a wild beast faced with her natural enemy, her red eyes burning. "...Brother, didn't have this...shoujo manga crap...in his porn...!!"

Sora wasn't sure what was making Shiro so mad. But come to think of it, sure... Ex Machina had used his porn as a guide to approach him. He himself didn't have a complete grasp of all the scenarios and content that had been in his collection. But if Shiro, with her photographic memory, said he didn't, then...presumably he didn't. Though one could not but shed a small tear at the fact that his little sister had memorized his porn.

"Reply: For this trial, unit sampled advice of woman..."

"...Hnguh? Uh, m-me?"

Since no one really cared about Sora's tears, Emir-Eins proceeded to point out the source of her information. Then something seemed to occur to her. She must have searched her memory and found no entry for Steph's real name.

"Request: Informal naming system not compatible with Ex Machina processing. Rename."

"Did someone finally just tell me to abandon my name?! It's Stephanie Dola!"

"Deprecation: Disclosing most useful information from advice of entity provisionally labeled Unknown."

Sora began to weep, bringing the total number of people with tears in their eyes to two, including Steph. Emir-Eins continued on indifferently.

"Elucidation: Master permits lies, jokes—but not lies to self."

Then, with a "Therefore," Emir-Eins smiled faintly.

Even Sora, who was so good at reading people, could just barely follow what she was saying. But in the end, he didn't know what it meant. She kept grinning. It was a declaration of war against all other women.

"Pledge: Until precise moment functional life of this unit ends, this unit will never hide her love."

"...————?!"

"—Uh, whaaa...?!"

Emir-Eins left Shiro and Steph speechless and pale as she turned.

"Estimation: If this unit restricts operational output—this unit can operate six whole years more."

With that, she faced Sora again and took an elegant obeisance with the implication, *See you again.* As for Shiro and Steph, she gave them a glance, with an expression that this time was clear. It was a sneer.

"Determination: This unit will not lose—to foes who are not true to themselves. Easy. No sweat."

Well, then. What's wrong? Smile, Sora, virgin, age eighteen. Ex Machina's still here! And just as you wanted, you've got your perfect stage equipment, and she's a girl! Not even a girl who thinks you're someone else, but one who's spelled out in no uncertain terms that she loves you. You've come all this way surrounded by gorgeous girls and women from many races, and yet, this is the first time one has said she loves you. Weren't you looking forward to this? Was this not the trope you desired?

It was just that…this girl seemed a little bit…off. Wicked enough to, for some reason, look at Shiro and Steph as if they murdered her parents. Imagining what would happen if Jibril showed up gave him the chills…and…another thing. For some reason, it seemed as if everyone was looking at him as if they wanted to stab him now… Hmm…

"Man…how *do* alternate-world protags maintain their harems?"

Sora decided that, at any rate, he wasn't up to it. That much he knew for now. Instead, he focused all his energy on how to get out of this situation.

■■■

This commotion now behind him…Einzig chuckled, acknowledging his jealousy for Emir-Eins. He walked slowly so as to record every bit of this scenery he might never see again. In this city, built up by their distant descendants, which could be expected to endure—

"…O thou. Ex Machina. Presumed to be individually named Einzig…"

—someone was standing there, so naturally to the point that it seemed unnatural. Out of place in a city of Immanities, yet, as if she belonged there. With her inkpot, a god in the shape of a little girl… Holou spoke.

"Thy advice hath enabled Holou to form a provisional hypothesis as to the nature of hope and wishes…methinks."

"…………"

As Einzig stood silently, overcome by a strange sensation, Holou heedlessly failed to get her words out repeatedly. What was it she wanted to say? What was it she wanted to tell him? She seemed to guess hundreds of millions of times and verify each guess—

"...Holou hypothesizes...she must convey *thanks... Gratitude!*"
Awkwardly, but with a smile, she got her point across. Einzig—
No, *Ex Machina*...replied:

```
"A god is a god for that she is a god.
Therefore, we shall never be able to
answer thy question."
```

Puzzled by this unprompted utterance, Holou cocked her head to one side. But even the speaker himself did not know its meaning any more than she did. They continued speaking as if their voices were merely being played back, their thoughts clouded by noise.

```
"But we shall reply to thy doubt. Doubt
is the heart. Therefore, thou who ques-
tionest the doubt art the heart."
```

Einzig did not know. None of the surviving units did.

```
"Thou art she who resolveth the will.
Thou art she who wisheth for hope. Thou
art she who is life in all who have
hearts. Yet, thou art she who doth not
perceive it."
```

Only one person knew the question that Ex Machina had been unable to answer for eons.

```
"Thus, let us now answer thy question
of that distant day."
```

```
"Our answer: If thou wilt hear us...we
will talk."
```

The question was known only to that god who had asked it, who now stood wide-eyed. It was an answer to Holou's former self, the Holou from a past far too long ago to conceive.

"...O ye, is it as suspected...? *Are ye the machines of that day...?*"

Holou gave a bitter smile. Even after filtering the noise, Einzig couldn't grasp what she meant. The machine man turned his head as he suspected a failure of severity exceeding that which had been detected by his self-diagnostics, yet—

"I must thank thee again. However— Holou...is fine now!"

He felt strangely convinced by Holou's smile. He left her just a narrow-eyed smile in return and slipped away into space.

"...Accursed Tet. Foul knave... Thou dare call Holou *too fast*?" Holou mumbled, grinning. It was just her now.

"How perverse! Holou is outstripped by her own creations!"

■■■

Loaded once more now, the memory, as ever, had a number of consistency errors. It must have been all the damage and logical faults: The data was inordinately abstract and fuzzy. But even Azril, no, everything that had been alive that day had heard it.

"*Nameless weak one—thou mayest hold thine head high, having truly proved thyself worthy to be mine enemy.*"

The last words of the god of war, commending his foe before he fell, were *as follows*. It is said that only the mere twenty-eight Ex Machinas, marred and smashed and broken from head to toe, recorded them...

"*...Challenge me again at any time, O weak one.*"

It could scarcely be believed that he was on the verge of vanishing, gouged of his ether, so steadfast was the simmering of the god of war as he declared war once more. It was all the machines could do to reply.

"*—You wish in vain, O fallen strong one.*"

But the god of war laughed it off as if amused beyond knowledge.

"It could not be that I might fall, and yet, it is. Aught can be. Tell your lord, O blades."

Yes—his words were not for Ex Machina, but for their lord. The weakest, whom the strongest had been forced to define as his natural enemy. The machines who had been able to gouge the strongest of his ether because they were the blades of the will of the weakest—now listened to his words for those who had forced him to no longer be the strongest.

"It was a fine match—and next time, I will win."

…With all due condolences to this god of war, these words could never be said. For the lord of these blades, the natural enemy the strongest of gods had recognized…that is: the weakest of all…the Spieler and the Preier…were no longer with us. For they had been succeeded by a different weak one—the two of Immanity.

——……

Far above Elkia, in Avant Heim, the city of the heavens, Azril sat on its edge, watching the machine man, Einzig, shift away. She remembered a story he had recently told her—one of her lord's final moments.

"—Azril. Do you mean to let them go?"

Avant Heim's question reverberated within her. She smirked.

"…What would be the point…? Lashing out at the blades that pierced my lord, after all this time…"

And rules were rules.

"I said I'd let them go if they gave an answer that tickled us. Aren't you tickled, Av'n'?"

Azril smirked more deeply at the hushed Phantasma and recalled.

—That day her lord was slain, he was…smiling. A broad smile had spread across his face—the first and last time Azril had seen such a smile.

…He must have been so happy. After six thousand years, she finally realized. After an eternity of ennui, he had met an enemy he could challenge with all his spirit…and lost. Still. He intended to win: *Next time, next time...* For his disciples to complain before such sublimity was nothing short of blasphemy.

"...For me to let defeat make me despair...I truly am...a false disciple."

All she had left to do was laugh. Azril just walked and thought:

"...The enemy of the strong...is the weak...? Hrmm... Hrm?"

...Sora and Shiro. Indeed, they were weak. The more strong allies came, the more strong allies fell before them. Their nature was pure—they *devoured the strong.* They were so weak... So weak you had to ask, *You have to go that far to win?* They were so foolish... So very foolish, and still they'd dared to challenge a god, and brought her down. Their weakness was beyond the ability of the strong to imagine, even to comprehend. Thus, they stood as the enemy of the strong, fulfilling their duty as the weak. Azril now believed she faintly understood them.

However—

"Hmmm? Then couldn't you also say, *the enemy of the weak is the strong*?"

The weak devised tricks, tactics, and strategies to combat the strong. But they devised them—always—to defeat an enemy too strong to beat fairly. Then was not the enemy of the weak—the overpoweringly strong, strength beyond the ability of the weak to imagine? Losing was not an option—they *devoured the weak.*

"...Nyaahhh, I dunnooooooo... Who should I root for?!"

As she walked, a thought popped into her head that made her clutch her head and squirm. They weren't the same individuals. They weren't even the same in form. Yet they, the weak, had succeeded them. And if someone took the place of the strong, who were left with the will to take on challenge after challenge—if, having tasted defeat, having learned of the weak, the strong stepped forth for *next time...* If these strong and weak faced one another once more, for whom should she root...? Azril writhed under the serious weight of this concern, until—*boom.*

"…I know! I'll just pick the side that's more *fun*. ♪ Nya-ha-ha! ♥"

Her head nearly exploded from overheating. Her thoughts ceased, leaving only a carefree laugh, full of hope, to ring through the city of the heavens…

■■■

Three days later, at last, the sign that read CLOSED FOR BUSINESS finally disappeared from Elkia Castle. Shiro had mumbled, "End of turn," as it went down, and immediately, all manner of national apparatus scrambled back into motion, breathing life back into the once-deserted castle.

"We'll be so busy… I don't even wanna think how much work's piled up."

Steph sighed in disgust, but the monarch rested on the throne with dignity.

"Hmmm! Bet you'll have to work especially hard, Steph. Meanwhile, we'll be doing the usual."

"…We can, count on you, Steph… We'll…do, *our* job…!"

"…Understood. Your Majesties intend to play as usual… *Hff…*"

They were playing games on their portable device even as they spoke, which made Steph heave an even deeper sigh. But—

"Well, yeah, you could say that…since that's our field."

With that, Sora and Shiro lifted their faces from their game console…at…

"It's always best to leave things to the experts. So we leave politics to the politicians."

There was a glint in their eyes as they looked over the people gathered in the throne room: the ministers and staff who had returned once the castle was reopened, along with some others as well.

"And so—leave gaming to the gamers. We'll solve problems the way gamers do."

Representatives of the commercial associations and guilds, even a number of lords, were in attendance.

"Hey, Steph. In strategy games, you only skip a turn…"

There was a distinct air of discontent, as the entire group appeared murderous while Sora and Shiro alone stayed jovial—as if mocking them.

"…when you've, got…tonnnns of free time…or if you're, *waiting* for something…or *both*. ♪"

Sora and Shiro's statement only made Steph blanch with the worst premonition she'd had yet. The two of them grinned at her and thought—

Expansion-oriented strategies were such a pain. Once your country got more powerful, you had to deal with all the new pressures from inside and outside, all the footwork. For instance…in this turn, they'd had nothing to do. They couldn't attack, and they wouldn't be attacked. But now with this next turn, that unbearably boring situation gave way to a whole spectrum of choices. That said, this new turn had a problem of its own.

—of the slight uncertainty as to whether they could survive. *But that's what makes it so thrilling.* Sora and Shiro grinned.

"So, Steph! This is our last chance. While we still can, draw us up a national missive."

"—Huh? Uh, y-yes…? T-to whom shall it…be addressed?"

Steph seemed confused by their disregard for the crowd's agitation.

"Mm. To whom…? Hmm, we haven't decided yet, but anyway, this is what should say."

Sora went back and gave it some extra thought… To whom *should* it be addressed? The fairy-girls, or the dwarf-girls, or perhaps they could even go for the dark horse? He considered with amusement who should be first—*for the loss*. Meanwhile, he dictated the letter he would have Steph send to them.

"Hey, dumbasses, need some help? How 'bout you thank us by giving us your whole damn country?"

Now back to the beginning.

Remember the law of increasing entropy? The law that it's easier to destroy than to build, easier to lose than to keep. Right, so… what does it mean to recap? To *recapitulate*. To settle the capital one has built up to build further capital upon it. How does one go about this? Well, normally, one would check one's foundations. This would involve a careful review of the status quo and a thorough survey for any existing problems. When problems are found, one must address them one by one in an assiduous process of correction. It's a painstaking operation.

Unfortunately, our two gamers despised games where they had to grind. As such, they dismissed this custom out of hand and opted for a mode that was easier and much more badass. So with that, let's get back to that spoiler.

————On this day. At this hour. Sora and Shiro, king and queen of Elkia, lost everything, in a *domestic insurgence*: the throne of the monarch, the position of agent plenipotentiary, their home, their power. They lost most everything associated with their royal authority, and about one month later—

—the country known as the Kingdom of Elkia *disappeared from the map*. It was the easiest and most badass method of recapitulation… Indeed.

The means to an end known as *destroying it all*.

It was as if to say, *I think this ought to be the fastest route.*

AFTERWORD

It was about eight months ago…

The year 2015 was drawing to a close. The man had finished his manuscript and had only the illustrations left. He sat with his drawing tablet, furiously scribbling away with his stylus.

He was desperate. Doomed. Perhaps even moribund. He had a cold and was operating on no sleep or rest. His already sorry state of mind had become even sorrier. Specifically, he would go to get a drink of water, stylus in hand, and then, for some reason, leave the stylus in the sink. There he was in his room, trying to draw with a cup. This is what it means to be terminally not right in the head. The man was encouraged to go to the hospital, even have brain surgery, but still he scribbled on.

The man's family was growing. His child's due date agitated him more than his deadline. He knew that when his child was born, things would not be the way they had been. His time for writing would be limited, as he could not press the care of a newborn babe solely into the hands of his wife. And so the man spoke to his editor.

"I promise to make the December release happen even if it kills me. Please give me paternity leave afterward."

The man was prepared for any unforeseen events— No. Under these circumstances, could any events be foreseen? He was ready to join arms with his wife, taking it one step at a time with their new child, searching for that new rhythm of life!!

...And the man made it through. He still had a mountain of work, some of which had to do with a separate anime project for another company. But for now, his most pressing task had ended... Now he had some space to face the unforeseen and rear his child while proceeding with further jobs. As the man reflected on this, full of emotion, there it was: a phone call from the anime producer.

"Heyyy, long time no see! I'll get right to the point, Mr. Kamiya— What do you think of an anime movie?!"
Heh. Heh-heh-heh, eh-heh-heh...
Was that a question? Did this person think the man would refuse? —No! They knew the answer perfectly well! In which case, the man could only give them what they wanted!!
"You don't even have to ask! Let's do it! I'll do anything you need!!"
The man answered immediately, and only after did he come to his senses.
"So...I have your word, yes? Now then...let's die together!"
Hearing the producer's voice echoing from the depths of hell itself, the man checked his scheduler and at last realized: *Well now, what to do about...this schedule......?*

...So!! I am that man: Yuu Kamiya!!
Having braved numbers of unforeseen events, and barely taking any time off during my paternity leave, I give you Volume 9! Things have been pretty heavy for a while since Volume 6, but I believe that now—yes, now!—this series is light once again! I hope you enjoy it!!

"But seriously, though! You sure had a weird way of writing this volume! (lol)"
......

…Uhhh, yeah… I'm not really sure it's a matter of *this volume*. But I guess you wouldn't know about the earlier volumes, being my *new editor*, "T"…

"I mean, you write the book and then you go back and shake the text up to make it 'light'? That's pretty weird to me! (lol)"

I—I guess you could…say that, too… Uh, well…mind if I add something, then? About the *second* unforeseen event…the *change in editor*.

Maybe my memories are getting mixed up… So let me check… There was previously a change in editor just before I gave you Volume 7, right?

"(*earnestly*) That's right! Don't worry, Mr. Kamiya! You're absolutely correct!!"

…Okay. So that was Editor I, who worked *so* hard so we could be on the same page through Volumes 7 and 8. Now this time, just after I turned in the first draft of Volume 9, it switched again to you, Editor T…

"(*firmly*) That's right. Relax, Mr. Kamiya. Your memory is fine."

…I…see. It's fine, is it…?

Then, this is a question I did my best not to think about until I got the manuscript in. But I guess it's time—so I'm going to ask, okay…?

I'm…just asking, all right, but…

—Could it be that no one wants to work with me?

"**Ah-ha-ha-ha!** …Oh no. It's really just internal circumstances… (*apologetically*) Sorry to put you through all the trouble."

Oh, I seeee! What a relieeef. ♥

—Also, could you tell me why you laughed?

"(*questioningly*) But, Mr. Kamiya, it seems to me that you handle switchovers like these just fine?"

You just blatantly changed the subject!! So people really *don't* want to work with me, do they?!

…Okay, look, let's see here.

I really depend on you guys a lot, getting your opinions and commercial perspective and all. So when the editor changes, it makes it really hard to build up that trust again, you know?

"…Right you are. I'll have to give my all to earn your trust, then. (*gulps*)"

Uh, yeah… I mean, no, that's not what I'm saying. See, it works both ways: You have to trust me—

"Oh, no problem there. My trust for you is maxed out at all times. (*smiles*)"

O-oh… Is that so? It's kind of freaky when you say that with your eyes wide open like that. Just what is the meaning of all…?

"(histrionically) Oh, Mr. Kamiya!! I never wanted to hear these words from you!!!"

Yikes! I don't know what I did, but sor—

"Do we need a *reason* to believe?! Mr. Kamiya, please don't say something so sad! I believe in you—(*firmly*) why should I need to justify it?!"

…

……

……Uh, yeah. Sorry about that. I guess you're right; we need to believe in each other if we want to get anywhere…

"(*straight-faced*) Yes, and now my trust is always *past* the maximum! My *trust that you'll deliver the next manuscript immediately*!"

…Sigh. Well then…now that I've resigned myself.

The next volume will be *No Game No Life: Practical War Game*—a spin-off, to be released in December…I guess? It's a short story/side story book. I'm writing it in tandem with Volume 10, so I'll try to get that out before too long, too! All the while, the *No Game No Life* anime film is coming along behind the scenes! I'll do my very best to make sure you enjoy it all, so please stay tuned!! All right, see you—

"(*serious*) Oh, one last thing, if I may?"

Wha—? Uh, yes…? What is it? I was just about to wrap things up all nicely…

"Well, it's just, I respect your taste and all, but as a former porno manga magazine editor, I have to say, that scene with the elementary school kids, you really should have made them the same age as the other characters. After all, at the end of the day, it's boobs that sell books. Oh, but I do have to give you props for the micro bikini—"

All right, see you later!!

"IF YOU'RE GONNA SELL MEDICINE, FIRST YOU GOTTA MAKE THE POISON; IT'S SUPPLY AND DEMAND. —ISN'T THAT WHAT THEY CALL THE BASICS OF BUSINESS?"

No Game No Life, Volume 10
—SHOULD BE COMING OUT AFTER PRACTICAL WAR GAME.
NO IDEA HOW THE SCHEDULE IS [CENSORED]

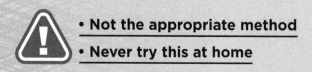

- **Not the appropriate method**
- **Never try this at home**

A NEW GAME IN A BIZARRE WORLD WITH ALIEN SPECIES!
PLAY, IF YOU DARE
No Game No Life
THE MANGA